ME, THE MOON

and Elvis Presley

●

Christopher Hope

ME, THE MOON
and Elvis Presley

•

MACMILLAN

First published 1997 by Macmillan

an imprint of Macmillan Publishers Ltd
25 Eccleston Place, London SW1W 9NF
and Basingstoke

Associated companies throughout the world

ISBN 0 333 59579 3 (Hardback)
ISBN 0 333 72203 5 (Trade paperback)

1 3 5 7 9 8 6 4 2

A CIP catalogue record for this book is available from
the British Library

Typeset by CentraCet, Cambridge
Printed by Mackays of Chatham plc, Chatham, Kent

The future is no longer what it used to be.

Paul Valéry

Material from Chapter 11, under the title 'Pogrom', first appeared in *New Writing 6;* Vintage (1977).

For Deborah

ONE

BUCKINGHAM – LUTHERBURG
1994–1949

CHAPTER ONE

1994

Pascal Le Gros told her: 'The past's *passé*. Junk it. And if you can't exactly love the future — at least try playing footsie-footsie with it.'

Mimi didn't disagree. But which past did he mean? She had any number. The child who had lived with Aunt Betsy back in the fifties, in the cottage at the end of Voortrekker Street where the tar gave out and a rutted sandy road left town for nowhere very much? Or the middle-aged woman with a preference for quiet colours, dark greens and muted blues who lived in the house now? Or the occasional layer-out in the little morgue over in Golden Meadow; or the Registrar of Coloured Births in the Town Hall?

These were just some of her former lives, all of them as intense as ever.

That was exactly Pascal's objection. She did not put her pasts behind her, where they belonged; instead, she ran them in reverse, ahead of her, like roads she might still travel.

'Always getting things back to front is pretty bloody dodgy,' said Pascal. 'Like a perversion, Mimi. So come clean. Stop living under an assumed name!'

That was the lawyer in him, still just about audible, —

dimly, briefly – because, like so much else, Pascal had forgotten all about it. He didn't care for history, personal or general. He said so, often. Pascal floated in the strong spirit of his certainties like a pear in brandy.

The name she lived under now was fictitious but it had this advantage over all her others: she'd chosen it herself: Mimi de Bruyn.

The trouble with Mimi, folks whispered, was that she did not appreciate the Change. Everyone talked of the Change, but it meant different things to different people. It seemed like some kind of fairy dust sprinkled on your eyelids so the world woke new and beautiful, and all the broken promises were mended.

It did no good telling Pascal that just about everyone lived under assumed names; because most of those who settled the country were pretty bloody dodgy themselves; runaway sailors, wandering Boers, wretched French Huguenots on the run, whom his own name recalled; and then there had been the throngs of slaves, named by their dim-witted owners from whatever came to hand: saints, animals, trees, even the months of the year.

He simply said: 'That was then and this is now. The Johnnie Februaries and Reggie Octobers. Forget them. You're deputy mayor. End of story. Mimi de Bruyn. That's the name you're known by now. So go for it! Face up to the Change.'

Mayor Williamson put it this way: 'Take the fall of the wall in Jericho. Big enough for you? Well, get this – we've seen the ascension of the servants to the seats of the masters. And that takes some beating. A miracle. We've been front row at the birth of a new universe.'

The number of new things people believed in the new

universe was quite bewildering. Bill Harding believed that Buckingham should stage the Commonwealth Games. Mr Moosah believed Jews were subverting the media. The Communist Party believed in mobile phones. Yet when Pop Harrhof back in the eighties bought himself one of the early models and went around on his tractor with this thing the size of a leg of lamb pressed to his ear, the Party condemned these instruments of Big Money and Neo-Liberalism and called for a boycott. But now the Party believed mobile phones were unjustly withheld from the labouring masses and demanded a cellphone in the hand of every comrade. The British Israelites, over in Nickleton, believed black women wanted to steal the superior genetic code of white men by robbing them of their sperm. Mr Moosah had once believed that every white man's house should be taken away and given to the poor. Now he believed in putting an end to 'dependency culture'.

When Mimi asked him how he could believe one thing six weeks ago and the opposite now, he got so worried about her 'lack of solidarity' that he consulted the Party Structures, which he always did when he wanted definitive answers; and the Structures advised as follows: 'Comrades Mimi, we are here, but you are there. And you can't get here from there. You must make the leap, you must let the old go.'

What they meant was: do as you've always done – but do it as if you've never done it before.

Pascal did it brilliantly. He completely forgot he had been an attorney who ran off with clients' trust funds and fiddled shares and salted mines and watered Scotch and sold it to the shebeens, and peddled windscreen wipers and time-share apartments in Margate and roofing felt, with his sidekick Mike the Spike. Pascal took one look at the future and bought shares.

The matter was decided because he said so. The rule was: anything would do as long as it did. And if in doubt, shout.

It was precisely one of those tricks that gave her trouble. That, and the art of the firm opinion. What did she believe in? She believed in the dead and that's what upset people.

Mimi locked her office in the Town Hall with its high white gable and oak beams. She and Mayor Williamson had adjoining rooms and shared the mayoral Ford. She'd never believed the mayor needed a deputy but the new council decided it was good for Gender. Mimi knew the Town Hall well enough – from years ago – but that had been in another life, another universe. No one spoke about it now.

The village lay rigid in the late afternoon sun; the wind had dropped, pale dust, fine as flour, clung to the window frames and to the forks of the thorn trees. The streets ran on a grid at harsh right angles, broad thorough-fares suited to turning ox-wagons. Upon the rocky flank of Spook Hill in letters a metre high, the town's name was spelt out in whitewashed stones. BUCK-INGHAM. Luckily the new name possessed exactly the same number of letters as the old one: LUTHERBURG. All the stones needed was a coat of paint and a little rearranging.

The air was so clear she could hear the kids in the new little makeshift school in the Old Standard Bank singing the old National Anthem; passing the Hunter's Arms she could see Pascal and Mike the Spike in the karaoke bar dreaming up schemes for putting Buckingham on the map; passing the police station she glanced into the charge office where Captain Nephew, now nearing retirement, walked about with his shoulders thick with gold stars. Who would have thought that this sixty-year-old police officer had once worn old leather flap pants with not even a button to his fly.

Mimi stopped a moment as she was passing under a huge dark willow. If she narrowed her eyes she met two people walking towards her. The woman was very erect, her high-heeled boots clipped the packed earth pavement like a pony's feet. The little girl trailing behind her mistress wore an olive walking-out frock. The child stared up into the willow as if she expected something to leap out of the tangled branches.

Mimi smiled: Aunt Betsy always thought of hunting or soldiering, and chose fawn or khaki or camouflage green when sewing outdoor clothes. She watched woman and child turn into the cottage at the end of the road and asked herself: 'Was that really *Me?*'

Then she followed them to the house they had entered.

Pushing open the green wrought-iron gate, its grille of lilies always so delicate in its heavy frame, closing it with the creak that sounded like a fish eagle's cry, pausing to watch the yellow monkey flowers open their mouths to the sun and drink it down; hearing the rusty gasp of the windmill in the field next door spitting a gout of water at a turn into the concrete cistern beyond the pear tree where once her friends would hide amongst the leaves and make love. One of those friends was dead. But that didn't stop her calling to Mimi from that very pear tree. And if she now turned and looked to the left she saw across the road the brick bungalow of Barnabas Basson, and he was dead, too. But that didn't stop him walking, or talking.

Inside her cottage smelt a little of liquorice and the old leather of the *riempie* stools, and of last night's fire. On the walls were Aunt Betsy's pictures and Mimi slept in Aunt Betsy's bed. Aunt Betsy had been dead some thirty years – but nothing had changed and Mimi changed nothing: not the Union Buildings picked out in coloured match-heads, not the samplers of gentle sheep on an emerald hill, nor the smiling man doffing his dark hat in a yellowing photograph clipped from the *Church Times* of 1949 and whom Aunt Betsy called the Good Doctor because he had led her people out of the land of Egypt and won them freedom after three centuries of servitude. And begun the Change.

The mayor said: 'My Lord, Mimi, we should send visitors. It's a period piece, *né?*'

But it was not the house that was the period piece. She wore under her skin the events of the past half century the way a tree wears beneath its bark rings of memories of past summer rains and winter droughts.

In the speckled bedroom mirror with the balding cupids embracing in the four corners, carved by Italian prisoners of war, she saw a round, smooth face with peach-yellow skin and hazel eyes, slanting slightly at the corners. The tilt to her eyes was the way of the country, going back all the way perhaps to the first people of the place, the Bushmen. As to the colour of her eyes, the person who claimed to have been her mother swore blind that she had an Irish lover who raced horses and drank barrels of porter. Now, if that was correct, and it was a big if (but people of mixed race were riddled with ifs) then she was part Irish and that might explain the hazel glint to her eyes, tiny flecks of light beneath good, strong lashes.

She also saw sometimes in the mirror, peeking over her shoulder, a little girl with springy black hair lit up, here and there, by a ruddy gold curl or unexpected blonde streak. The girl was wearing the oddest khaki smock or dungarees which swam on her. But then Aunt Betsy always held that indoor clothes should be large enough to 'grow into' and loose enough to allow the skin to breathe.

The child in the mirror was cheeky; sometimes she lifted her smock and revealed pants sewn from a bag of Miller's No. 9 Grade A flour, stamped in blue, and drawn with brown butcher's string.

Mimi said: 'Oh, I wish you wouldn't do that!'

The child stuck out her tongue.

'Is that really *Me*?'

Pascal thought these visions were bloody dangerous.

'Old world's gone, Mimi, overs-cadovers, finished and *klaar*. Isn't it? So what's your problem?'

And she said: 'No brakes.'

When the wandering shearers who rode their donkey-carts across the empty desert wastes climbed a hill, someone had to run behind the cart and jam a rock behind the back wheels when the going got steep; otherwise the fragile load of pots, kettles, kids went rolling backwards. Her mind did the same – ran down to the very hollows of the past; and lay there among all the ghosts she had known, and been.

Pascal said: 'Hells bells! Take a trip down memory

lane, by all means. It's a free country. But remember, *lane*'s the operative word, Mimi. It's not a bloody motorway.'

But she couldn't get the hang of short trips. She tried to swallow the rule which said: 'That was then, this is now.' But it stuck in her throat like a fishbone. Someone had to speak for the dead. And there were so many, many dead, not least her other selves, calling to her across the years. She believed that while she could remember them, the ghosts stood a chance. They needed her to fight for them. Memory was her weapon. Unless the ghosts were remembered there would be no peace. It was her responsibility. She couldn't let go the girl in the mirror until she had someone to put in her place, to take her forward – a future for her past.

She was at the mercy of her voices; they could call at any time, just as she began reading the lesson in church, when she was chairing a committee for Health and Gender, and there were the signs: a slight rolling of the eyes upwards under the lids; a downward tweak of the lips.

People knew; they sighed, they gave the tight smiles they usually saved for Englishmen, foreigners, Jews, epileptics and whispered: 'Mimi's gone. No brakes!'

And she could see them, scrambling to the brow of the hill and watching as her memory rolled her all the way back – to the beginning of her life, to a time before she'd even been Me.

CHAPTER TWO

1949

Her mother took her to the farm of Barnabas Basson and his wife, Arletta, out on the road to Zwingli, and warned her that if she didn't work hard, Boss Basson would beat her with a whip.

Boss Basson felt he had done well by taking in the child of a drunken woman and training her as his house servant. The woman had been prepared to deliver the child up for good but she wanted a bolt of yellow cotton if she was to disclaim all further rights. This was her 'book price'.

It was far too much.

So, like the goods they bought from Levine's Central Dealer, they took her 'on appro'. If Arletta approved of the child, they would talk about a booking-in. Later. If not, she would be returned.

They set her to cleaning the kitchen and polishing the cans of paraffin which fuelled the fridge, of which Arletta Basson was very proud. The child made a mess of it and she was put to simpler tasks: cooking, scrubbing floors, making beds. She got two meals a day; pumpkin, porridge, maize. They reckoned her to be about seven and began wondering why they'd bothered – she being too skinny to lift a bucket of water, or polish the old

yellow-wood floor to the decent gleam it deserved. Had
they been conned by the drunken woman into buying a
pig in a poke?

But the Bassons had not returned her. They did not
simply throw people out. Barnabas had not got rid of
Daisy, their old cook, when the cataracts steadily cover-
ing her eyes finally closed out the light of day. He'd had
an idea. Jackals had been very active amongst his sheep,
and he was losing five or six lambs a night.

So it was that Blind Daisy was appointed to watch
over the flock in their stone kraal over in Leopard's Hole,
half an hour's walk through the rocky fields, beyond
Bushman's Drift. The child was appointed as Daisy's
guide. She would carry the water and the bread and
perhaps a slice of cooked pumpkin or squash, wrapped in
an old tea towel emblazoned with a picture of the Union
Buildings in Pretoria which celebrated the Act of Union
of the four provinces of South Africa in 1910.

As they prepared to leave for the sheepcamp at sunset,
Daisy would cry out: 'Well then – where are My Eyes?'

The child leading, with Daisy's hand on her shoulder,
at first sobbed all the way to Leopard's Hole as she had
never been abroad at night and the rising of the moon
and the blazing fury of the stars, so clear and cold,
frightened her and she would scratch her head as if they
scattered on her some dust that itched and irritated.

Blind Daisy always began their walk by asking the
child to tell her the star patterns and then explaining
how, long ago when animals were still people, the
Praying Mantis, who was the Hottentots' God, made the
moon by throwing his shoe into the sky, and that the
stars were once girls like her with shining hair. Eventually
My Eyes stopped sobbing; it was part of their routine.

Approaching Bushman's Drift, it was Daisy's turn to be scared and she held tightly to the girl's shoulder; in the drift were the bodies of many Bushmen shot by a Boer commando years before, and every now and then spirits would fly up out of the ravine, crying for the decent burial of their bones, and bewitch passers-by.

The child shivered but she was not really scared of the great gorge of rock and thornbush. The hugeness of the night sky and the powdery choked brilliance of the stars frightened her more. Though she was pleased they did not go too near the edge of the drift where the rocks ran madly down through reeds and scrub to the river bed far below.

Once in the sheep kraal they would stop the gaps in the stone walls with ashbush and settle themselves in a corner of the wall for the night. The child crept close to Daisy's comforting bulk when she heard a rustle in the darkness amongst the sheep moving like little pale clouds; she had seen what the jackal did to a lamb, how it tore at head and tail, gnawed its feet, left it half eaten, sometimes half-alive in the cold dawn light, and she was tempted to shut her eyes very tight and blot out the sly, prowling murderer.

But Daisy pinched her, saying: 'If My Eyes are not open, what can I see?'

She would prop open her eyelids with her fingers, staring into the darkness where the smudgy sheep sighed and chewed. And if she saw the slightest movement she dug Daisy in the ribs and Daisy would throw back her head, open her mouth very wide to show her teeth and begin barking: hard, commanding yaps that sent the sheep scattering in cottony confusion. Daisy's bark was so real that, with her eyes closed, My Eyes believed a great big guardian collie sat beside her. Often she did not know if she was asleep and only dreaming she was awake when Daisy's warning blasted across the sheep pen at intervals through the night – like the pulse of cicadas or distant thunder – but she knew she was safe, as one was safe under a roof when the lightning flashed and the thunder cracked, sheltering in Daisy's warm softness.

At first light, so crisp that icicles sometimes stuck to Blind Daisy's lashes like sugar, My Eyes opened her eyes, and nothing was said; they shared bread and water and the remaining squash and then, with Daisy's hand on her shoulder, the child led the way back to the farm.

Then came the hunting season when Boss Basson would clean his Mauser the night before, and wake at five to receive his hunting partners for an early breakfast of coffee and rusks – the custom of the Buckingham Hunters before a day's shoot.

It was as one of the hunting party, sitting in the kitchen, that Aunt Betsy first saw the thin, silent child with the round face and pointed chin, barefoot, wearing a cotton dress in the first nip of an autumn dawn, approaching with a bamboo tray of coffee held high on her chest. But not high enough to reach the big oaken kitchen table where the hunters sat blowing on their hands and checking their ammunition.

The girl had time to consider this problem because no one paid attention; the hunters were busy. Like kings with gold coins. Bullets before bread, they said in the Lutherburg district. Men carried wads of ammo in their shirt pockets. Bullets bought respect, power, pleasure, sport, blood, justice, good health. Sticking their hands into their pockets and coming up with fistfuls, shining like cash in the firelight. You saw your face in the brass jacket of the bullet and you knew who you were. Bullets made brothers.

Springbok were the targets, and pheasant and guinea fowl and duck. Yet Buckingham Hunters' Club also dedicated itself to hunting out certain predators, like the lynx. The Karoo lion had vanished many a year before. The black-backed jackal was almost gone. Which some thought a blessing. Others recalled the wild Bushmen, hunted to extinction, a great success, really. But what a loss to sportsmen throughout the region.

Setting the tray on the floor, the girl went into the yard and came back rolling a chopping block, the bole of an old willow. The image of the girl remained with Aunt Betsy all day. Her tongue clamped between her teeth, she balanced on the chopping block and slid on to the table the heavy tray and dark blue enamel mugs edged in darker blue. The men sipped and played with their treasures.

It was this Aunt Betsy was to remember some weeks later when, out in the field, after a day's hunting and a good bag of springbok, she stayed with the men around the fire in the evening, and Barnabas Basson laid his hand unexpectedly on Aunt Betsy's knee as she sat sipping coffee by the fire. They called him 'Bananas' for the curious mottling of his cheeks, a flush of blue-black shadow along his jaw and a slightly jaundiced pallor.

Without putting down her mug Aunt Betsy hit him with the stiff edge of her right hand below the cheekbone and when he cried out she flung the remains of her hot coffee in his face. Never a word was said. But it began the war that followed the end of the war between the

English and the Germans. What is more, it was plain to those present that Bananas Basson had got off lightly. Aunt Betsy had stopped this side of killing him and the coffee burns blended into the mottling. So nothing really changed. Yet it was something that had repercussions for everyone, for ever. Even if no one ever spoke of it. Always a sign of something taken very seriously in Buckingham.

Bananas Basson, as he wiped the scalding coffee from his livid face, seemed to divine something of Aunt Betsy's thoughts. For it was now that he made a curious and spiteful offer – as though he wished to make up to her and undo her at the same time. Since Aunt Betsy was so interested in that scrap of a girl who was bloody useless, to be honest, then she was welcome to take her off his hands. Her mother had put a book price on the girl and he knew where her mother might be found, back in Buckingham, in Silver Street.

He did not say that the asking price was a bolt of yellow cotton, enough for a year, if you went carefully. Nor did Aunt Betsy say that she was interested in his offer. But she did not say no, either.

When Aunt Betsy met the woman and arranged a book price of six stones of coldwater soap, all the district laughed. Basson saw it as a monstrous conspiracy of women. It worked and worked in him, along with Aunt Betsy's fist by the fire, the scalding and his very own offer. Now trumped.

Day after day he sat on the step cursing her softly for a dried-out old leather-prune, drained of juice, hairy as a hound. Witch. Hellbitch. The dark mottling across his cheeks that gave him his nickname, now mixed with coffee burns, set up a polka-dot effect when, whip in hand, he came galloping into the yard one evening yelling at the girl to get out into the open where he could see her and My Eyes felt, yes, now came the beating her mother had warned her about. Blind Daisy wasn't ordered into the yard but she came anyway, refusing to let go of My Eyes's shoulder.

Perhaps that saved her from the beating but it was worse for the blind woman shuffling beside her and crying: 'What is it you see, My Eyes?'

But she didn't say, couldn't say because at that moment Mrs Basson came running into the yard shrieking that any damage done to the servants and they would have fed and clothed and housed them all in vain; and trying to wrestle Basson's rifle away from him. Basson jumped up, shouting: 'No, man – Arletta!' and hit her across the face and began pushing her into the bedroom. Behind the door Mrs Basson was screaming and then they heard the sound of the belt or a whip, and Mrs Basson screaming again until she gagged loudly, probably because her husband buried her head in the pillow.

When they came outside again her eyes were dark and her lip was bleeding and she went away without a word. Bananas picked up his rifle and sat on the front step with a bottle of cherry brandy. He'd take a few pulls and start shooting at tin cans ranged like crows along the top of the fence. Old Daisy kept asking what was happening and shrieking each time the rifle went off. Basson potted cans; he finished his bottle, then with a wave of his rifle he abruptly told them to start walking *bloody well right now*.

My Eyes walked steadily, feeling Daisy's hand tightening on her shoulder each time the gun sounded, and hearing her begin to growl the sheepdog warning low in her throat.

The bullets kicked up geysers of dust at their bare feet. Splintered shale stung their ankles. My Eyes was not really frightened. It was better than being in the dark sheep kraal, stalked by jackal and lynx she could not see. Better the bark of Basson's rifle, because shots were the real thing and she could see, with a kind of approval, the stones leap when the bullets clipped them.

'He's aiming to miss,' she whispered to Daisy.

But Daisy was growling so loudly she didn't hear.

With each step My Eyes felt stronger. They were leaving and the boss would not stop them. She reckoned it was maybe two hours' tramp to Buckingham. If Basson did not kill them then they would get there. All she had to do was to put one foot in front of the other.

CHAPTER THREE

1994

On a June afternoon, cold and bright, Mimi de Bruyn was among the first to see him sailing down Voortrekker Street in his whites. Anyone else might have taken him for a pasha, a strolling pope, a fat cricketer. All pretty startling in dusty Lutherburg and equally unwelcome.

Mimi thought of something else; he didn't so much arrive in Lutherburg, he arose; like the moon, and she remembered a snatch of the old song: 'I see the Moon, the Moon sees me.'

Except that he didn't see her. At least, not then. He had eyes only for himself. Creamy flannels, crisp tennis shoes, a vast ivory sweater, its V-neck edged with bands of black and purple; colours of some minor long-gone provincial tennis or cricket club perhaps, draped over the hill or hummock of his belly.

He went bowling down Voortrekker Street, a shape-changer from the start: he was a shimmering moth in the window of Levine's General Dealers as he paused to comb back his thick eyebrows; a fat creamy flag fluttering in the fluted, brass-panelled, bolted doors of the defunct Joffe Brothers & Sons, Chandlers – and in the windows of the Agricultural Co-op he paused just long enough to plaster the shiny milk canisters with the huge woolly label of himself.

People stopped whatever they were doing, as they might have stopped to watch an eclipse and, squinting against the bright sun, observed him sailing on his silver way down Voortrekker Street to alight at the Lutherburg library, which shared a room with the Co-operative Burial Society, in one of those boxy, somehow brazen buildings of the thirties, tiled in marine green, just beyond the Post Office.

'He waltzed in,' according to Julia La Rochelle, town librarian, 'requesting the complete works of the philosopher Hegel – in a good Afrikaans edition.'

The vast man proffered a limp handshake: 'Pascal Le Gros.'

He struck Julia as a colossal aubergine on legs. His purple cheeks, scored with veins like rosy rivers, rose up on either side of his nose.

'So I said to him: I'm afraid you'll have to take whatever edition I can lay my hands on. Please remember, Lutherburg is a long way from anywhere.'

This was undeniably true. Lutherburg lay on a great plateau, a vast, rocky shelf strewn with rocks and scrub and dotted with sheep. A consuming summer sun vaporized its meagre water supplies and baked it dry. In winter bitter winds froze the fence menders' fingers to the wire. Driving fast, always dangerous on the rudimentary dirt roads, you took an hour and a half to reach anywhere. And anywhere wasn't much. Just another god-forsaken hamlet – Bushman's Bend; Compromise; Scorpion Point; Abraham's Grave; Pumpkinville; Mutton Fountain – of which Lutherburg set the inescapable pattern. The rocket nose of the Dutch Reformed church steeple, spiky over the bluegums, marked the centre of what folks called 'Lutherburg proper' – the white town; half a dozen streets under the brown bulk of Spook Hill.

Its smudgy, larger sister called Golden Meadow, the brown town, lay beyond the municipal shooting range, hidden in the smoky haze of a thousand dwellings. You'd never know the other town was there until Friday evenings when the farm labourers spent their money in the bottle store and reeled around the streets fingering their knives, launching mock karate kicks at each other, and falling over.

Nothing much happened in Lutherburg by day, nothing at all at night: that was the story. After sunset, even the drunks went home because brown folk, officially, were not allowed in the bar at the Hunter's Arms – and white folk, unofficially, said it was the seat of Satan; and only the shriek of the police siren, announcing another stabbing in 'the Scheme' as most called the brown town, might sometimes break the brilliant silence of the starry night.

Despite all this, the librarian resented the pale stranger's disdain. Lutherburg people were seen as pretty odd, even by their neighbours an hour down the road. But they weren't apologizing. Bugger that! Pascal Le Gros had been in town five minutes and he was giving speeches. Well, there had been civilized settlement in Lutherburg for a century and a half, since the first wagons from the Cape creaked their way over the snow mountains and the Scots Presbyterian pastors brought the light of Christ to the wild Bushmen. Why come to Lutherburg, wondered the librarian, if your tastes ran to Hegel in good Afrikaans editions and you wore white a lot? Khaki was the only sensible colour, it did not show the dust.

CHRISTOPHER HOPE

But Pascal Le Gros never accepted the remoteness theory. His clothes said so. He said so – to Julia.

'I beg yours. But isn't it time we stopped thinking of cities as the centre of the universe? I've got family in Miami. I've got friends in Douglas. I've bought the Hunter's Arms. This is the late twentieth century. Great changes are afoot. Let's catch the spirit of the times. Wake up, people! Before Lutherburg goes down the tubes. Just another Karoo relic, like the dinosaurs.'

Julia La Rochelle was no pushover. She had been electoral officer in the first open elections ever held in Lutherburg, when old Theo Tromp stormed into the Town Hall where voting was taking place, waving a rifle and calling her a traitor to her race, and demanding she halt this devil's orgy. The old man's farm workers stopped voting immediately they saw Boss Tromp and doffed their hats and tried to look as if they were doing something harmless like queuing for their pensions in the PO, instead of preparing to vote out of power men like their boss.

Julia greeted Boss Tromp politely – he was her godfather, after all – warned him politely that carrying weapons in the polling booth was an offence, and then had him arrested.

The arresting officer was Mr Tromp's nephew, Willie Tromp, who in his twenty-year career had never taken a white man into custody. Arresting his uncle had untold effects on Constable Tromp who got a taste for it in much the way that the starving may acquire a taste for human flesh. He began arresting white men all over the place, for jaywalking and parking the wrong way and speeding through town, even though the dusty empty streets of Lutherburg seldom saw three cars a day.

Julia La Rochelle let Pascal have it from the hip. 'If you think we're so hopeless why come?'

'I'm here,' said Le Gros simply, 'to put you on the map. To get this town taken seriously by the world beyond. The world of work, and business. I come to celebrate its tranquillity, its profound peace. Yesterday I took my car and a bottle of Scotch, parked up at the dam and watched the sun set. And I had a vision. I saw paradise! But what good's paradise unless it's on the map? I see renaissance. I see city types, sick to death of car-jackings, muggings, rapes, shootings, flocking to find peace. Perfect peace is the gift of Lutherburg. The roads are good. I see coach parties from the Cape. Good books by the fireside. Civilized cuisine. Know what a hub is? Like Heathrow Airport, in London; that's what's called a hub. Paris, it's another hub. OK? Well, us too. Look at that little airstrip, out by the rifle range. Only needs a good sweep – and somebody to scare the donkeys off the runway – and Bob's your uncle. 'S virtually an international airport you've got there. Namibia's just up the road; not to say Namaqualand and Botswana. Plus my friends from Douglas; they'll all be flying in. I see us as a staging post for desert ventures. A refreshment station of the heart. Lutherburg, the hub. Use it or lose it.'

The voice was like the man, round; big and fat and loud, like a red and yellow beachball, it went rolling into the corners of the library, bouncing among the samples of funeral furniture; polished grey marble headstones, plastic blooms under glass bells, granite Calvinist crosses. His voice had something rich and shameless about it. Two children, reading Danielle Steel novels in the corner beside the display of brass casket handles, lifted their eyes to this apparition and immediately lowered them again, hot faced, as if they had just heard a rude joke. In a town where everyone wore muted clothes, khaki or ochre, yellow or old rose, this shining icecream man with the mauve face and the big voice was somehow shocking. And even Julia La Rochelle, who took no nonsense from anyone, found herself accepting a pink printed invitation card:

HAPPY HOUR at the HUNTER'S ARMS.
Strawberry Daquiris Our Speciality,
Unaccompanied Ladies: Half-Price.

'I told him straight: people will ignore you.'

Pascal inclined his huge head in gentle scorn. He put a hand on his waist, he did not really mince but there was a hint of a pirouette as he turned first one hip, then the other: 'Think so?'

'I'm telling you.'

'Then they'll be ignored right back. I don't need them. I'll pull a better class of guest to Lutherburg. Guests appreciate a show of culture. Hegel this week, Raymond Chandler the next. A good mixed bag. Soon, they're dropping into your library. We all benefit. Remember – the Hunter's Arms always goes one better.'

'He'd been moving steadily down the street,' said the librarian later, 'calling at the butchers and the Co-op, ordering stock for the hotel. I was last on his route so I got the book order. How many books did he get on a ticket? Three, I told him. Fine, he says, one ticket for me and one for Mike. That's my partner. Count on us for six tomes weekly, for our reading room.'

*

He swept back up Voortrekker Street under full sail, reported Bill Harding, the last Englishman in Lutherburg and an expert in nautical matters. He'd been building a yacht in his garage for years. But the Lutherburg dam hadn't had a drop in it since the big drought began four years before, and the sea was five hundred miles away, and no one expected him ever to get the thing out of his garage. So the billowing progress of Pascal Le Gros from the library to the hotel was the closest many in Lutherburg came to seeing a regatta.

The Hunter's Arms stood across the road from the Co-op, the Volksbank and the old synagogue, and diagonally opposite Bokkie Bok's Butchery and the old Anglican church. It dated from the time of the British Empire when Lutherburg had been called Buckingham. It possessed a fine red verandah, facing the street; and leading off the rooms on the second floor a series of balconies, adorned with wrought iron railings depicting in intricate patterns wildlife of the olden times: the Karoo lion, the black-backed jackal, the hunting Bushman bow and arrow in hand. The hotel roof had once been black slate but it had been replaced with corrugated iron, the same ruddy colour as its verandahs. The hall smelt of dust, insecticide, linoleum and the musty hairy odour of the mounted heads of springbok, kudu and eland in the entrance hall. And when Maureen's two elderly, shambling, incontinent Dobermanns Bruce and Brad were installed, also of dog.

Regular guests were few and far between. Salesmen travelling in sexy brandy glasses or bar coasters sometimes slept over; once a month the bank inspector, up from Cape Town to check the books of the solitary branch of the Volksbank.

The reason why local people never ventured into the hotel went back a way. The Hunter's Arms was Satan's hostel, said the first true Calvinist Dutch Reformed pastor to come to Lutherberg since the Afrikaner conquest, back in 1948. And no subsequent pastor had relaxed the rule. Mothers warned their children about it, young girls averted their eyes when they walked by. Behind its yellow walls there was flirting and lovemaking and all manner of orgies. No respectable woman ever entered its portals. Officially the place was always empty.

In truth, a lot of folks used the place. Local farmers, slipping through the back door, drank thirstily in the public bar, lounging on the oaken counter, scuffing the brass footrail. Brandy and Coke for starters, cold beer chasers to wash the dust from their throats. But no one said anything about that. The Church also used the forbidden hotel once a year, and organized a teetotal reception; people sipped coffee and orange juice and pretended to be somewhere else, and anyway, this was Church business, so it must be OK. On Friday nights local rugger-buggers, blonde giggling girlfriends in tow with make-up thick as face-armour, sneaked in the side door and watched TV or played noisy games of pool and made a beer last all night. But then they were young, weren't they? – and the young must have some fun.

But it was never a gold mine. The Hunter's Arms had gone from bad to worse over the years as a succession of inept owners tried to break down the walls of hostility and reserve which gave out the message that *never never never* would decent folks visit the hotel: and tried to get customers to settle their outstanding bar slates. Tradition had drinkers chalking up weeks of credit, then swearing blind they'd never taken a drop. It was even harder to make folks pay for smashed glasses, or guys pogo-ing up and down the staircase; or shooting out the lights, or wrecking the tabletop felt when they abandoned their snooker games and began shoving cues up their nostrils; or rode horses into the bar after the gymkhana.

None of this was seen as notable. Or very bad. It was the other, older reputation that did for the Hunter's Arms; the traditional rumours of incest, of bestiality, of wholesale fornication, always located in the hotel; a mystical, garish belief, all the stronger for being without evidence, passed from one generation to the next and continued to confirm the worst suspicions of the Hunter's Arms. The rumours were harder to refute because no one said, or perhaps even believed, they were true, but they were traditional and Lutherburgers had enormous respect for tradition.

The town was unaware that the hotel had changed hands once again. One day, out of the blue, Pascal Le Gros and his friends arrived in a red Nissan pick-up. There was Mike the Spike, a little, lithe man with dark hair and hurt eyes. And his girlfriend, Maureen, who wore big hairpieces and liked exotic arrangements, an elaborate beehive or a well lacquered bird's nest – and had a laugh like a pneumatic drill. The town said probably they slept three to a bed.

Pascal Le Gros had meant what he said about jazzing up the pub. That evening, a banner, painted in red on white sailcloth, billowed between the pillars supporting the upper floor verandah. The invitations Pascal had pressed on people around town were already out of date. He'd upped the offer.

HUNTER'S ARMS HAPPY HOUR
Daquiris half-price: Ladies Free!

The Volksbank across the street closed early, as if fearing trouble. The headmaster of the private whites-only school at the top of Voortrekker Street marched his pupils to view the banner and marched them back to the little school and locked the doors. 'Sodom has come to Lutherburg,' he told the children, his bible open and he gestured to the world beyond the concrete wagonwheel fence. His little charges stared. Until then it had been believed that Sodom was in Zwingli, an hour away, where people visited each other at night and partied for entire weekends.

The regular drinkers at the Hunter's Arms witnessed what happened next. Bill Harding had dropped by for his customary two whiskies before climbing back into his BMW and driving the block and a half home to his dinner. He was chatting to Jimmie Judd, the ex-cropspray pilot who lived with his tiny withered wife who wore blue and was inclined to drop to her knees and pray in public for her husband's soul, before dragging him out of the bar and back to their cottage under a palm tree on the edge of town. JJ drank anything and he drank fast, putting away sweet sherries like there was no tomorrow. In the months to come, JJ would retell the story to anyone who would buy him a drink.

They'd had the place entirely to themselves. Despite the big ad flapping in the breeze an hour passed – 'And zilch guys pitched,' JJ used to say, 'not a sausage. *Niente, niks.*'

Outside on the front steps, fluttering under the bare bulb that lit the entrance like some huge furious moth,

Pascal moved backwards and forwards. The wind got under his hair and into his flannels. The wind got behind the banner, tore one of its moorings loose and momentarily wrapped it around him like a shroud.

'Like a bloody walking mummy, true's God!' JJ made these little chewing sounds when he was amused.

Nine o'clock came and still no one pitched.

It looked like Julia La Rochelle had told Pascal right. The town was going to kill him stone dead and throw him to the jackals.

JJ always liked to remember what happened next: 'Pascal walked into the street and you know those guys sleeping it off behind the abattoir, the layabouts and alkies and the deadheads who stand about on the corner of Voortrekker and Leibrandt, hoping heaven'll fall in their laps? Just hold out your hand to the white man . . . Well, up he goes to them and says: "Free drinks, guys!" Well, in two ticks the bloody bar's popping with meth-heads thinking is this or is it not fucking Christmas? And knocking back strawberry Daquiris like they were going out of fashion!'

Pascal's Happy Hour caused a worse sensation than anything in town since the elections. Because the next night brown people, who usually drank on the street, were again sitting at the ornate bar counter, their toes on the brass footrail and Maureen was serving them, admittedly sporting a neat little parabellum pistol in a white leather holster, but even so a city woman with nice manners – fixing drinks for township people.

There was one change: this time they were paying for the privilege. And Mike the Spike was slapping cash in the till, saying: 'Let's hear it for the Jewish piano!'

Later, Pascal made a speech about the new spirit of

democracy and how he welcomed it; he welcomed, also, with every ounce of his being, fair shares for all in our upcoming rainbow future. He said the new Lutherburg was the hub of the country. Above all, he just wanted to say he believed, passionately, that the bar belonged to the People and the People belonged to the bar. At which everyone cheered a lot and fell over.

Next day, Dominee Greet came to see Pascal. Tall and dark with a line of midnight blue stubble around his jaw, like some narcoleptic Mexican bandit plagued by visions of hell. There were stories about Greet; that he was getting as angry as a cobra, but there were few signs of the deep internal agitation which was to sweep the Dominee down paths none could imagine. Pastor Greet made the usual disclaimer about not wanting to interfere in another's business, before letting Pascal have it between the eyes.

The town was concerned. By what right had Pascal invited township people into the bar?

'Use it or lose it,' said Pascal. 'You tell 'em that, padre. I wrote an invite, didn't I? They didn't show. So I took action. This is the new Lutherburg. We had elections, OK? No more separate amenities. Open access for all.'

Dominee Greet did not wish to be drawn on the politics, and said so very sincerely, and asked also that Pascal please mustn't think he was speaking for himself. He was speaking for the whole town. Dominee Greet now unpeeled his zip of sharp little bright teeth behind lips open no wider than a knife, in a smile that reminded Pascal of the anteater's curious apologetic pose as it dives into the termite hill and sucks the colony into its maw. Had he ever told Pascal how much he loved statistics? So he would relate a little story free, gratis and for nothing.

The Hunter's Arms had never made a profit and if Pascal squeezed his margins any further by giving cut-price drinks to street loafers he'd go bust. And, what's more, white farmers on whom the bar depended would never enter a mixed bar, never drink with these people. They'd never be back.

Pascal closed his heavy, veined eyelids wearily. 'So ignore me. I'll just give you more to ignore. I can't lose. What I stand for, padre, is the spirit of the times.'

Next day Mike was at work.

Mike the Spike had once been in liquor, then roofing felt, and then windshield wipers – but his start in life had been carpentry. With his tools belted to his waist, he was soon at work on what they called the Next Stage, while Pascal brushed up the menus at public meetings:

'Staff learns how to flambé; staff learns to use fresh ingredients and not think any rubbish will do; staff knows the old days are dead and the new world begins here! Do you read me, you funny people?'

And the brown cooks and cleaners stared at him with huge frightened eyes.

Pascal stalked through town informing everyone about the Next Stage, the transformation of the residents' lounge. Mike was building a new bar counter, faced with pink buttoned leather, running its full length from the fridge to the sound system where the CDs towered; there was Jim Reeves, Pavarotti, Country favourites, Tom Jones and Manhattan Transfer. Next came lights; pink and blue spots and some good mixers. Karaoke facilities were on order from Kimberley.

'State of the art, no pissing about,' said Mike the Spike. 'As good as you get in Jo'burg. Better. Whole world's gonna hit the new karaoke bar.'

'Chances are,' said Pascal, 'my friends will visit from Miami. Our karoake bar will cater for discerning tastes. The farmer who cares to bring his lady for a Chicken Breton of an evening. Or visiting politicians in need of peace. In a word – the cognoscenti. I'm training my kitchen staff in the ups and downs of fine cuisine. Mulligatawny soup on winters' nights; Hegel on the coffee table and karaoke in the saloon bar and anyone who gives me uphill's out on his neck. The Hunter's Arms reflects the spirit of the times. Open amenities, sure, but no forced mixing. Standards at all times. A dress code. No thongs. No tank tops. Those wanting to piss it up and spit on the floor can do it in the public bar – where they can be effing and blinding to their hearts' content.'

Dominee Greet began a campaign: 'Brown drunks belong in jail.'

But Constable Tromp simply wouldn't arrest brown people any longer. Since he'd collared his own uncle in the polling station, only whites would do. And when he carted off the visiting Volksbank inspector, tucked under his arm like a parcel, crying to be put down, the campaign died.

Then Pascal put the boot in. He began saying that what had happened in the Hunter's Arms was a little miracle of sorts. He'd struck a blow for reconciliation between the communities.

Mike said: 'You mean between us and the drongos?'

Pascal shook his head at Mike's crudity. 'Where, before, was one bar there are now two, where there was discord, amity.'

Really and truly! thought Maureen, this guy's the biggest bloody shyster *ever*.

But she had to admit it seemed to work. People began saying, *ja* well OK, fine — so long as nothing's really changed, why not? Amazingly, the Women's Federation decided to hold a mid-morning coffee session in the saloon bar. Pascal talked of the big breakthrough. Mike he designated greeter-in-chief and told him to settle the ladies in. Once they were comfortable Pascal would arrive and say a few words of welcome.

They trooped in, led by Elsabee Dippenaar. Mike made sure all his little fancies were stowed out of sight; the Scotch with the novelty label the guys always liked — *Fuck Me!* — and the girlie barmats and the cunning Chinese glasses which revealed tiny copulating lovers in the base when you reached the end of your double brandy and Coke.

He needn't have bothered because the women turned blind eyes to the bar and pretended they were somewhere else. When he saw to his dismay that they'd brought Pastor Greet with them, Mike rooted around for some religious music, just in case. Elsabee Dippenaar announced that the new head of Health and Gender on the Municipal Council would address them on 'Talking to Each Other'.

Mimi de Bruyn arrived, very nervous; the mayoral Ford she shared with Mr Williamson had been taken by Mr Moosah who was addressing the Structures on 'Marxism: The Next Thousand Years' in the Masonic Hall over in Zwingli. Mimi had wanted to walk to the hotel, but the mayor felt it would give the wrong impression and so they used the Trans-Karoo Taxi Service, in fact a battered Nissan Centra and she protested at the fare: 'Five rands — for two blocks? That's robbery!'

'Normal activist fare,' said the young surly driver, who wore a Harlem Globetrotters T-shirt and mirror shades. 'Support the struggle, comrade!'

'But you're a taxi driver now, not an activist,' she said.

He shook his head: 'I'm an activist who's been redeployed in the business sector.'

Elsabee Dippenaar, speaking from the karaoke platform, formally welcomed the deputy mayor and even though she'd called her nothing but 'Mimi' for years, now started calling her 'Miss de Bruyn', with a nod of surprised approval on the last syllable as if either she couldn't quite believe it herself, or she couldn't understand why she'd never thought of doing so before.

The women in her audience turned their faces downwards, fiddled with their fingers, and flushed deeply. They felt now, for the first time in their lives, that they were singled out, a threatened group, they were white women of the town and the tables had been turned because the others had the town now. It was very awkward, this. Ma Lamprecht could remember when Mimi de Bruyn was just a little booked-in child in sheepshead slippers. And Fluff Breda swore to herself she wasn't going to be talked down to. Ria Joubert reflected that just because you entered a donkey in the sweepstakes didn't make it a racehorse, did it?

But they were also aware that Elsabee Dippenaar, with her five farms and her Toyota Landcruiser and her fine herd of merinos, had a new way of speaking – 'a knack', she called it – when faced by people like Mimi. If the Queen of the Karoo had it, then they had all better acquire the knack. It was a great challenge. Speaking to people like Mimi was once easy as winking.

But now with the Change no one knew quite what to

say any longer so they stared, fascinated, at Elsabee who seemed to have worked it out:

'I'd like to thank the deputy mayor for making time in her busy schedule to come and talk to us about talking to each other, which is what we must do if we are to heal the wounds in our community.'

And still they thought: but this woman was nothing but a clerk until five minutes ago; and a deacon in her church, certainly – but that's the brown church. And some of us remember that she never even had a father or mother and that crazy old Betsy raised her; yet now, here she is with a 'busy schedule'. She's up there and we're down here to get our noses rubbed in it.

Mimi stared at her audience in mounting panic: women in hats; women she'd grown up alongside, known all her life as pale white girls, seen but never spoken to; women she was once afraid of and who were now afraid of her. After saying in a trembling voice how happy she was to be there, she simply froze. It was awful to think they suddenly feared – worse, hated her, where once they'd never even noticed her. She had always been there but she hadn't mattered. Now she was important, more important than any of them had ever been. There was, in the fumbling fingers in their laps and their eyes fixed on the floor, a bitter reproach.

Mimi understood. She looked at herself standing up to speak and heard herself ask, like them: 'Who does she think she is?' And wanted to shout to them: don't you know? It's me!

Flawlessly, smoothly, as if he'd not been listening to what she had been saying but only waiting for her to stop, Pascal Le Gros was welcoming them to the Hunter's Arms, urging them to Pull Together, take the God-Given

Chance to become Rainbow People in the New Lutherburg.

The fact that Mimi had said no more than five words was not held against her. On the contrary. Her audience was relieved and even grateful, already the speech was taking a glow of kindness. For it was perfectly well understood that everything was now very different, that no one was any more what she had been. But Mimi hadn't gone and rubbed their noses in it. They pressed her hand and said: 'Well spoken, Miss de Bruyn!' and surprised themselves at how natural it sounded to call her that. Perhaps they were getting the knack?

Then Dominee Greet said a prayer – even though he'd warned often enough he wasn't having brown folks in his church, Change or no Change: didn't they have their own church? – even if he prayed with long teeth, nonetheless he prayed for God's blessing. Then Mike played 'Just a Closer Walk with Thee' from his Elvis Gospel Collection; and though nothing was said, people felt the spirit of the times was settling on Lutherburg.

CHAPTER FOUR

1950

In her cottage at the far end of what, until just the week before, had been Marlborough Street, Aunt Betsy was making soap. She was busy scouring with river sand her heavy iron 'roaster', a blackened cauldron, scrubbing away until its grey throat gleamed. A fire pulsed in the waist-high hearth. Chunks of sheepsfat with the texture of oily carpet felt and powdery ashbush and caustic soda stood ready.

She rested a minute at the old stinkwood kitchen table to catch her breath. Settled her aching muscles into the chair whose seat was made of interlaced *riempies*, strips of leather that creaked comfortably beneath her weight; she'd shot and skinned the kudu and sliced the thongs for this chair with her own hands. Everything in her life, her house had been more or less the product of her hands. She kept no servants, she asked no favours. Neighbours stepped off the sidewalk when Aunt Betsy went by in her black boots and her broad shoulders strapped into black bombazine or dimity.

A witch, some said, with her water-divining and pill-pushing and her frank belief that the leader of her Party, Dr Malan, the Good Doctor, was the messenger of God.

A bitch, insisted Barnabas Basson, her neighbour.

Now she coupled the cauldron to the chimney chains and swung it into position over the fire. What once she'd found easy now took all her strength. And that was why she'd decided, at last, to take those steps which everyone, her brother Arnaldus in particular, had been urging for years. Time she got some help around the house.

She mopped her red face on her crimson apron. A surprising snatch of colour in that dark kitchen, painted in two shades of vegetable green. Two walls were spinach, the others lettuce. The greens had started from the same gallon then ran out two walls into the second coat, and time and her kitchen fire had made the difference.

She'd painted those walls ten years before, while war was raging overseas between the Germans and the English. And it seemed very likely that the Germans would win. Aunt Betsy, alone in her cottage at the end of Marlborough Street, across the fields from the brown folks' graveyard, caught the excitement. A celebration was called for. And so she had a mind to redecorate her kitchen. The old thick cream paint that covered her walls and ceiling had turned toffee-coloured over the years and was flaking in patches like an Englishman with a bad case of sunburn.

But with the coming of war, there was no question of buying new paint from Levine's General Dealers over on Empire Road. Or Joffe Brothers and Sons. Aunt Betsy was for the Party of the People. And the Party, urged to remember its duty by its leader, the Good Doctor, called on patriots to boycott shops run by English or Jews, or non-patriots.

In a place as remote as Buckingham, lost on an enormous lunar plain of stunted shrubs and small rocky hills freckled with chunky sunsplit rocks, where it took a week to reach town by wagon from some outlying sheepfarms, a boycott of shopkeepers was not easy. But this was a holy struggle. Neighbours lent each other sugar and salt and a volunteer took the bus once a fortnight – hours on the dusty roads through the gorges and mountains and into the big town of Beaufort West where there were stores run by one's own kind – and stocked up on soap and salt, needles, flour and bullets.

However, from time to time a pedlar in his little donkey-cart trotted down Marlborough Street, his canvas sail creamy with the dust of the country roads, after weeks touring distant farms and settlements, and the neighbouring towns of Eros and Compensation, Pumpkinville and Scorpion Point. A little man with ginger whiskers and the sharp face of the meerkat, strong shoulders and short legs; a gaberdine jacket and a blue sailor's cap, greasy and ringed with sweat. He didn't have a name. He was the smous. Never got any older. Just shorter and his eyes brighter.

From the smous a patriot might buy without letting down the side. The pedlar had been just a boy when he had landed at the Cape of Good Hope some time towards the end of the last century. Somehow he'd got himself a cart and donkey, headed up country, hawking lead and needles to the remote Boers of the Karoo.

True, the hawker was Jewish; but not 'normal Jewish', like the Levines who had General Dealers. Better still, he wasn't English. Where he came from no one could say. South America maybe. Most thought the smous was 'Peruvian'. It didn't really matter; he spoke the taal, like a proper man; knew the country roads; sheep-dipping, wool prices and foot-rot. The long flat landscape seemed to expand sideways as it ran towards the Snow Mountains, shimmering under huge bright skies. But the pedlar could tell each bush and stone, each tenant farmer, trekker, poor-white squatter in the vast, lonely district, better than anyone but shepherds and wandering shearers.

The smous urged his ghostly dusty donkey down Marlborough Street, followed always by a cloud of children, buzzing like flies, and chanting, 'Slowcoach, slowcoach – here comes the cock-a-roach!' For he sold something for everyone. Even if no one had a whole penny to spend. A farthing bought two big nigger balls which, pouched for hours in bulging cheeks, changed colour a dozen times. For those without even a farthing, you could sniff for free. His cart reeked of peppermint oil, black shag tobacco, biltong, sugar and snuff and the little pink sugar lozenges beloved in those parts by old and young because they lingered on the tongue and cost so little and smelt so sweetly they were called 'ladies' breath'. Also fans of shining needles; bales of calico, dimity, flannel, cotton. Satins in colours it was wicked merely to contemplate; coolie pink and electric blue.

People loved to watch Aunt Betsy haggling with the smous. Only person in town to take something off him for nothing. Or the price of a bullet or two. The pedlar fancied himself with a rifle; always boasting about how he could knock down a brace of Egyptian geese with his eyes shut or take a springbok at full tilt. One sweet head shot, the smous would mimic with thumb and forefinger, and he had biltong for a month. He'd never been sharper. No, sir! Never in his life. And anyone who thought different was welcome to try him.

Aunt Betsy would nod and chew on her rather hairy

upper lip, then she would fetch her rifle and they would shoot canaries out of the mouth of old Isaac the Lame. Old man, skinny, wrinkled, half blind. Close on a hundred, it was said, and you could still see how the slave-shackles he'd worn as a child had bent his left leg like a pipe cleaner.

Like most things, the news that farmers were ordered by the British to free their slaves reached Buckingham decades late and took a while before it got enforced. People didn't hear, didn't care, and when they were made to hear, they took their sweet time about obeying. That was Buckingham for you. Deader than the dinosaurs that once ran around the veld there. And trickier than the bloody Bushmen who owned that part of the world till they got shot out. Buckingham, forever seeing its arse, they said over in Zwingli and Eros.

Took years to be enforced, actually. When Isaac's shackles were removed, it was ten years too late for his leg.

Anyway, he had advantages. Being half blind, he didn't flinch when the lead flew. Aunt Betsy stood him up against the thick whitewashed wall of the old jail as they reckoned his dark profile gave a better sighting on the canaries in his mouth: hollow tin tweeters you filled with water and whistled through, high and sweet. Six for a half-penny, in red or green. Old Isaac would water up, stick the whistle between his lips, turn sideways and give a bubbly trill. Then the game started.

First the smous would lift his rifle to his shoulder and pot the canary. A slug tore its head off and Isaac seemed like a statue, spouting water. Aunt Betsy next. Sudden death, loser paid forfeit. The Peruvian was good. But Aunt Betsy was cool, easy, lethal. Didn't fire so much as let loose the round, breathed it on its way. Nineteen straight canaries was the record. By the end of a session their slugs had scooped a crater from the fat mud wall, deep as a soup plate, just in front of Isaac's nose. If ever she lost Aunt Betsy generally paid forfeit in her best watermelon preserve and fatcakes. But mostly it was the smous who dished out – he paid with sherbet all round; or he handed out liquorice pipes, very stale and lovely after weeks in the sun. Sprinkled on their bowls, to resemble glowing shreds of tobacco, were fiery-pink sugary hundreds-and-thousands.

Some folks were not too happy about allowing the only black man in town to mark target. If word got round the district, who was to say you wouldn't get a flood of kaffirs in Buckingham looking for cushy jobs? No blacks here, they said. Bad enough dealing with the useless brown folks already crowding out the place.

Aunt Betsy pointed out that Isaac earned no cash; he got given only the canary the loser missed. And after some thought people reckoned this was probably fair enough.

So it was that when Aunt Betsy had a mind to redecorate her kitchen, the smous offered two half-gallon cans of premier paint, sea green, lead-based, for just half a crown. But she just fixed him with her pale blue eyes and let him see that she wasn't being jewed, not on a Monday, not on a Sunday. A florin for both. Or no deal. The pedlar had the meerkat's way of standing bolt upright on his heels and scouring your face as if it were an horizon.

He took the deal and then showed her his tomato red cotton. Even though Aunt Betsy shrank from its rich, flagrant rawness, a million miles from her life and habits, a red that recalled Satan and his pomps, and the blushes of ruined girls, yet she could not resist. Something of the war fever got into her and she shelled out a full sixpence for a bolt of the red worth not more than twopence, tops, from which she sewed a pair of crimson curtains for the front room and her apron, and sat proudly in her new green kitchen to celebrate the satisfactions of war and the coming victory over the English for which most decent folk hoped in their hearts.

The kitchen fire glowed nice and steady on its waist-high platform of brick within the blackened chimney breast. Aunt Betsy fed in more fat and swung the heavy round roaster on its metal hook back into the heart of the blaze. She felt the strain now.

Her brother Arnaldus had been urging her to modern-ize the primitive arrangements of her cottage – mud walls daubed with lime-green wash, rusting tin roof, reed ceiling and goat-dung kitchen floor where brother and sister were born before the fire.

'Brick up that hole in the bedroom wall for heaven's sake, Sus!'

He meant the alcove carved into the wall where, behind apricot curtains, she still slept in the closet-bed in which their parents died of the great flu of 1918. Why still cook on the kitchen hearth like a trekker? This was 1950? Get a servant. A stove.

'If it serves, it stays,' she said.

She went on chopping her own firewood under the pear tree, stored it in the woodshed beside the lavatory, behind a screen of cacti. She shot for the pot. Used her old .243, the local sprinkbok rifle. She had a better repertoire of headshots than anyone around, except maybe the smous, dropping her quarry sweetly, with an unspoiled hide. She salted and hung her own biltong and no man in Buckingham said a word against it, though none would have dreamed of allowing their wives in the veld.

And when at the end of the day the hunters pulled out their peach brandy and gathered around the fire, Aunt Betsy sat down too, though she never touched the hard stuff, sipping coffee, fiendishly strong, sweetened with three spoons of condensed milk.

And when, one night, as it is reported, Barnabas Basson, known as 'Bananas' for the curious mottling of his cheeks, well into his brandy, rested his hand in a friendly fashion on her knee as she sat sipping coffee by the fire, she damaged him so badly he had never forgiven or forgotten.

In the beginning, around '40, '41, the war had been going so well. Then, all of a sudden, they heard that the Germans were losing. And the local English in town became quite insufferable and it seemed that God's people were destined for yet more decades of damn Anglican rule. She had heard that Germans killed Jews, and did not believe it. Concentration camps, Aunt Betsy knew, were an invention of the English, designed for the extermination of the Boers.

Stirring her cauldron, Aunt Betsy saw to her pleasure how the liquid turned thick and full. A good soap needed will, patience and muscle. Praise the Lord! The English might have won the war, just as they had won the war against the Boers. But in victory, the English did not thicken up sufficiently, were unwilled and came to naught and God was not mocked. They had lost the peace.

Just three years after the war ended, the English of Buckingham who'd thought themselves so la-di-da lost the election, were out on their necks and the people chose their own government for the first time ever led by the Good Doctor. Free at last!

The Good Doctor's famous Victory of '48 was no more than two years old and yet the changes for the better were already to be seen. All her life she had lived in Marlborough Street. She lived now in Voortrekker Street, having arrived, at the age of sixty, at an address which united her with her ancestors. The people ruled now and the new policy was to favour the indigenous: the new municipality had a new slogan: 'We name our own!'

And soon, if the talk was true, Buckingham itself would wear a new name more suited to modern times. Buckingham, a town much mocked for the stubborness of its inhabitants – 'six streets under a hill and six hundred knuckleheads under the influence' – was now pushing its luck, but *seriously*, said smart alecs in Zwingli and Eros. Fancy changing the names of your streets. Jumping on the bandwagon, seizing on the Change, just to show you were better than everybody else in a hundred miles. Absolutely blooming well *typical!*

They could say what they liked: Marlborough was no more. George Street, upon which stood the Hunter's Arms, the old synagogue and the Anglican church, was George no longer, and had become Leibrandt, named for a freedom fighter in the struggle against imperialism, a man who just like Buckingham's own John Joubert had blown up bridges in the war.

Swinging the pot out of the chimney she set about skimming the excess fat from the surface of the oily sludge with a wooden ladle. Then carefully tipping the cauldron on its stout chain, she began decanting blue-veined, glistening liquid into six of her second-best baking tins waiting on the table, each snugly lined with hessian. In these long deep containers she cooked jaw-breaker toffee specialities for missionary mornings and church fetes, and her fly cemetery with its fine sheets of pale pastry between which slept the little black currants.

Here was the crucial time. The aromas – ash, acid, fat and sacking – blended, strong but not unpleasant. The soap must now cool but not become too cold. It must be ripe, like a cheese. Ready for the knife. It took a practised eye. When it had achieved the consistency of butter she would take the big black butchery knife, sharpened on the whetstone behind the kitchen door, and with a wristy delicate surgery divide the slab of soap lengthways into six long sections.

While she waited for her soap to ripen she went to her bedroom and dressed in black skirt and white blouse and little jacket made of black crêpe. She opened the red curtains and sunlight fell on the photograph of the Good Doctor doffing his dark hat. She'd drawn her curtains while busy with her soap; as if it were the fruit of some secret recipe. In fact, soap she made each month and she owned a good supply. But this soap was different; it had been commissioned.

Across the road stood an empty field and in the distance the skinny wooden crosses and stone memorials of the Coloured graveyard. Until the Good Doctor came to power, white and brown folks tended to be buried in a single graveyard, down beyond the cypresses that marked the town border, with a good line between them as was only proper. But the new Dominee said it had to stop, and the new town council moved the brown cemetery to a strip of land right across the road from Aunt Betsy's.

Arnaldus was forever twitting her: 'But Betsy, man! How can you live facing a graveyard?'

The dead were never troublesome; they did not interrupt the view, which stretched for twenty miles or more to the shimmering Snow Mountains in the south. Sometimes, briefly, on Sundays during the war, a lot of Coloured boys came home to be buried and the graveyard was crowded with weeping families and brother soldiers raising flags, firing salutes and bugle-playing, all of which she could have done without. Aunt Betsy felt sorry for the mothers of these fallen soldiers, but she had to say that brown boys fighting in an Englishman's war made even less sense than good Boer boys dying for the King.

All that stopped when the war finished and things got normal and quiet and slow again. In 1945, like switching off the wireless, the bands and the music went away. Just a distant little group sometimes showed up nowadays, outlines knife-sharp against the enormous sky, following a coffin on the back of a wagon. And there was rhythm to those burials, something almost reliable, like the wheeling, rusty blades of the iron windmill in her backyard, each turn of which pushed a gout of water with a choked little splutter into her oval stone reservoir beside the pear tree. Across the road now, this morning, nothing passed or moved. The heat haze shook the wire fence and her only observers were half a dozen wild-headed tumbleweeds which had flung themselves into the fence and stuck there like white-faced spectators.

*

An hour later, Aunt Betsy pinned to her dispensary door a notice written in indelible pencil: NO VISITORS TODAY.

Carrying her stones of soap wrapped in sacking in a wicker basket, covered with a tea towel of the Union Buildings, she set off down the sidewalk of baked earth, stepping around the trunk of Nephew's willow, shaggy and dark and huge in the centre of the pavement and from whose heavy canopy of trailing branches there came no sound this morning.

Looking neither right nor left she marched down Voortrekker, passing in turn Levine's General Dealers; Williamson the blacksmith; Joffe Brothers and Sons, Chandlers & Feed Merchants; Karoo Choice Butchery and Mesdames Hair Salon – none of which places she patronized, preferring the new all-Afrikaans Co-op established by the new government for the new Dispensation.

She quickened her step passing the synagogue. An old habit. The dangers of the world, said the pastor, were symmetrical. Thus the house of the Jews stood opposite Satan's kiosk and the home of strong drink. Aunt Betsy thought the dominee sentimental. It was not symmetry – it was biology, justice. These *Joode* were fading fast, like the English before them, because their time was up.

Down on their knees a group of maids with fat tins of Cobra polish were buffing to a gleam the broad red stoep of the Hunter's Arms Hotel. The hotel shone, it beckoned like a fancy tin of jujubes, brash as lucky packets lolling in Sampie's Café window, wicked as pedlar's trinkets; it might be Gehenna – but how it enticed!

The synagogue, by contrast, with its wooden walls and corrugated iron roof, always in the past so richly kept, looked scuffed and bruised. Maintenance was hard in

Buckingham, and costly. The winds screeched across the rocky, barren, baking hillsides and slammed into the town, autumn and spring; the heat blistered paint and the winter cold cracked pipes; and all the time the fine dust of the desert choked every opening. The Jews of Buckingham were always calling theirs the largest temple this side of Calvinia, and they looked after it lovingly. But it needed a lick of paint and its face was split by the sun, putty was falling from window frames, the tin roof lifting.

As a girl, her mother was always warning her never to pass the synagogue on a Saturday when the Jews were inside. Children had been known to vanish into that wood and tin temple and never reappear.

Now it was the Jews of Buckingham who were vanishing. Betsy could remember, before the war, crowds of worshippers on the pavement outside the synagogue on Saturday mornings. Those who gathered outside now were no more than a dozen: the Levine family, six in all; and the three Joffe Brothers, minus sons. Israelsohn the lawyer came, plus the occasional prospector from over Nickleton way; and once in a blue moon, the little smous might join them, if he happened to be passing through. The feed merchants Dr Sam and Issie Joffe were still trading. But the sons, to whom their trading notice so proudly referred, had gone. Sam's boys heading out for the Kimberley diamond fields or the goldmines of Johannesburg. Issie's only son, Bennie, lay in a grave in the Western Desert.

Aunt Betsy passed the new Volksbank, a recent addition, a bulky arrangement of modern orange brick, managed by one Hoopoe Laurens. Red nose and curly brown hair, he made a speech when the bank was opened with a prayer by the pastor, Dominee Havenga, the first

49

true pastor since the English occupation. Until then they had to share one with Eros and Zwingli. For decades, declared Hoopoe Laurens, it had been the Jews, the English and the foreign mine-owners who squeezed the lifeblood out of the poor. The Volksbank was the people's bank, designed to make capital available to struggling farmers and their tenants and to redirect the resources of the state towards the dispossessed.

When Hoopoe said 'dispossessed' his voice rose sharply, like the cry of the bird which gave him his nickname, and several tenant farmers, too dumb to know that Hoopoe was the man to save them, laughed. But decent people soon shut them up.

Next door was Karoo Choice Butchery with its sheep carcasses twisting on steel hooks in the window, glowing like rich scarlet candles larded with waxen fat. Behind Karoo Choice, a young butcher, 'Bokkie' Bok, had built a new abattoir and freezing facility with a loan from the people's bank. This was regarded as a masterly move because right next door, the last in the line of buildings on Leibrandt, was the small, grey-stone Anglican Church of St Augustine, where the English worshipped.

They weren't too happy these days. Oh, they'd been pretty on top of things when the war finished and their side won and they'd rubbed people's noses in it. But that soon passed. Come 1948 and the boot was on the other foot, Good Doctor Malan and the people's party ruled in democratic fashion, and the fancy rednecks spilling out of their oh-so-English parish church, built with his own hands by a bishop, adorned by the only green lawn in Buckingham, watered from their private borehole and planted with beds of pansies, delphiniums and roses, once so used to having everything their own way, now stepped out of church and walked almost slap-bang into Bokkie's new abattoir.

Although no slaughtering took place on Sundays, last week's blood and offal and dung was in the air and declared, fair and square, that things were changing. 'Phew, what a pong!' churchgoers sometimes said. It was the height of their rebellion. Some Anglicans, like Bill Harding, tried to pretend differently; they went on talking about Marlborough Street and George Street and told themselves that this new government could not possibly last and our chaps would knock their chaps for a six just like Monty did to old Rommel in the Desert War, up north in Egypt.

Aunt Betsy turned right now and walked along Silver Street which no one had bothered to rename perhaps because it had never possessed a street sign. It led towards a patch of small whitewashed cottages, each marked by its sturdy fat-bellied bread-oven chimney, some with sky blue doors, some with gables, many with a single window often broken, stuffed with rags against winter winds and summer dust knifing across the plain. Carved into the red earth, alongside the street, stopped with slabs of shale to make primitive sluice gates, were irrigation canals which were fed, not from the town reservoir up on Ghost Hill, but from a hidden spring over which a well was built beneath a conical stone roof like a Chinese hat. Traditionally in Buckingham, water was twice a day flushed along these roadside canals into small fields where the people of Silver Street cultivated maize, beans and green vegetables.

Aunt Betsy surveyed the scene and decided that two things made this neighbourhood different to any other: the medley of activity and shameless exposure. She repeated the word to herself. An unseemly, messy, barbarous medley which should not occur in a town, whitewashed and still, clean and proper, lying like stones a child has tired of playing houses with and thrown away upon a vast lunar plain, high and cold, stretching away as far as the eye could see.

In Silver Street nothing was still or private. Everything was on show. It was all rumpus and dirt. Crumbling cottages and yellow barrel-ribbed curs, foraging pigs, a traffic of goats and mangy sheep wandering without supervision or purpose, trampling through dusty gardens, reeking backyards, vegetable patches – and everywhere barefoot, darting children, as ignorant as the goats of fences, boundaries, decent concealments.

Her lips thinned to see among the old men taking the sun on rickety bentwood chairs a few who had once been proper Europeans! It did no good for them to raise their hats. 'You can't fool me!' said Aunt Betsy. They were the dregs of poor-white life – bankrupts, squatters, derelicts, drunkards – but also victims of the previous regime. Discarded people. Casualties of the long war which began with the wholesale slaughter of women and children in English concentration camps, the torching of farms, the cutting off of the mother tongue; and ended in the final humiliation – loss of identity in the termite heap of Silver Street.

Well, the days of denial and derision were over. Aunt Betsy's fist clenched in her pocket. Free at last! The Good Doctor had arisen. The Lord be praised.

She found what she was looking for at the last cottage in Silver Street. In the doorway a woman with a bloated face and very small eyes waited, resting her hands on the shoulders of a girl of about six.

Aunt Betsy strode briskly up the path, stepping over two bantam hens pecking grimly at a mess of cabbage leaves. To her left was a small dusty peach tree; and against the fence a lean-to of sacking and tin which she took to be a henhouse or goat pen. The woman gave off wine fumes like a stove; the eyes she fixed on the basket were swollen. The child wouldn't look at the white woman. She was wearing a stained gingham frock and rudimentary slippers fashioned from the scalps of sheep, pulled inside on, still showing the indentations of nostrils and eyes.

Aunt Betsy lifted the tea towel: the drunken woman blinked, nodded and they moved indoors.

When they emerged minutes later, the woman held the basket and Aunt Betsy had the girl by the hand but she appeared unwilling to walk and began crying.

Suddenly, a furious barking began and out of the sagging lean-to beside the fence crawled a round dark woman in a white headscarf, who was baring her teeth and growling. The child cried all the louder and the dog-woman roared back; so realistic were the gruff yaps and snarls that Aunt Betsy feared she might be attacked. But after the salvo of growls, the creature sank back on her haunches.

'Back! You rubbish!' screamed the drunk woman.

'Where are you, My Eyes?' the dog woman called to the peach tree.

And Aunt Betsy suddenly realized she could not see.

The child still wept, but silently now, because the woman who said she was her mother had picked up a stick and was advancing on the creature who was groaning to herself: 'What will happen to me? What can I see without My Eyes?'

Tightening her grip on Aunt Betsy's hand the girl tugged at her, pulling hard, perhaps hoping to prevent the beating she feared was coming to the dog-woman whose despairing barks floated after them. And it seemed to work because behind them there was silence now; though neither looked back.

Down Silver Street and into Leibrandt, without a word, Aunt Betsy's long strides and the steady beat of her boots on the baked earth pavement intercut by the hasty clip-clop of the sheepshead shoes. The child was frantic and yet utterly quiet until they were passing under a dense and tangled willow in Voortrekker Street and the air above their heads exploded: a flash of yellow, a glimpse of beard, a belly of some size, a pair of veldskoen shoes falling to earth and the girl screamed and clutched Aunt Betsy's skirts.

'Shush your mouth. It's only Nephew!' She patted the terrified child awkwardly on the nape of her neck.

Out of the tangled branches had sprung a ragged man with blond whiskers, yellow bandanna at his throat and old Boer skin pants, the sort you clapped closed and fastened in a knot.

'Where's Auntie off to?'

The girl risked a quick peep at the blond giant who'd jumped out of the tree. Nephew was what you called little boys whose names you'd forgotten. Here was the biggest small boy she'd ever seen. Aunt Betsy spoke to him as if he wasn't much more than a child.

'It's plain as the dirt on your face,' Aunt Betsy replied, 'where we're going. Home's where we're going.'

'Who's that?' The young man nodded at the girl, opening his pink lips and showing a line of strong yellow teeth.

'A child of the bush,' replied Aunt Betsy, 'previously boarded out on the farm of Barnabas Basson. Sent by a wine-soaked mother to skivvy for a family who starved and whipped her and sent her into the fields at night with her blind companion to scare jackals. A waif. A scrap. If she hadn't got away it would have been tickets.'

'What's she called?'

Aunt Betsy turned to the girl, frozen in her shadow. 'Well?'

The girl said nothing.

'We're not saying, at present,' said Aunt Betsy.

Nephew considered this. He always liked to be told, needed to know, made it his business to find out what was going on. People who approached Nephew's willow braced themselves for his descent. When he leapt from his perch amongst the branches they fed him a titbit of information here and there. Not as they might have given money to a beggar. Nephew was not that. But rather as you might pay a toll upon crossing a bridge. The sense of solidarity was so strong in Buckingham after the Change that it seemed more right than ever not to abandon Nephew. Now was the time to build the *Volk* and this tree-dwelling boy, whether one liked it or not, was part of the nation.

Nephew's parents had gone off one day, no one knew where. The boy grew up a stray on the streets and when he was about twelve he took to the willow on Voortrekker Street; sitting on a wooden platform he'd constructed, fifteen feet up, reached by a rope ladder. He'd grown into a burly teenager and was as mad as ever but, for all his affliction, he was one of them and in need of protection. Not a clown or a fool, as the old guard made out, not a typical addlehead. The English joked that the Boers produced in numbers, not a primitive, a lunatic, but a poor boy whose mother and father had discarded him, and who spent many hours each day among the willow branches and passed his nights in a shed in Bokkie the butcher's yard, a place of safety paid for by the Women's Church Federation.

Passers-by flung him his titbit and felt they had paid their toll. Nephew hit on another idea: someone must need to know what he learned from those who passed by his willow; so he told the police.

Often they could not see the point of his obsession. Nephew's questions were personal. He asked young men if they were walking out, women if they were in the family way. He saw it as his duty to challenge, in particular, any brown shearer or traveller who passed beneath his willow.

'Have you stolen meat? Or firewood? Whose tobacco are you smoking? Don't lie to me, you bloody Hotnot! Quick! Who do you work for and where are you going?'

He would make his victims turn out the money in their pockets, count it, examine their packs; warn that he had his eye on them and at the least sign of trouble he'd be down on them like a ton of bricks.

This sort of thing the police had no objection to if it kept him amused, but they could not see what good it did to pry into more intimate matters. What did it matter if someone was pregnant? Or which boss you worked for? Nephew said sternly they didn't know the half of what went on and you had to watch people like hawks.

'How much did Aunt Betsy give for it?' Nephew nodded to the girl.

Aunt Betsy told him to mind his own business.

Nephew examined the girl. She wasn't worth much, he

said. His father had once booked-in a young boy for a twist of tobacco.

Nephew's father had been a drunkard who abandoned the boy when he took off for the diamond fields. Nephew was forever boasting about the bargains his absent dad had struck and how, even now, he was panning for gold in Barberton and would soon be as rich as Barney Barnato and they'd live in a house with a toilet and a paraffin fridge and go to the seaside for their holidays. It was pathetic, but people in Buckingham shared Nephew's pain because everyone needed someone to believe in. That was precisely why they had elected the Good Doctor – to rearrange the unbearable and to give hope to the people.

Aunt Betsy considered the small, round, tight-lipped face, dark curls cropped close to her head, skin the palest of pale buttercup. Yes, closer to nine, she decided; she'd seen tiny urchins who were already in their teens.

Begin as you mean to go on, she told herself, and gave the girl the black soap cauldron to scrub, showing her how to scour it first with sand, telling her it would be ready when her own face peered back at her. Not before. When it was ready they would wash.

Later, she took her to the woodshed and showed her the large and the small axe and chopping block; the girl was to prepare kindling and light the fire each morning at dawn. Water was drawn from the stone reservoir in the backyard behind the pear tree, supplied by the windmill scraping and squeaking away in the field next door. A flight of stone steps led to the reservoir.

'If I go up the steps and I lean over to scoop the water, will the snake eat me?'

It was the first thing she had said. The child's voice was polite, interested, not particularly fearful.

'What snake, child?'

'The watersnake. There's always a snake living in the bottom of a waterhole.'

Aunt Betsy frowned and pulled her upper lip like she did before she went shooting against the smous, then she rubbed her nose with the back of her hand, and lastly she rubbed her fingers on the powdery stones of the reservoir wall. Eventually, she said that hers was a Christian house. What was more, all her life she had been in the business of finding water and never once come across a snake in a well or a reservoir. Just those that ran naturally around the place, and were common as dirt in any Karoo place come summertime: yellow cobra and puff adder. But snakes in the water? Certainly not. Not in this house.

At least the girl was talking. Aunt Betsy asked her name. But all she got was a long stare. She was sorry now she'd not asked the mother or whoever the woman was, back in Silver Street. But the woman could barely stand and stank of cheap wine. She had paid the agreed price and fled.

'What's your age?' Aunt Betsy held up her fingers and counted them. 'Seven? Eight?'

The girl studied her sheepshead slippers.

Aunt Betsy shrugged and went on with the education. Here was the privy. And she could see the wooden seat was too high to reach, so she placed a boulder as a stepping stone. Aunt Betsy changed her mind, again. Maybe she was not yet nine. Eight years might be closer. A slow eight.

Back in the kitchen she boiled water, filled an enamel

basin, stripped off the filthy gingham dress and tossed it into the fire. She was appalled to find the girl wore no undergarments. She had laid in a few things in preparation but no underwear. Now what must she do? She handed the girl a piece of blue cold-water soap and told her to scrub herself, which she did, keeping her large eyes on Aunt Betsy's face, and the suds ran over her ribcage like cream.

Aunt Betsy sat at her treadle machine and sewed a pair of underpants from a flour sack – Miller's No. 9 Grade A, stamped in blue – and showed the child how to tie them at her waist with brown butcher's twine. She dressed her in a blue pinafore, ordered in readiness from the People's Co-op in Beaufort West. She instructed her not to go about in her hideous sheepshead slippers. With her own hands she prepared supper; bread, buttermilk and a slice of ham and a handful of dried apricots.

She demonstrated how she wished coffee prepared in the morning; how the beans were to be milled in the old mincer clamped to the table edge and the grounds sprinkled on the muslin sieve stretched across the mouth of the coffee jug. She would sleep in the window seat by the fire. At dawn she would return her blankets to the old stinkwood chest beneath the kitchen table and then revive the fire. To all these directions the booked-in child answered not a word. Aunt Betsy took away the paraffin lamp and left her staring at the fire, and went to bed, hoping she had not been rash.

She was woken by reverberations reaching into her cupboard bed, through the heavy taffeta curtain. Aunt Betsy lay there feeling she was inside a music box that grinds out a grating tune. She identified sobs and chokings which spilled into the cold air and shook the mud walls.

Aunt Betsy let the grief run on a while, then suddenly she pounced, calling out sharply in the darkness: 'Who's there?'

The weeper choked on the question, and shut herself down, stage by stage, to a hiccuping, snuffling, breathy silence. For a moment Aunt Betsy thought her gamble lost. Then from the other side of the kitchen wall, borne on a sob turned hiccup yet carrying also a hint of outraged surprise, the voice said clearly: 'It's – me!'

Aunt Betsy nodded, satisfied. 'Very well, Me,' she ordered, 'now go to sleep.'

CHAPTER FIVE

1994

Everyone in Lutherburg knew the world had changed –
even if they didn't yet know what it meant when they
saw the sign on the road into town: WELCOME TO
BUCKINGHAM.

Elsabee Dippenaar protested to Little Boy Williamson.
She was being robbed of her history. Lutherburg was a
name dear to the hearts of the people, a holy name.

'Why change?'

'Why not?' said Mayor Williamson. 'You people did it
all the time.'

'That's different.' Elsabee's pretty face flushed with
anger.

'We're not changing the name, really and truly.' The
mayor was enjoying himself. 'We're just going back to
the old one. The real one.'

And that was the trouble: one side hating it, and the
other side lapping it up. The brown town dancing in the
street and marching and calling out Viva Democracy!
and telling each other that the future had arrived and
everyone would be living in big houses with a Mercedes
outside the gate; while the white town walked about and
muttered, wept in the street like Baby Vermaak – very
confused and feeling a bit ill.

People asked: what was going on? Once, you had addressed problems in a clear, no-nonsense fashion. But now these problems put on fancy outfits, gave themselves big names, sat down uninvited in your front room and it hit you like a shotgun blast: Jissus! *They*'re not the problem any longer – *we*'re the problem now.

You looked at something; it stared back at you, apparently unchanged, but you knew that nothing would be the same again. It made people queasy; it wasn't anything you could put your finger on – it wasn't quite nausea and it wasn't vertigo; this was a time-born disease; a nasty attack of the futures.

And however much people said they didn't really mind that the old days were gone, in their hearts they yearned. They felt lost. In the old days identity derived from geography: to know who you were, you asked: where am I? An idiot could do it.

Over *here* was Lutherburg, the white town proper. Well, white by night, anyway, because brown guys came to work here by day. Clean, simple, straightforward, honest place. Khaki shorts and shaved hair and crimplene frocks and the police van patrolling, and nothing moving on Sundays but the tumbleweed. Six broad streets, straight as arrows. The church; the Co-op; the hotel; the bank; a little dorp resting peacefully under Spook Hill, on the flank of which was your town's name, spelt out in creamy painted stones for all the world to see.

Over *there*, beyond Spook Hill, lay Golden Meadow: the brown town, the Scheme, dusty wasteland, guitars, drunks, knifings, rapes, incest – hundreds of tiny tin-roofed brick houses, sandy streets and swarming kids. Had been like that for ever; or at least since the early

fifties when the brown folks were moved out of Silver
Street and real time, Lutherburg time, began.

Marking the border between Lutherburg proper and
the brown town was the police station; if ever you got
lost, you looked for its towering radio mast like a spear
stabbing the sky and you had your bearings. You were
here and they were there and you never went there from
here.

Different spaces; separate places. 'We know where we
are,' said the people of Lutherburg proper; they oiled
their rifles and went to church and were happy in the
comfort of distance, sweetness of borders, sanctity of
orders, and a world that ran on Lutherburg time.

As for moving with the times, forget it! There were
laws against that.

Then, suddenly, the world came off Lutherburg time.

What had been small symptoms, minor unease, name-
less dread, shivers in the night, whistling in the ears, now
grew into a full-blown epidemic, like the Spanish flu of
1918 that wiped out half the population. Lutherburgers
looked at the future and it made them shiver. It was
horribly familiar.

They remembered those dinosaur prints embedded in
rocks outside Levine's General Dealers; mute reminders
of the aeons when this part of the great Karoo, now a
vast sun-baked scrubby plain, had been a soggy inland
lake ruled by terrible carnivorous lizards.

There were also, in the smoky overhangs high in rocky
clefts in the hills, pictures of eland and the long-lost
black-maned lion and wild horse, chiselled into the rocks
by other vanished owners of these lands – the Bushmen.

There were in the bush tumbled gravestones of those

British invaders who made war against Dutch farmers, won Lutherburg for Queen Victoria and renamed it Buckingham. Poems on their headstones and stones on their breasts to keep the jackals away. Long, long forgotten.

Too many reminders. Too many extinctions. Now they felt themselves heading for prehistory. People asked themselves: 'So now what?' And they watched everybody else to find out if someone had a method of dealing with the Change. A lot of Lutherburgers felt like Baby Vermaak, who wept in the street before she came to terms with things. But you couldn't have the white town blubbing and Golden Meadow laughing. Besides, the guys over in Zwingli would say they were a lot of *moffies*.

Elsabee Dippenaar, otherwise known as the Queen of the Karoo, was defiant: 'I'm for change: so long as we maintain standards.' She gave that knowing smile of hers which in better times had sent people crazy at her arrogance and her monied sweetness but which they found consoling now – because it showed she was touched too. She owned a huge spread out on the Compromise Road – Cape Dutch mansion with four snowy gables; hundred thousand hectares of prime land, herds of prize merinos, plus other farms to spare: she was far too rich and too regal and too kind to worry about anything. Elsabee's way, and it had been very successful, was: if in doubt, build a farm school. At the drop of a hat, she supplied and paid for books and teachers and addressed her farm workers kindly but firmly on the need to stay off the booze and plan their families better.

But the new council in the new Buckingham scorned

her efforts; the new rulers were not nice, they were not grateful; they were barely polite; they issued Elsabee with this instruction: never mind the sermons, whose standards do you mean? Get your workers' kids into proper school in Buckingham, or else!

Elsabee freaked. First they changed the name of her town. Now this! Sweet smile faded fast. For someone who'd never said more than 'Gosh' and 'Oh, Heavens above!' to start shouting: 'Fuck you, *meneer!*' at the new mayor was quite an eye-opener.

But the mayor laughed and said: 'Hey, now we're talking!'

If the Change made Elsabee Dippenaar talkative, for his part Dr du Plessis was struck dumb. How did you talk to these people? After forty years as district surgeon, this relaxed, even arrogant man, who never fussed about anything or anyone very much, was speechless.

Dr du Plessis's speech impediment was specially frustrating because he needed to have a word with Saul, his gardener. But the reason he needed to speak to Saul was the very cause of his loss of voice. It seemed that Saul, plain simple Saul in his blue overall and his brown felt hat and his slow sucking on his ancient pipe, that same Saul who had worked in the doctor's garden for twenty years, in the old Lutherburg, was now health officer in the New Buckingham. It was a bloody marvel! He didn't know one end of a zinnia from the other. What did he know about health?

Worse was to come. It was said that Saul spent the mornings taking evidence from people who considered Dr du Plessis a lethal menace. Patients spoke of a lousy diagnostician, arbitrary with his drugs; they said he was lazy, cruel and neglectful. The crippled, the comatose,

CHRISTOPHER HOPE

the bleeding, even the dying had to be brought to his surgery, preferably between nine and noon. And even then the doc might not pitch until the patient had passed away.

There were rumours that the Health Committee were going to report him to the Medical Council.

The doc needed to put the record straight. This was a country practice, right? Win some, lose some. Budget no bigger than a flea's ear to stock his dispensary. So what did they expect – Harley Street? These things he wished to discuss with his gardener.

But what the hell to call him? Saul always addressed the doctor as *meneer*.

Now *that* was an idea! *Meneer* . . .

So he tried. He put his heart into it. He practised in front of his mirror. And in the mirror, it worked; but the moment he tried a *meneer* anywhere near his gardener the word died on his tongue.

He sat now on his stoep with its yellow shutters, watching Saul clipping the Virginia creeper; opened his lips, licked them, cleared his throat and . . . fear grabbed him – what if *meneer* sounded too servile? What if the neighbours heard him?

Perhaps it would be better to stick to Saul's surname?

Something like: 'Listen now, um – how's about we have a little chat?'

Fine – except he didn't know the man's surname. It seemed funny to think of him as anything but Saul, simple Saul.

Meanwhile the rumours multiplied and the doc grew terrified: he was to be sued for damages by relatives of the dead; he faced prosecution for gross negligence. One day he couldn't stand it any longer so he downed a couple of brandies, waved to Saul, secateurs flashing among the palm leaves, and pleasantly but firmly called: 'Oh – ah – *Mr* Saul . . .'

It should have been fine. A bloody good compromise. Exactly the right note. Respectful – but not obsequious. Formal but not fawning.

But the stupid old fool pricked up his ears at the 'Mister' and goggled around the garden trying to work out who the boss was talking to.

It made him want to weep. Forty years doctoring in Lutherburg and he got kicked in the teeth by his gardener.

Dominee Greet reacted to the Change in spectacular fashion. He had succeeded Dominee Havenga – and that was difficult. Havenga, the Hammer of the Heathen, had been more feared than typhoid in the district for his crusades against drink, tobacco, raffles, television, Sunday sport and loose women. Dominee Greet's individuality lay in his reverence for authority; the Church and the bible and the police. It made what he did all the more sensational.

On that extraordinary Sunday morning, up in the pulpit with its white leatherette trim, as he was reading to his congregation the bit in the Psalms about those who become a portion for foxes – usually his cue to start praying for any farmers suffering from jackal raids on their lambs – the truth suddenly hit him like the wrath of God.

Baby Vermaak, watching horrified from the front pew, closed her eyes and began shrieking. 'Dominee, put your clothes on!'

It was too late. He had torn off his long black toga and flung it into the pews with the gesture of a footballer who has won a big match, and he stood there in his black braces shouting that Lutherburg was a harlot's house.

'I Tertius De Doorns Greet will lead my little flock into the high stony places to worship the Lord as He has commanded, without alien adulteration. Those who cannot take any more of this brown and white mixing must please follow me!'

Down the aisle he marched and out of the door with about thirty worshippers behind him, splitting Lutherburg, brother and sister and wife and husband, right down the middle.

He started up his own church, the Reformed Reformed, right there in St Augustine's, which hadn't opened its doors in years because its congregation had shrunk to just one member. Bill Harding was the last Anglican in Lutherburg. He was also the only member of the Anglican Council and in that capacity, he agreed to sell the building to the Reformed Reformers for a couple of thousand.

Dominee Greet then removed the stained glass windows of English saints and the portrait of St Augustine and the Boer War standards of defunct English regiments, and anything else that reminded him of the hated enemy, and opened his doors; he offered purity, racial separation and the preservation of the white man's sperm from black robbers: a belief the new Church shared with the British Israelites, over Nickleton way.

The Dutch Reformed Synod, in far away Cape Town, sent a young, bright new minister, Gerrie Niemand, to take over the real Church but the schism between Reformed and Reformed Reformed was too deep for repair; on Sunday mornings their choirs competed to see which could drown the other.

When Bill Harding saw the congregations that Greet pulled on a Sunday he reckoned the Anglicans had blown it.

'Those bastards never liked us. If I'd known the striptease padre was going to make it big, I'd have charged him double.'

So did the future infect and inflame people and send them mad.

Even those who said they really liked the new Buckingham and welcomed the future and rejoiced that we were all part of the rainbow nation and formed joint ventures with important brown partners and told the *Zwingli Advertiser* that anyone who didn't like the Change was white trash and should go and live in Australia – and Pascal Le Gros said all these things – yet even *he* had a bit of trouble.

His dream was a theme park with a difference: a unique safari park for a vanished people, a vast reserve where Bushmen tribes who had once roamed the region would reclaim their 'lost dignity' in a hunter-gatherer habitat.

'Themed in Khoi-San motifs to make a living eco-tapestry,' he wrote in his application for planning permission.

It was going to happen right outside town, in a joint venture with the mayor's brother, Baba Williamson – it would be new, it would be progressive; it would be a sensation!

But the new planning committee in the new Buckingham was giving him no end of uphill. What would he do to keep the little blokies off the booze? Would he employ locals on site? Would he make sure tourists didn't patronize the San? Was he the right man for the job – or should someone more 'indigenous' run the show?

Strangely enough, the one person in Lutherburg who should have been in serious trouble with the Change seemed fine. This was Gerald Wright, the ex-spy. No one would have known he was an ex-spy if Elsabee Dippenaar hadn't dug out those old pictures from Sunday papers. There he was, a bit fatter perhaps, with funny, long English hair at what looked like a *braaivleis* in some cramped damp London garden. A pleasant, pudgy bloke forking steak into his mouth and lifting a thumb to the camera. At the time he was masquerading as an exile, a fighter for freedom; fooled them every step of the way; blew holes in the enemy command abroad and returned in triumph as Captain Gerald Wright, secret agent. Later, he received a medal from the President.

Marie Smit, the first brown teller over at the Volks-bank, handled his business; she called him very refined and said he drew a pension from the government – which was now the government he had betrayed. It came through every month and was paid into his account.

People wondered: how long can that last?

People also wondered: refined? How would she know? Marie lived with her mother in a shack out on the Compromise road with rubbery springbok skins on the floors, and the only clock was a big plastic wristwatch with a butter-yellow dial hanging on the living-room wall and a toilet in the corner of the garden.

Then someone saw them walking together by the

dried-up dam outside town and he had his arm around her. What was his case? Nothing made sense. The world was moving too fast. Once they would have known what to do, now they hadn't a clue.

He seemed a refugee from another place. It was almost impossible to think of him as a great agent; he was too plump, too ordinary. He was seen at the gymkhana eating curry and rice; the mechanic, Errol, at Lutherburg Motors, reported he had trouble with the disc brakes of his Mazda. If Doc du Plessis had divulged he suffered from piles, it would hardly have been more banal.

As it happened, Doc du Plessis said: 'It's crazy having people you've hardly ever seen running the show, while real locals get kicked into touch.'

There was a good deal of sympathy over this. Take Mayor Williamson . . .

He claimed to be local. Ha! Local, my eye. That dark wavy hair, the white teeth, sallow complexion and funny wispy moustache. A dead give-away. He could claim to be pure brown until he was blue in the face; he belonged to Bombay not to Lutherburg. Professional trouble-maker. Run out of Zwingli, locked up in Springbok, he'd jumped on the political bandwagon. Thick as thieves, his lot, with the Communist Party and the Hands Off Cuba Committee.

And didn't Littleboy Williamson drink in the new karaoke bar in the Hunter's Arms with Gerald Wright? The very man who had once laboured to bring Williamson's comrades down on the bones of their arses! Yet he was happy as larry, boozing with the bigwigs of the new Buckingham.

'Honestly,' Bill Harding asked the bar, 'doesn't it make you want to honk?'

Pascal pursed his full lips in his craggy red beet face, two pink hoops poised above a little cherrystone chin hidden in the flesh of his jaw:

'I know nothing about politics. I'm just a simple entrepreneur. But I think we can do business with Gerald Wright.'

At first there was a lot of opposition to this idea. It was suicide to speak to Wright. The guys he'd betrayed were running the country now, for Chrissakes!

'If it's the difference between doing a deal and extinction, what then?'

Pascal lifted and dropped his great head; he glanced across the street; he closed his grey, slightly bloodshot eyes. 'Who wants to go like the Jews?'

Across the street stood the synagogue, wooden walls and wrought iron grilles, pretty arched windows and black corrugated-iron roof. Once the Jewish traders of Lutherburg had been big in leather and calico and pins and pickles. But then the Co-ops came to town, stuffed with government money. They rigged prices, throttled the competition and killed open business. The old shopkeepers dwindled and vanished to the goldfields or the diamond mines. The synagogue had closed in 1955; it was home now to a dusty collection of fossils, petrified wood and ferns in rock.

Pascal pressed his point.

'We need to talk to the other side. Tricky – but our friend seems to have cracked it. Friendly with the mayor; making a play for that girl in the bank.'

'Career move,' said Maureen.

'What's wrong with career moves? Don't knock them till you've tried. This whole town better make a career move. And fast! If some people can do it, people you never thought could ever, ever join the twentieth century before it ran out, then we can all change.'

'Excuse me,' said Maureen, 'but who?'

'Take our Bokkie the butcher,' said Pascal. 'He's adapting.'

'Don't be silly,' said Maureen. 'He's a crochety mean old man.'

In Karoo Cuts across the road, Bokkie Bok the butcher, forty years in the business, pencil-thin, monosyllabic, wearing an old blue sock on his right hand as a glove, spent his days serving bags of pre-packed frozen sausage, neck of lamb and liver from a huge, ancient Frigidaire to queues of threadbare customers. Mr Bok raised that blue hand and the customers stared at it like it was a policeman's truncheon or a traffic light. And the butcher told them what he thought of them.

'You should eat bloody vegetables, and lots of greens and rice and stuff you can afford. Look at you! *Bladdy* Hotnots! Not even a coat on your backs when the winter winds start, yet you must have meat. Always meat. Only meat. Are you surprised you're so bloody thin? It's a wonder more of you don't bloody starve to death.'

'Sheez, does he give those woodheads what bloody for!' said Mike the Spike.

'Do you know what it takes to change the habits of a lifetime?' Pascal demanded.

'Tell me,' said Maureen sweetly. 'As much as you know.'

'Since the Change, Bokkie's customers are running things.'

'They still starve, don't they?'

'Yes, but now he doesn't blame himself. Now he says: "Want a job? Go elect one. You're free!" Once, we were responsible – but now everyone's free to starve in their own way.'

'And that's better?'

'Look, it's not perfect. But it's a start. Right? Bokkie doesn't have to feel bad any more. It's the new honesty. That's going to be my approach to our friend . . .'

'If the new honesty is so wonderful, why's everyone poop-scared to say anything? So utterly confused, and pissed off?' Maureen demanded. 'And what makes you think James Bond will do anything for us?'

'Look, he wants to belong, doesn't he? Don't you, don't I?' said Pascal. 'You can see it in his moves so far. You can see it in his eyes. He wants friends. He wants to fix himself up in the world again. He's got to deal with Change. So he makes love to Marie; that squares him with the brown guys. But at heart, he's one of us. So if we're smart, we give him the chance of coming home. He's a natural go-between. And I'm going to have a chat to him, now-now.'

Not everyone was sure about this. Maureen rolled her eyes. But they remembered Pascal had relatives in Miami. He'd sold time-shares in Margate; he was, well, *modern*.

Above all, they remembered the Jews.

Mike got the general mood. 'If we don't do something, we're for the high jump. We're already on our knees. But they want us to roll over. Come the end of the cal. month, it's not payday no more; it's doomsday. Cheers, *totsiens* and goodbye.'

'I'm not being written off,' said Pascal. 'And I'm not rolling over. OK, *manne*?'

Mike the Spike spoke for everyone in the bar.

'No way, José.'

CHAPTER SIX

1954

People in Buckingham knew that things were really changing when a sign went up on the road into town: WELCOME TO LUTHERBURG.

The new mayor, Pompie Joost of the farm Brak Water, a man with rolls of neck red as beef under a dark brown felt hat, consulted his council and it consulted the Party and the Party consulted itself and decided, unanimously, to return to their town the name it had when Scots missionaries first settled in the district, fought off the Bushmen and brought religion to the wild high Karoo.

That the English, still smarting from their electoral defeat, should make a helluva song and dance was only to be expected. But Mayor Joost was appalled to learn of murmurings among the brown folk over in Golden Meadow.

It was the rank ingratitude that angered him. These people had spent their lives dead drunk or begging for handouts. Give them houses and water and a church hall and pensions and jobs and what did they do – bitch!

'Did anyone ask us how we felt when the English named our little town after the palace of their King?' demanded Mayor Joost of council members and, to a man, the members roared: 'No!'

In fact, Mayor Joost's men shouted 'No' twice. Once because Bill Harding was up before them to read out a petition signed by 'Concerned Citizens' and it was fun upsetting the English. And then they did it again just for the hell of it.

Saying no had always been important – Mayor Joost and his men said no to raffles and Sunday sport and street traders; no to black fellows and Asians and Catholics and communists and queers; no to liquor, lipstick, liberals, missionaries and fancy women.

But saying no to Bill Harding was not just a duty, it was a pleasure. Tall and dark, his airforce pilot's moustache grainy with sprinkled sand on his upper lip, his hair coaxed into an important quiff like frozen black milk, Bill claimed to be just as patriotic as anyone. Hardly convincing, though, was it? Most decent patriots had sat out the war, rooting for a German victory – and wasn't his own wife the daughter of a local hero? Elsa's dad, John Joubert, had blown up bridges all round Buckingham to sabotage the English war effort. Well, then, Harding should show a little sensitivity.

How much did he love his country? someone asked.

Bill said he supported the resettlement of brown folk; keeping the streets white by night; fighting communism and maintaining his country as a bastion of Western Christian civilization. Would that do?

'We're beginning to feel like second-class citizens.'

Someone muttered: 'About time too.'

He appealed for sympathy: 'English is under attack; when do you hear a word of it in the Co-op or the bank or the Council?'

They clapped.

Bill was getting mad. Bloody rockspiders! They could barely string three words together in their own language, never mind the King's English. He unfurled the petition:

'We, the undersigned, appeal to you: don't throw the baby out with the bathwater.'

For some reason the pseudonyms of the petitioners brought out the worst in his audience: 'Desert Rat' and 'Oscar bravo' and 'Fed-Up-to-the-Back-Teeth' had them in stitches. When he got to 'King and Country' it brought the house down; they whistled snatches of 'God Save the King'; they saluted. It was awful.

Then Mayor Joost thanked him for his petition and warned that in future there would be more order, more organization, more freedom. After years of oppression, the *volk* would govern. End of story.

'We'll protest,' Bill warned.

'Do it!' challenged Mayor Joost. 'We've got the guns.'

'Well, at least don't change the name of our town.'

'We're putting back the true name,' said Mayor Joost, 'stolen from us by you.'

'Just like you pinched council funds,' some heckler yelled to a storm of applause.

'What do you mean, *me?*' Bill yelled back. 'I've never ever been on the bloody council!'

'Well, OK. Not you personally, maybe,' Mayor Joost said, 'but somebody ran off with the moolah.'

When the Good Doctor stepped down as leader because his health was failing Aunt Betsy refused to believe it.

Me found her frozen in the passage outside her bedroom, staring up at the photo of the Good Doctor doffing his hat. With tears streaking her cheeks she asked Me: 'Does he look sick to you? He doesn't look too bad to me.'

So fierce was Aunt Betsy's denial of any leader but the Good Doctor that it took her neighbour's child, Baby Vermaak, named for her pink fresh cheeks, vivid in orange tutu and blue scarf, practising in her garden a dance-chant of welcome to the new leader to be performed by the children of Lutherburg School, to convince her that there was a new leader: Mr Strydom, Lion of the North. She reckoned kids don't lie and so it must be true.

She turned the Good Doctor's photograph to the wall, took to her bed and ate only pumpkin and celery for some time.

After a suitable period of mourning, Aunt Betsy went and inspected the portrait of the Lion of the North hanging in the new Municipality, a cool and whitewashed mansion of oaken beams under snug thatch, modelled on an old Cape Dutch homestead, with big shuttered windows and generous gables.

It had been given pride of place in the courtyard. A tray of glowing marigolds, below the portrait in its gilt frame, formed an altar so positioned that at noon a burst of sunlight fell fullsquare on a patch of wall where he was standing stiffly, arm on the back of a chair: looking more like an angry eagle than a lion, thought Aunt Betsy, with his high forehead and quiff of hair and clenched, angular jaw.

She flicked her fingers as if they had been scalded, murmured, 'Ay yai, yai!' – went home and lay down and called Me to rub her feet.

When Aunt Betsy's feet ached a deal after a long day's

march across rocky koppies prospecting for water, Me rubbed them with arnica oil; first her mistress must have her handsome buckskin boots pulled off so that she might prop herself up against the teak bedhead, her grey steel, pot-scourer curls reposing on the big feather bolster, directly below the old hand-painted psalm of 'The Lord is My Shepherd', in which blonde angels danced among the shepherds' crooks and the curlicues of ornamental letters went looping to and fro like lost lambs across green meadows below a shining city on the hill.

The child would sit on the bed opposite Aunt Betsy, brace her back against the baseboard and in her small brown hands take up a foot, huge and pink as a Christmas ham and, placing it carefully in her lap, rub in the yellow oil, beginning with each toe, moving to sole, arch, ankle and heel. In the beginning Betsy guided Me but soon she had only to nod approvingly, applauding the strength of the small fingers reaching for the tendons as they dug into the aching instep. 'Yes – that's right!' and she would crumble into sleep.

Me was about thirteen now, rounding out, pale apricot in complexion with dark lashes and a full mouth. While Aunt Betsy was definitely sixty-four, lithe as ever, her muscles very strong but going to sinew in upper arms and calf, her grey hair still thick. Except at night when she spread it on the bolster in a shower of steel rain, she wore it pulled into a small bun above her shirt collar. Her chin was a little more pointed, the hairs on her upper lip a little snowier.

So they slept, top to toe, and Me cradled the warm white foot, smelling of arnica, against her belly and in the morning she prepared coffee and neither referred to the night before, even though Me may well have turned in the night, crept closer to Aunt Betsy and rested her head on her small bosom just as, long ago when out in the sheep pen and the jackals prowled, she crept under the skirts of Blind Daisy and heard her ribbon of warning barks floating up to the moon.

And it was not unknown for Aunt Betsy as she lay sleeping to shift her hand on to Me's swelling breast, so smooth to touch, so heavy in the palm, and rest it there a moment, in pleasure or pride, who could say? For she felt both. Me had proved to be so excellent an investment and Aunt Betsy took as good care of her as she did of her gun, her horse or herself.

In the five years they had been together Aunt Betsy had grown to be very pleased with her deal. The girl proved quick in the dispensary where Aunt Betsy handed out medicines, and soon knew goitre may be treated with rooibos tea, and quinsy with milkweed.

Young Dr du Plessis, in the big house with the yellow shutters and the tin roof across the road from the Standard Bank, called her 'our Hottotot healer'.

'Only the walking wounded,' said Dr du Plessis, 'take Betsy's bush-quackery.'

'It's a wonder his patients can still walk by the time they get to me,' returned Aunt Betsy.

At the girl's first bleeding, Aunt Betsy showed her how to stuff a cotton pad between her thighs and secure the tapes in her pants with a double knot. When Me's breasts became so prominent they could no longer be ignored, Aunt Betsy rode the bus into Beaufort West and returned with two heavy brassières of khaki cloth. She scorned such frills herself and wore, strapped across her small breasts, only a length of cheesecloth knotted below her right armpit.

Since Me had walked away from Silver Street she had never been back. But some things did not change. On the first Friday night of each month the farmers came to town, in dog-carts, ox-wagons, tractors and new Dodges, wagon wheels spitting pebbles, steel treads mashing the fine red dust into a smooth powder, making a peculiar chalky squeal, as if the soil cried out. The farmers came to take Evening Communion with their wives in black bonnets and sleepy, barefoot children, well wrapped against the cold, shaven skulls sticking like tortoises' heads from their sheepskins.

Then the children of Golden Meadow swarmed like flying ants down Voortrekker Street, racing each other to swing open the big farm gates that still stood at the door of the town and never looked left or right. Watching from her seat on the green wooden bench behind the monkey flowers on Aunt Betsy's stoep, Me remembered the prizes to be won from the white Christians: watering the horses got you a half-penny, a pencil or a slice of bread, and – best of all – silver paper, still smelling wonderfully of the sugary smeary vanished chocolate but more precious than pennies because what she did was to take a glass marble or a ball-bearing and fold the silver paper around it in a rough envelope; then she popped the silver cocoon into an empty matchbox and rattled it gently for about half an hour. At the end of this time, if you had done the job right, you slid open the matchbox to find, shining within, like a slug or a small silver sausage, your walking ball which when balanced on your palm or your forearm turned head over heels with a lovely, lolloping stately tread, as if alive.

It was understood, since she came to live with Aunt Betsy, that she was not to join the other children. Never to run blindly into the street because, in these times of triumph and new prosperity, spanking Fords and big lorries – Lordy! sometimes as many as one a day – snorted down dusty Voortrekker Street where only a year before a single lorry in a week had been amazing.

Wool prices rocketed and by 1954 a pound of decent stuff was fetching close to one pound sterling. Farmers got fat, their limousines larger and more of them followed the example of Barnabas Basson, who built a townhouse of biscuit face-brick and steel window frames right across the road from Aunt Betsy's cottage and parked a new powder-blue Ford outside the garden gate, and painted a carport bright green, the colour of their new money, and spent whole days sitting on his stoep, or ringing around the neighbours to talk wool prices.

It was said that Arletta Basson had asked her husband if she might learn to drive and he'd said no: if she learnt to drive she might wish to go somewhere.

A little girl in a white pinafore, a blue ribbon in her shining hair, cleaned the windows. Aunt Betsy said the Bassons had got themselves a kitchen maid:

'Brought her in from the backyard, and taught her how to live in the house. Some people's so fancy these days they'll soon not be pissing unless someone holds the pot.'

The Bassons got a taste for town life. Soon they went to the farm only at weekends to check the foreman was sober, the workers awake and the sheep well.

Aunt Betsy's lip curled: 'Stoepfarmers.'

Me wondered why the Bassons should bring a girl out of the backyard into the house. 'I've always been in the house, haven't I?'

'Ah, but that's because you're not a kitchen maid.'

'What am I then?'

'You're a bargain.'

The smous came to town only every other month now, and his stock was a shadow of the treasure chest of old; no silks, cotton, brandy and needles. A few stale liquorice pipes; some watermelon conserve. No children followed the little donkey cart with the tarpaulin curtains down what had been Marlborough Street.

Increasingly the Co-op killed off business. Patriots shopped there. Dominee Havenga, Mayor Joost, attorney Haarhof set an example. Crimplene dresses in acid green and custard yellow, dungarees, dusty magazines and plastic flowers. And the smous and the storekeepers watched farmers, fattened on wool sales and government credit, pay twice the going price for second-rate bombazine and gingham and coffee. Old Mr Levine at the General Dealers had spent years hoping against hope that the Good Doctor's victory would be short-lived and he and all his kind would fry in hell. But the Doctor seemed to go from strength to strength.

When the Doctor stepped down at last, he was followed by someone far worse: the Lion of the North.

Old man Levine took to his bed and, after saying, 'Better the devil you know,' turned his face to the wall and pined away.

Mr Joffe was claimed by polio. *Polio-tics* some said it

was. Bill Harding relayed his last words: 'The shadows have fallen and will not lift in my lifetime.'

'Max Joffe knew a thing or two,' said Bill, still bitter about the petition. 'We're buggered with the Happies running the country.'

The old traders closed, one by one. Joffe Brothers & Sons went to a farmer who kept the name and sold windmill parts. Levine's General Dealers went to a councillor named van der Merwe, who kept the name and sold bridles, candles and paraffin. And the Austin Princess in which Mr and Mrs Levine had taken celebratory rides, like Lord and Lady Muck on Toast after the English won the war, mouldered under tarpaulin in the yard because the time for their kind of Jewish English capitalist fun was past. Now it was the turn of the people who ran the new Lutherburg.

Once upon a time death sent shivers through the community. One less and already so few and the desert so big! But in the new Lutherburg, the decline of the English and the Jews was just one of many causes for celebration since it was not possible to be truly free while either was around. The Anglicans were shrinking fast. But the Jews were beating them to it – the synagogue was down to a congregation of three, plus the travelling pedlar on the rare occasions he hit town by Thursday. The question was: should the council vote fresh land in the Jewish cemetery, beyond the screen of cypresses in the corner of the graveyard? Luckily this was not necessary because, in the case of overspill, there was a good amount of space left in the Anglican section and they would never notice.

*

Finding death useful was just one of the ways people celebrated the birth of new Lutherburg.

Mayor Joost celebrated by knocking down the empty houses in Silver Street and turning the first sod on an extension to Golden Meadow, intended for brown folk who'd missed the first wave of resettlements.

Every brown family had the sacred right, declared Mayor Joost, to move from cramped and filthy ghettos like Silver Street to new brick houses on the Municipal Scheme, as fine as anything white people had – better, some would say – with lights and running water and a church and a rugby field, all their own.

And Dominee Havenga thanked God for progress; and thanked the Minister responsible for brown housing in faraway Cape Town, and thanked the police for ensuring that resettlement took place without incident.

These were heady times.

Dominee Havenga celebrated by tearing down the old church which had stood on the corner of Paul Kruger (formerly Jubilee) Street and Oxwagon (formerly Victoria) for a century or more: a whitewashed, broad and capacious building of cool yellow shadows and carved stinkwood pews, with a small annexe at the rear for brown servants. Now the browns were to have their own church, Dominee and his committee felt something good and modern was needed for the Dutch Reformed faithful of new Lutherburg.

A special prayer meeting of thanksgiving for the coming of the new Lutherburg and the successful demolition of the church and solution of the Jewish problem was held at the site of the new church on the corner of Kruger and Oxwagon and everyone clapped when thousands of orange face-bricks arrived for the new church, plus steel windows and a pulpit with white leatherette trim, and a huge weathervane, the biggest cock on any church in the entire region.

The new church rose rapidly, with a steeple that looked for all the world like the nose of some sacred spaceship straining for heaven. It was very modern and serious and set to stand a thousand years. Like the government and the country – and the Party and proper patriots were full of joy.

The Dominee had a few quiet words with Aunt Betsy on the first Sunday she took Me to the new church. Aunt Betsy must please not bring the child. It wasn't modern.

'They have their own church now, in the brown town.'

'But she's with me! How can she go to that place there?'

After that Aunt Betsy no longer attended the new church and she sometimes muttered to herself when they walked past its important steeple that things were very, very strange. That she was a *vreemdeling*, a foreigner, in her own town.

Things got stranger still.

When the smous showed up on a rare visit, Aunt Betsy stood old Isaac the Lame up against the wall of the jail house, a pink canary clamped between his teeth. Amazingly, Aunt Betsy lost, paid forfeit in watermelon candy and it felt almost like old times.

A few days later, Mayor Joost informed her that shooting against the smous must stop.

And when Aunt Betsy asked in her coldest voice: 'Oh, and why so?' the mayor cited as reasons the damage done to the jail wall by the fusillades, and the false encouragement given to foreign natives in search of easy work in Lutherburg.

'Sorry, Auntie,' said Mayor Joost, 'but Auntie must now realize it's time to say no.'

'Oh *ja*?' said Aunt Betsy. 'No to what?'

'To people like Isaac the Lame. We don't do their jobs, OK? They don't do ours. Find a white person to do it. It's the modern way.'

Aunt Betsy went to Titus Labuschagne, the road mender, who lived in a hovel in the mayor's backyard and offered him the job. Titus stared at her from beneath his sweat-stained khaki hat with honest astonishment:

'For that job you need a bladdy hotnot! I'm a road mender!'

Next time the smous came to town Aunt Betsy told Me to stand against the wall in her own backyard with a pink canary sticking out of her mouth, and shot the pants off the smous and he paid up in nigger balls and it really was almost like old times.

Mayor Joost hurried round and said he was very, very sad. Using a brown girl to mark a white target was actually worse than using black Isaac. It was against the law.

And he told the smous: street hawkers were not allowed in the new Lutherburg. The Party planned to return the streets to proper people and not see them jammed with *sammie* fruit sellers and hoboes and *skollies* and highwaymen and bandits and beggars and matchstick sellers.

'How d'you know we were shooting?' asked Aunt Betsy.

'I got my sources,' said the mayor.

Next morning Aunt Betsy saddled Balthazar, and with Me mounted tightly behind her, she headed for the big willow halfway down Voortrekker Street.

'Hey, big mouth, get down here!' Aunt Betsy shouted up into the tree.

Me stared into the hairy green tangle and shivered for no one replied and yet she knew the treeman was watching. She could smell his skin pants.

Aunt Betsy slipped the safety off her rifle and aimed into the branches: 'Right now, boy. Or I'll put a round slapbang in the place where the monkey keeps his peanuts.'

With a rush and a huff Nephew leaped from the green cover above their heads, and stood before them bright and glistening as an unshelled snail.

Aunt Betsy could scarcely contain her astonishment.

'What's this – all washed? And combed? Where's the wedding?'

For Nephew, usually so ragged and hairy and smeared with dirt, was uniformed from top to shining toe in brown boots, khaki shorts, lanyard, tunic, and there on his head was a peaked khaki cap.

Nephew reached for Balthazar's bridle and saluted proudly. His square face beneath its cheesy hair was alert.

'You told them about Me and the smous?'

'Yessir! He's not herringfolk.'

Aunt Betsy took out her Chinese clasp knife and began fingering it in a reflective way. 'You never did know what's what, Nephew! So far's I know, herring's a fish. How can we be fish?'

Nephew says proudly: 'Nephew knows what's what. He knows more about comings and goings than anyone. Like who's had who's baby and shouldn't have. Nephew knows. Right back till way back when. 'Cause I asked and looked and remembered, so now I'm Special Constable Nephew, on the lookout for doings.'

'What doings?' Aunt Betsy is really puzzled.

Special Constable Nephew holds up a stiff forefinger and pushes it rapidly back and forth through the splayed fingers of his other hand, like a sewing-machine needle.

'Imm-o-rality!'

Nephew nods towards Me. 'Is *it* going with Auntie?'

Aunt Betsy's answer is to test the blade of her clasp knife on her stubbled cheek; the red Chinese dragon on the clasp has a fierce golden eye and flaming hair, and the heavy dark grey blade is as sharp as the whetstone can make it. Suddenly she reaches up and with a single slash slices a fistful of switches from the willow. Nephew ducks.

'Of course she's going with. To Van Wyk's farm out Compensation way. So what? Me's mine. I take her where I want.'

Nephew lifted his chin and chirped like a songbird: 'Work reserved for Herringfolk may not be done by persons from other groups. It's the law. I think Auntie must come along with me.'

Nephew made a grab at the reins. Aunt Betsy's hands moved so fast Me heard only the cry; then the willow switches were back under Aunt Betsy's arm and Nephew's cheek showed a catspaw of livid welts and Balthazar was moving.

Nephew was running behind them, crying for them to stop.

But Aunt Betsy dug her heels deeper into Balthazar and they were trotting. Me felt very strange. In her belly, a little sick, a little sad because she knew Aunt Betsy had seen him off. But it wasn't the same. Oh, what was happening in the world? Old Isaac the Lame might not mark target; the smous might not sell his wares; and yet a wild boy who lived up a tree was suddenly Special Constable Nephew.

There was something even worse: for the first time ever, Aunt Betsy was scared.

Aunt Betsy leading, with willow rod held before her, Me traipsing behind, for much of the morning they walked the Van Wyk farm under a sun blistering the blue metal heaven. But the rhythms were bad. Three to five square miles Aunt Betsy tramped with nary a twitch of the willow rod. Me followed with water bottle, dried figs and soda bread for their midday meal, which was taken in the shade of a giant anthill.

Aunt Betsy baffled, furious at Nephew's questions, his new uniform, his barefaced cheek, muttered to herself a stream of questions. Who was anyone to tell her how to use Me? Where was the farmer in the district who did not uphold the principle that what's mine is also Me? He might talk of his lambs, his crops, his fences. Just as his wife talked of her kitchen, her cooking, her shopping, her babycare, her housekeeping. But the farmer himself did not shear or sow or wrestle with the jagged bales of barbed fencing wire. His wife did not cook, or shop or mind the babies or clean the house. Of course not, they had people to do that for them. And those people were not just theirs, they were *them!* Had farmer and wife done those things themselves, far from winning praise exactly the opposite would have happened: pity, scorn, and contempt would have been heaped on them for being too poor or too ignorant or too mad to have such things decently done.

She tried the willow wand again after lunch; nothing – in three hours. The small bright sun was dropping like mercury in the pale blue glassy sky. Enough. The trip back to town would be long. Tossing aside the switch she began loading gear into the saddlepacks. When she looked again, the girl had picked up the switch and was mimicking her movements, holding it like a prod, tight into her belly and taking little steps along an invisible, impossibly narrow line, swaying in an effort to keep her balance, as if walking a tightrope. She was clumsy and a bit silly yet something of the point of the exercise must have occurred to the girl because she avoided areas where Aunt Betsy's firm boot prints showed in the crusty sand between the rubbery succulents.

Loading billy-can, lunch box, pegging stakes, mallet into the saddle bags, she smiled at this primitive aping of her method: this sliver of the mother mirror. She watered Balthazar, tightened his girth strap, and was about to tell the child to straighten her shoulders and walk like a human being and not a billy goat when Me screamed, threw the switch high over her head and raced back blubbering.

It took her some minutes to coax the girl to retrace her steps, several more to persuade her to take hold of the wand once again. Almost immediately she tasted water; the switch giving the most profound bow. Judging that the child was again on the verge of hysterics, she hammered in a marking peg without saying a word, and they set off back home.

Five miles on she tried Me again. The girl struck water inside ten minutes in an old pasture, between two long lines of drystone walls which Aunt Betsy had always felt must be good for deep level springs because ancient

Bushman beads and arrowheads littered the freckled rocks but where the weeks of walking had not shown so much as a twitch.

No doubt about it, the girl had the gift.

Lutherburg had a problem.

'A moral dilemma,' according to the mayor.

It seemed neither fair nor right nor sensible, for many better people had tried divining and failed, yet this girl had the touch, the skill, the knack, better even than her Mistress – the orphan, the stray, the six soap bargain, was finding water where no water was ever found before. And in a world where the rains fail every five years, or so, and the sheep die in dozens, the diviner is the farmer's friend.

Everyone talked of the miracle. They said – this kid walks the land on Bobby van Wyks's place and the wand swoops earthward and suddenly they have a borehole up and running, pumping several thousand gallons a day across his lucerne.

It was a very great thing.

Trouble was that other towns asked if they might borrow her. Everyone agreed this must not happen. So the mayor and the farmers made a plan.

Me may prospect their lands but they will assume she is only an extension of Aunt Betsy. When Me discovers water she will report it to Aunt Betsy and Aunt Betsy will tell the lucky farmer. This way there can be no misunderstandings. No one wants Eros and Compromise and Zwingli going around saying that Lutherburg needs a brown kid to find water.

On the other hand, Me is pure gold, say the farmers.

They want her to find more boreholes and, when she arrives, they ply her with cake and buttermilk to keep up her strength. But their distrust is never far away.

And even Aunt Betsy has a slight problem because the child has funny ideas. She believes that all fountains, wells and even garden taps have their resident subterranean snake. She hears him slaver. If you insult a watersnake, calling him old fat black man in the hole, he can draw in his breath and slurp you down into his deep home. His coils are all colours of the rainbow, and he squeezes moisture from the sand and rock. To those he favours he gives water. Those who ignore or abuse him, he snatches into his lair. When Me handles the willow switch, the serpent smells it, licks his lips and draws the stick downwards.

'That's why the wand dips.'

'Bushman relics. Ghost stories!' snaps her mistress.

'Does Aunt Betsy know why her stick dips?'

It became a battle between them and, because Aunt Betsy was scared, she did something very strange; she arranged for her to go away with the Dominee. This puzzled Me; if they might not visit the new church why did Aunt Betsy want her to go with the Dominee?

Aunt Betsy said: 'Don't argue, child. That's what you need to stop a sin – a pastor.'

Me left the house with silent Pastor Havenga, bible in one hand, paraffin bottle stopped with a rag in the other. The Dominee led her to the very place where she had begun. For the first time since the day Aunt Betsy arrived with her basket of coldwater soap Me was back in Silver Street. But she did not recognize much – many of the cottages had been razed to the flat stone slabs that had once been the floors; others still had walls or broken roofs. The graves in the cemetery had been abandoned, crosses sliding under the long grass, the relentless sand. What had been fields of maize and beans and squashes were dusty husks; water no longer ran down the irrigation sluices.

Me stood beside the well, capped with the Chinese hat of red tiles. Pastor Havenga read from his book about crushing the head of the serpent, and then asked:

'Who owns this well?'

'The watersnake who lives in a fine dry cave miles underground and keeps the spring flowing. He spits it out when he's pleased and bites it off and swallows it into his belly when he's cross.'

She was going to say she would not stand too long by the well for the snake sometimes claimed children and marked them with his spittle so they came out in bumps and welts, worse than a horsewhipping – when Pastor Havenga yanked the cloth of the bottle and poured shining liquid into the throat of well.

It was a very special poison, he told her, guaranteed to destroy serpents.

Me shrieked and tried to grab the bottle which fell and smashed, quite empty, and then she tried to throw herself into the well and Dominee had to drag her, spitting and clawing, to Aunt Betsy who stuffed her with sleepy-tree-tea until she passed out.

For a long time after that she woke in the night, screaming. The snake was angry. It was going to punish them all. Aunt Betsy tried to ease her wild dreams with dandelion tea. But this time Aunt Betsy could not help. What helped were the nightsounds Me heard in her head as she lay in her bed.

There was, as always, the shaggy palm tree in the field

next door, creaking in the wind; the windmill rustily pumping a gout of water into the stone reservoir by the pear tree. But these were old friends. Now there was a new sound. A giant wailing in the night; a huge noise that started up after dark and seemed to paint the sky; it rose and fell; it blared and softened; it went on until late; she could listen to it whole, like the wind or the rain; or she could concentrate on its parts; they were guitars, dogs, screams, laughter and clapping. It must have been there all the time she had lived with Aunt Betsy. But only now did she hear it. It was the after-dark voice of the brown town where she had never been, never so much as thought of before the Dominee killed the watersnake. It was a bit frightening in the way it tore through the night. And crowded into her ears. It was strong. It excited her. It woke her up. It made her well.

And when she was well, she refused to touch the divining rod.

It was bloody annoying, Lutherburgers agreed but, on the other hand, it sorted out an tricky problem. No smart-arse from Zwingli and Pumpkinville could go around claiming that the new Lutherburg needed a brown girl to find its water.

CHAPTER SEVEN

1994

Pascal bought a five-page spread in the *Zwingli Advertiser* and said it would feature 'Buckingham-the Hub!' and took a collection to pay for it and when people complained he said it cost big bucks to become a hub – if you were doing it properly and paid editorial was the way to go – the Gulf States did it all the time . . .

Mike the Spike got out his camera and people stopped by to hear Pascal shouting orders to Maureen who hung over the top floor balcony, wrestling a line of international flags, whipped by the fierce Karoo wind.

'My dear, the Stars and Stripes looks like old washing. Where's Germany? And little Taiwan has her knickers in a twist . . . Oh never mind, better show the Chinese flag, anyway.'

To Mike he said: 'Shoot me from the waist up. We're putting our best foot forward.'

The photo session went on all day and at the weekend the *Advertiser* was bursting with pictures. Pascal beneath international flags: 'Entrepreneur Gears for Foreign Tourists'. Pascal inspecting the new computer in the Farmers' Co-op: 'Town thanks Entrepreneur'. Pascal switching on the sprinkler system on the rugby pitch: 'Seismic change in the New Buckingham, says Entrepreneur.' Pascal shaking hands with Gerald Wright: 'Buckingham "The next Hub" says ex-civil servant.'

'I was never civil service, exactly,' said Gerald Wright.

He and Pascal were drinking beer in the karaoke. The ex-spy was nervously fiddling with his bar mat, centring it on the mahogany surface with neat, fussy movements, only to move it an inch left or right and square it off again, digesting what Pascal had just asked him.

'Why me?' he asked in his high-pitched voice. 'I'm new around here.'

'We've seen you, there by the dam. With Marie Smit. You're dipping your wick, right?'

Wright considered this. He moved his beer mat to and fro as if it were a large truck and he was practising a difficult parking manoeuvre.

'We're engaged,' said Wright.

'Great! You've answered your own question. Why me? Because you're in good with Golden Meadow. With what I call the other side. You know them. We don't.'

'But they work for you.' The ex-spy pulled at his beer. 'Your own chef's local affairs officer. And the health guy works in the doctor's garden. You see them every day.'

'They're staff, OK. When they're staff we can't talk to them – and when they're not staff they won't listen to us. Christ, we don't even know what to call them half the time!'

The ex-spy thought it over. Then he smiled, showing small white teeth, like a rabbit's.

'If you knew who you were asking, you might think twice.'

'We do know.' Pascal spoke with what he hoped was

real warmth. 'That's exactly why we want you to be our bridge. We want to work with them.'

'You want to use them, you mean.'

The ex-spy drove his beer mat forward a few inches and reversed again: 'What you offering in return?'

'Mutual interests.'

'Won't do. Self-interest is a better bet. You're not the only ones poleaxed by the Change. They're also flailing around. One day they're shepherds and shearers. The next they're running a modern town and it scares them. Why not give them the benefit of your experience? You tell me, I tell them. That info's tradeable.'

And the white folks, when they heard, thought – *brilliant!* That Gerald Wright, he's not bad – they said. Pity about Marie, mind you, he deserves better. And they told him how things were done when the town was run properly. Even then, they thought – well, the bastards didn't have a clue. And if you did it by numbers and took them through tendering, planning, revenue, they'd still probably fuck up. But who cared – as long as it got them a favour or two in return.

'If you're going to stick a Hottentot in a Cadillac, may as well teach him to drive, hey?' said Mike.

Pascal and the ex-spy met up at the dam once a week and sank a bottle of brandy and the information began to flow. The business with Doc du Plessis was first to be sorted. The spy relayed the deal:

'Early retirement. Nothing more is said. Lots of people are doing it. Look at Bill Harding over at the PO. So here's the offer – grab the cash package and head on out.'

The doc asked: what if he didn't go?

The spy reported back: 'Then they'll have his head on a platter, hide on the wall and his *derrems* on the washline.'

'That's blackmail,' said the doc.

Pascal said it wasn't so bad – when you thought of the alternatives. Prosecution. Struck off. Maybe jail. Give and take – that was the nature of a good deal.

Then there was Tookie Theron, big farmer over Red Hills away. He had these squatters he wanted to kick off his farm because they didn't use the toilets he built for them. But the squatters were also the land tenure committee now – and they wouldn't order themselves to move. So what to do?

Again, the spy negotiated a deal. Free housing for the squatters for life. And then the cops would pull assault charges against Theron for whipping kids who looked after his sheep.

Fair enough?

'That was years ago,' said Theron. 'Anyway, everyone did it.'

Time to make an example, came the reply. The cops were dying to press charges to show they were also modern and building bridges, and Tookie was top of the list for a little sail up shit creek.

There were mutterings about the value of the bargains struck and Maureen summed up the feeling when she said they were hardly seismic, were they?

Then the deal came through on Pascal's Bushman Reserve. The planning committee didn't turn him down, they limited him to the employ of one San person – for test purposes, for a month. After which they would assess whether they needed someone more indigenous to run the show.

Just for a moment Pascal's feelings showed:

'*More* indigenous? Who do they want – Chaka Zulu? I got Baba, the mayor's brother, as my joint-venture partner. He's one hundred and one per cent indigenous.'

But when he saw how Mike and Maureen and Doc du Plessis and Tookie Theron took the news of the Bushman deal, he got a grip on himself and said it was not bad thinking, actually. These were modern times and hunter-gatherers were entitled to consideration. He'd press ahead and try out a sample.

'How can you have a Bushman Park of one? Poor little guy. He'll die of loneliness,' said Maureen.

'No – well – *ja* – fine. You'll see. One's enough to begin with.'

'They're all dead anyway, Pascie,' said Mike the Spike, 'round these parts.'

'So? We'll import.'

One evening Mayor Williamson called at the karoake bar, sang a couple of choruses of 'The Green Green Grass of Home' and, in bridge-building mood, Pascal bought him a whisky on the house. After a couple of refills with Pascal wondering: was the mayor freeloading all night? – Williamson whispered that he owed him a favour.

'In the strictest confidence. For your ears only. Our Finance Committee's been sifting through the town's accounts. And, oh boy!' He shook his right hand, as if flicking water from his fingers: 'We found a mountain of cash went west, when you guys were in charge. The old guard had their snouts in the trough. Up to their piggy ears. Lucky we knew where to look, isn't it, hey?'

Pascal felt cold. He didn't like being included. But it didn't matter. The mayor was right. Maybe he wasn't old guard. He wasn't 'you people'. But he was in it – up to his piggy ears. End of story. He sat there thinking it over, sometimes pulling his enormous nose, nodding, sipping his whisky.

'How d'you know where to look?'

'We have our sources.'

And the mayor, with a wink, slipped off his stool and was gone.

For an hour Pascal did some singing. On his own because, as if they knew some sort of leprosy had arrived, the bar stayed empty after the mayor left. He'd been doing Dean Martin songs, and he wore a tux and a white tie, spotted red, like a mushroom; his belly strained at the buttons of his coat and his face was bruised like an old rose. He'd sung 'Volare' over and over and when he got to the 'Oh-oh-oh oh' bit he felt almost unbearably sad.

Now he sat drinking Mike's Indonesian Scotch and he didn't stir when Mimi de Bruyn came in and sat down beside him and ordered a port and lemon. The deputy mayor was wearing a leafy skirt and jacket and shoes, with a golden fleur de lys brooch at her throat, a hat with two tall peacock feathers and a little black lace veil. Altogether, with her sweet and rather grave expression, she was a handsome woman.

He peered blearily at her.

'Why you all dressed up like a lettuce or some kind of bloody fern?'

She was smiling at him. It was a gentle smile, but he didn't like it.

'You taking the mickey – or what? Go ahead, I don't care.'

Mimi found usually there was something comforting

about his quivering jelly-buddha calm. Not now. He turned his grey eyes on her and she saw to her distress that he was close to tears. Angry tears perhaps, drunken sorrow, but shocking all the same.

'So you going to tell me what you all dressed up for?'

'I've been to a wedding,' she said. 'Didn't you know? Gerald Wright married Marie Smit this afternoon. Over in Golden Meadow. It's our first rainbow wedding.'

'Nice one, Gerrie. Good career move!'

Two red spots in the middle of his plump cheeks glowed like warning lamps.

'Hey, listen, Chief or Comrade or Your Worship – or whatever, I'm just a simple entrepreneur. Right? I ask a guy to build bridges. I look to him for trust. How are we going to get on with the other side if we don't trust? Can you tell me that, Mrs Deputy Mayor? So I trust – and he boots me in the nuts. That Gerald Wright; he's a bloody spy!'

She tried to check her amusement. 'But yes. That's what he is. What did you think? We knew it – you knew it.'

'We've been infiltrated.'

Her smile went on but Pascal heard the edge to her voice.

'You've always been. Every house in town had one, two, three spies. You didn't see them because they were dressed as maids, cooks, nannies. But they – we – saw you. Your kids, your beds, your secrets. If someone got pregnant or someone killed himself, we knew almost before you did. Only we couldn't do anything about it. Because we weren't really there. You were the ones who did the doing.'

'He made fools of us.'

She shook her head. 'He didn't need to. What hurts is that you're not *doing* any longer – now you're being done unto.'

Pascal let out his breath, shook his head as if to banish the memory; he flapped his purple jowls, he rubbed his nose. He was drunk but that didn't help. Even drunk, it was true. The old guard were outgunned. Worse, out-smarted. What a bunch of woodheads! What a collection of prize paw-paws! And not just now – *then!* When the guns and power and tanks and God were on their side – they'd blown it. Couldn't even get oppression right. Couldn't make it work. Too lazy, yes – and too stupid. They'd done their horrible best – as the new Nazis or the great white terror – but they lacked true talent. They'd pissed it up against the wall. No – they'd got someone to piss for them. They were too dim to wear jackboots and pass water at the same time. Well, that was over. All they could expect from now on were walk-ons, bit parts – minor clowns, useful idiots, entrepreneurs. Who cared?

Pascal said: 'Well, bugger me!'

Mimi did something strange then. She reached out and put her hand on his shoulder. He gave no sign he'd noticed it but Maureen, pushing her head around the door, got the fright of her life.

She ran upstairs to Mike and told him straight: believe it or not – the deputy mayor was sitting in the bar with her arm around Pascal.

'My Lord, hey Mikey – what a bloody *place!*'

CHAPTER EIGHT

1955

When Me was forbidden the shooting range, Aunt Betsy took her into the veld and soon she could lay down accurate fire with the heavy old Mauser. With her own little .22 she split wooden clothespegs which Aunt Betsy lofted like pigeons.

The neighbours were very concerned. It was not nice to see guns in the hands of servants. Bananas Basson said to Dominee Havenga: 'How am I supposed to feel, hey? Across the road from me, it's not master and servant what I see – it's old maid and coloured child living like family.'

Dominee agreed. Transformation and patriotism, these were the stuff of the moment. It was odd that Aunt Betsy did not understand, given that her brother was a senator in the government.

Arnaldus drove an Oldsmobile with white leather seats and a shrunken head swinging from the rearview mirror. His wife, Ina, had the first integrated kitchen in Beaufort West.

'The sink,' said Arnaldus, 'is built in.'

The son, Nico, was at boarding school in Pretoria. He was said to be even more modern than his father.

Lutherburg was moving ahead at a great rate. No

brown people remained in the town proper. Mr Israel-sohn, last Jew in town, loaded the ark and the sacred writings and a forest of candlesticks into his Morris Traveller and drove over to Beaufort. The synagogue closed its doors. The Anglicans of St Augustine's might assemble for Sunday morning service and evensong but numbers were down and the minister came over from Beaufort only twice a month – and the smell from Bokkie Bok's butchery was as strong as ever.

Yes, things were looking up.

Only Betsy had failed to move with the times. Me went on sleeping in the nook above the firewood, when she did not stay in Aunt Betsy's bed, after soothing her feet.

Some brown folk remembered, when they saw her following Betsy down Voortrekker Street.

'Her ma gave her to Auntie for six stones of soap. That soap washed away many a year ago, but the girl goes on, oh yes.'

But the children of Golden Meadow, feeling she must be some sort of strange European, blushed when they saw her watching them chasing prizes on Communion night and looked away when she caught their eyes.

Me wasn't exactly lonely – Aunt Betsy was strong company – and, besides, she found friends of another sort. To the windmill and the palm tree and the many-voiced brown town creature that sang and raged after dark, she added the moon, seen through the small window beside her fireside bed. She'd found it cold when she and old Daisy scared jackals but if she looked into it on the full, a face looked back at her, now smiling, now stern; dependable, singular, firm, in a sky where the clouds of stars were simply blazing dust. Her other friends expected her to listen to them: to the moon she could talk and it listened to her.

Since the exorcism, Aunt Betsy was taking her to church again. They sat in the back row where servants belonged before they got their own church and Me bowed her head when the pastor led prayers and she saw again the shining poison pouring into the well. Several children had died and everyone, except the pastor, knew why; he claimed it was typhoid. He offered prayers of thanks for the new prosperity of Lutherburg; for the improved sewage services; he thanked the Lion and his government for doing God's work.

Me prayed for all this too but she liked it best when the organ thundered; she found if she clenched her teeth the music played along her jaw-bone.

Bill Harding pitched up one morning asking: didn't Aunt Betsy want to get on the party line?

Bill had been chief pole-planter with the PO ever since he came out of the airforce. He and two brown chainmen walked the empty country between Eros, Compromise, Pumpkinville and Scorpion Point – and from Mutton Fountain to Abraham's Grave – in all weathers. Setting off from the PO, always Pole Number One, followed by the chainmen who dragged a line of heavy steel wire, forty-four yards long, measuring off distances: one chain's length between poles on main road lines; two lengths for farm lines.

The poles Bill planted strode across koppie and gorge, from the Karoo to the Kalahari, and remote farms, hamlets and baking rail sidings which hadn't spoken to anyone in years were suddenly jabbering away. An operator handled traffic in a little room in the Lutherburg PO. It was easy. You cranked a handle and he put you through. Every house had its own ring-code. It was a triumph of science and shoe-leather.

Bill offered to put Aunt Betsy on the party line.

Aunt Betsy fetched down her shotgun from the top of the yellowwood cupboard and spat on the stock, polishing the wood with her fraying red neckerchief.

'What for?'

'Someone might want to reach you. With news.'

Aunt Betsy broke open the piece, unloaded and dropped the cartridges into the pocket of her red flannel shirt and blew down both barrels.

'Good news keeps. Bad news always got fresh horses.'

That was Betsy, stubborn as rock, backward as a Bushman. Stiff-necked, straight-backed, seen passing the chandlers' yard, followed by that odd child, now surely too big to be living like a kept cat, a caged bird, in the dark little cottage?

So when the bad news came, folks tended to say it was her own self she had to blame; at least she might have heard the news in the privacy of her home if she'd gone and got a phone when Bill Harding offered her one. Instead she'd had the news on Basson's phone. He had not crossed the road himself to tell her, he rankled still for the coffee attack and the loss of Me, so he sent February, his gardener, to call her.

At first, Aunt Betsy simply could not understand how February knew they wanted her over in the hospital in Beaufort. To her certain knowledge he'd never left Lutherburg. And she was baffled when he lifted his hand to his ear and made revolving motions. Finally, he had to pull her across the road and give her the heavy black

Bakelite receiver in her hand and press it to her ear because her inclination was to turn over the mouthpiece and stare at it, as if the squawking voice buried deep inside, like the cry hidden in a doll's stomach or the warble in the tin canary, was amusing but not important, a trick for children.

The distant voice in her ear told her that her brother Arnaldus and his wife Ina were dead.

Aunt Betsy sewed what she called 'graveside clothes'. For Me, a khaki suit, which gave her a vaguely military air, and a hat like an inverted soup bowl. Aunt Betsy chose flowing black muslin. She baked fly cemetery, syrupy *koeksusters* and fatcakes.

When they clambered aboard the bus to Beaufort the driver, red-eyed, hair heavy with Vaseline hair cream, would not let them pass. 'Can Auntie tell me – what age?'

Aunt Betsy regarded him severely. What difference did it make?: 'Sixty-five.'

'I mean her.' The driver snapped his ticket punch irritably at Me. 'Auntie's daughter.'

'Not my daughter.'

'So who then?'

Aunt Betsy thought it over. The other passengers, awoken from their long-distance daze in the baking bus that smelled of its red leather seats, looked on silently at the thin old woman in black and her girl, carrying cake tins stacked one on top of the next, like hatboxes, a tower taller than herself.

The driver upped the stakes: 'Servants can't ride on this bus. It's the law. Sorry, Auntie.'

The passengers knew a poker game when they saw one.

Aunt Betsy squared her shoulders and pushed a pound note at the driver: 'She's my granddaughter.'

The driver stared at Me for a long while but he took the money. The audience let out a collective sigh and settled back in their seats. Bluff called, and lost.

For the next few hours they crawled up bumpy farm roads and crunched through the gravels of streams, with just enough water to wet their axles. Aunt Betsy balanced the box of fatcakes on her lap, because fatcakes bruise. She was angry. What was happening in the world? Tree-dwellers in buckskin pants were suddenly Herringfolk; bus drivers told you your business; and a person could no longer call her servant her own.

The farm cemetery lay beneath three towering blue-gums; a sign on the wire gate read RESTING PLACE FOR GOD'S CHOSEN. About twenty people stood around the graves; whites stood closest; farm servants waited under the trees. It was seen as curious that Aunt Betsy should place her maid beside her, and the other mourners let her know how queer it was by keeping clear inches between them.

Arletta and Barnabas Basson were there; they had arrived in their big blue car and did a lap of honour in the farmyard. They had brought the maid Me had seen cleaning the windows of their townhouse, the one Aunt Betsy said they were 'kitchen training'. She had a pointed chin, pale face, pink dress and pink ribbons in her dark curls, and stood amongst the servants.

Arletta Basson fixed Me with a look as if to say: 'Be careful, my girl, I've got my eye on you.'

Me gazed at two dark shafts cut into the earth. Where the spade had sheared the iron-hard ground, the lips of the shafts gleamed like metal. Over the shafts was draped a grass-green carpet, like an itchy lawn, smeared with clods of earth. And into the lawn were cut holes, like big post-boxes.

The coffins stood huge before the minister who said: 'The Lord giveth and the Lord taketh away,' and everyone answered: 'Amen.'

Everyone except the boy. He was fearfully calm in his school uniform of grey shorts and green and blue striped blazer. Me had never seen so much hair. It began as a fat cowslick rearing over his forehead; at the back of his neck it gathered over his collar in a folded tail she had seen on Egyptian geese but never anywhere else; men she knew wore their hair cut short, and shaved fiercely over the ears. She never even thought boys had hair; yet here it was piled up and greased, the comb marks running sweep after sweep through the blond stack.

Let down on ropes, the first coffin was posted through the letter box in the grassy carpet. Aunt Betsy was crying. Me wished she could feel sadder herself but Arnaldus had never meant very much to her. A big man with a red nose who when he looked at her said: 'My Heavens, Betsy – when're you going to get rid of this stray?'

The second coffin tipped its shining face like a mirror, and showed her her own and she was astonished to see tears on her cheeks.

Afterwards everyone sat in the big front room of the farmhouse drinking coffee and ate Aunt Betsy's fly cemetery and fatcakes off plates, balancing on their knees. They were subdued, even a bit angry. Not just the death but its manner perturbed them. Arnaldus and his wife had been driving home from a big wedding over in Scorpion Point when their car left the road at Bushman's

Bend. So empty is the hot dry country between Luther-burg and Beaufort that it was three days before they were found – bolt upright – with the radio playing selections from the Don Elliott Sextet.

The mourners looked for consolation. It was a damn miracle that they hadn't been robbed by passing natives. At least their boy was away at school. Yet if this happened to a senator, it could happen to anybody. It hardly seemed fair, really. And they stared at old Aunt Betsy. There was her brother, a big shot in the govern-ment. Dead. And here is his sister, still living in a mud cottage with dung floors, no lights or water, keeping a booked-in child – and not even putting her out in the backyard. What a family!

Some of the men drank brandy and the Bassons showed off their maid. Her name was Childie and she was not a bad learner. They stood her in the bay window and made her show how clean her teeth and nails were and she thanked them both.

Bananas Basson said: 'We're giving Childie a leg up. By making her a kitchen maid.'

'Childie gets on a chair before we come to town and she soaps herself all over,' said Arletta Basson. 'Until she's as clean as a Christian can make her.'

'It's a gamble,' said Bananas Basson, 'taking a girl out of the backyard. You can get some very bad bargains. I know folks who've picked up something for next to nothing and lived to rue it.'

Aunt Betsy poured herself a cup of coffee, walked over to Basson and stood there, blowing on her coffee, and folks moved carefully out of range because they knew she was daring him to tell her: just what had she lived to rue?

Basson began to sweat. The dark patches on his face grew darker, islands of yellow skin gleamed and the mottling that gave him his nickname began spreading over his face. Next thing he was yelling at Childie to get the hell into the yard, shooing her out of the room, saying she was supposed to clean his bloody car!

Everyone knew Basson was running, not chasing. His car was shining clean.

There were times when Me was proudest of Aunt Betsy because she was stronger and wiser and better than anyone in the world.

CHAPTER NINE

1994

Elsa Harding, the pole-planter's wife, found him in a pet shop in Beaufort West. A little lime-green budgerigar, salt and peppered at the throat. A quiet little fellow, neat in movement, cruelly locked up in a blue and white cage with a pair of hoodlums: a macaw who screamed like a cop siren and a ragged blue parrot, both with the hot-eyed stares of men who fight in bars.

The salesman saw her smooth, scrubbed face and straight grey hair and took her for a hick from the sticks. Auntie must buy the parrot, he kept saying — he sings the old National Anthem.

Typical Beaufort bighead, the salesman, Elsa decided — but not far wrong about her. For thirty years she'd taught separate Sunday-school classes for brown kids while Bill worked in the Post Office. Then came the new South Africa. Lutherburg turned into Buckingham and no one wanted some white auntie teaching Sunday school to brown kids over in Golden Meadow. Then Bill took 'the package', the bundle of cash the Post Office paid white guys to leave early, bought a little BMW and they both retired.

Even as she got into the car outside the ironmongers, when Bill did a three-point turn and hooted loudly, and balanced the cage on her lap, she knew what was coming.

The red desert dust enfolded the BMW, as they roller-coastered through the dips in the baked dirt road back to Buckingham.

'I speak under correction,' Bill's sharp voice climbed higher in his nose the way it always did when he spoke under correction, 'but bloody hell! If you want a pet, why not a big biter? A mastiff. Pit bull. Alsatian. Anything that'll chew the arse off a burglar. But not a little bitty bird with a big nose.'

Elsa said, in the firm, flat voice that had stopped the pet-shop man in his tracks: 'No, thank you very much.' Then she lifted the green baize cover and peeked at the little chap sharpening his beak on a piece of cuttlefish and blew him a kiss.

She named him Roy, after her father's old lawyer, Roy Liebenberg, who had helped Pa that time in the war when he went to jail. Pa's mother and sisters had died in the concentration camps where the English locked up Boer women and children. When the Germans went to war against the English, Pa had blown up every bridge around Lutherburg. Her Roy had the same kindly way of cocking his round head and twinkling at her, as if he knew a lot more than he let on.

Bill Harding liked to say that pole-planting was hard graft but regular as religion. And thanks to him everyone just about – except mad ones like old Aunt Betsy – all over the vast district, got their first crank-handle phone.

Strangers took a while to fix their ring-code in their ears. Many a young bride, fresh from the city, jumped for the phone each time it rang, wept because the calls were always for someone else, stopped lifting the receiver for weeks, until one day a runner arrived from the Post Office saying that the exchange had been ringing her code daily – why didn't she answer her phone? But once she knew her ring, she was in the loop.

It might have turned people incurably quizzy. Like folks were, over in Scorpion Point and Compromise. Except that Lutherburgers hated gossip worse than strong drink and listened in to the conversations of others only when they absolutely had to. Besides, just knowing what people were saying to each other didn't mean shooting your mouth off. On the contrary. It meant keeping more to yourself. Let some hopalong from nowhere-much come to town popping with questions: did Dominee Greet really tear off his toga in the middle of Sunday service? Is your new mayor truly a bloody Indian from Bombay? What's this about Pascal Le Gros opening a casino in the Hunter's Arms? – and he hit the traditional stone wall: 'None of my business. Search me. Buggered if I know. Better ask my husband . . .'

Elsa's habit was to put Roy's cage on the windowsill during the day so he could watch the street. At night he slept on the piano under a green baize cover to keep him snug. All day long they'd nuzzle and kiss. Each time the phone rang – and it rang many times a day with passing traffic she never even noticed any more, just calls to other farms, other families – Roy stopped swinging on his trapeze or pecking his bell or sharpening his beak, and cocked an ear. And when she called out the destination of the call – the police station, the Pastory, the Hunter's Arms – so did Roy. Soon he was saying: 'Who's a pretty boy then?' and trilling a dozen different ring-codes perfectly, followed by their owners' names. Easy as pie. He was a great talker, she could see that.

'You're a clever Royboy!' she told him. And he nodded and blew her a kiss.

She tried to make Bill like him. She taught Roy respectful phrases like 'Evening, sir!' but it did no good. Bill retreated more and more into his workroom with his boat, stuck a sign on his door, a bird in a circle with a rude red line through it, and never showed his face till it was time to leave for his sundowner at the Hunter's Arms.

He'd been working at his boat ever since he'd left the Post Office. He took the plans from *Yachting Today*, drew them on the wall, scaled down the twenty-four to sixteen feet; still worked in the old measurements, using simple materials: hardboard, nails and alkaline glue. One fine day, Bill swore, she'd be ready: he'd launch her on the dam, hoist the sail on her twenty-four-foot mast and cast off, eight passengers aboard.

He knew there was no water in the dam. A decade of drought had left the great mud-wall dam outside town a flat and grassy pan over which the springbok scampered. But the rains would come again, the lake would be six fathoms deep, like it was in the old days when you could sail for a mile or more. 'One day,' he vowed, 'just you bloody well watch!'

Come sundowner time, Roy perched on her shoulder they watched Bill backing the BMW down the drive. After thirty years on his feet he wasn't walking anywhere ever again. He'd made himself that promise when the Post Office paid him off for being too male, too pale, too middle class for the new Buckingham; and gave his job to a bunch of brown guys, the new affirmatives.

So he travelled in style now. Cruising two blocks at ten miles an hour, window down, arm over the door jamb, along Voortrekker — he still called it Voortrekker, none of this bloody Democracy nonsense for him – and into Leibrandt Street which was now Freedom Street, and pulled up in front of the Hunter's Arms; thank God that at least had kept its name.

Bill drank two whiskies, never more, for precisely one hour, perched on a bar stool directly beneath the mini-garden of Japanese parasols in pink paper, just left of the mounted kudu head with the crumpled horn. Nursing his double Johnny Walker and soda, chewing the fat with Pascal Le Gros. Come seven sharp, he drained his glass, said: 'Well, duty calls . . .' and then he was out to the BMW and home to the wife and supper.

Roy always greeted him respectfully on his return with their phrase for that day: 'Welcome home, Mr Harding,' or even something nautical like 'All shipshape and Bristol fashion, Captain!'

But Bill would not make the slightest effort and tended to get really shirty and he'd bark back: 'Who asked you, beakface?'

It made Roy unhappy to be spoken to in that tone. Elsa poured her heart into his care; he rode on her shoulder and sat on her finger; she rubbed her cheek against his and kissed him. He was her friend, pupil, child, her Royboy. So quick and lively and loving! With Bill, she always knew what he was going to say next.

She never knew what Roy would say next.

He loved having her read to him and it was one morning, as they sat together paging through *My Big Book of Tribes*, which had belonged to her old dad, and she was showing him the little apricot Bushmen toting bows and arrows, who once lived around Buckingham until they got shot by the farmers, that Roy did something very clever: he began picking out the tribes by dress and ornaments, and saying in his/her little boy-girl voice: 'Two Bushmen, three Xhosas and a Shangaan.'

It was her neighbour, Baby Vermaak, who made the next discovery. Not only did he count, he could subtract. After just one lesson he knew that four Hottentots take away two Bushmen left just two Hotties! He was like a maths prof, said Baby. He should go on TV, actually.

Soon all sorts of people were dropping by with pictures torn from *Farming Today* or the *Zwingli Advertiser* and the *National Geographic*, just to test him out: Maoris rubbing noses, Bangladeshi farmers in a paddy field, kibbutznik in an orange grove, Innuit harpooning fish, sumo wrestlers thudding together like bread dough. Roy lapped it up. You only needed to hold the picture up to his cage bars, tell him who he was looking at, give him another glimpse and he knew it.

He hopped up, fixed it with his bright, round eye and sang out: 'Four spear carriers' or 'Two Jewboys' or 'Six pansies', exactly as you'd told him, in your own voice.

Soon he was doing everyone from Dominee Greet to Pascal Le Gros – perfectly.

You couldn't fool him by trying a bit of disguise. Cut out a yarmulka and stick it on a picture of a Griekwa herdsman and Roy sang out: 'One Hottie!'

'He knows, does Roy,' said Elsa proudly. 'Put a hat on a Hottentot and he's still a Hottie.'

But his best trick was scaring the street. When the municipal workers clocked off at five and wandered past the house, on their way back to Golden Meadow – because, after the Change, everyone still lived exactly where they had done before the Change, except for Mimi de Bruyn, and she was odd – Roy would pick out the different groups passing his window, calling out the score: 'Two Bantu, six Coloureds and a Hottentot,' and he followed each identification with a couple of bursts from his repertoire, a sleighride of ringing phones.

It worked every time. The pastor or the butcher loved to hide behind the curtain and watch these guys damn near leap out of their skins when someone yelled at them in Sergeant Nephew's voice, or with the hollow boom of Pascal Le Gros. And there was no one to see – just this little bird in his cage on the windowsill.

Roy did ethnic groups; he did new categories, too. When the brown foreman who had replaced Bill Harding at the PO and five pole-planters marched past the window, he called out: 'Six affirmatives!'

A university down the coast heard about Roy and sent a bunch of professors to observe him doing his stuff. There'd been work on dolphins, they said, and parrots and chimps. But never, never, budgerigars. There was, of course, the Clever Hans Syndrome to watch out for. It had to do with a counting horse. The profs wanted to be sure Roy was no Clever Hans so they watched him in action on the windowsill and were incredibly excited by his talents. And privileged. And proud. Elsa was as good as Doctor Dolittle in talking to an animal. She appeared to be communicating with a non-mammalian creature without cueing or prompting.

They begged to be allowed to study Roy in controlled surroundings. Elsa said maybe later but not right now, she loved him too much to let him go anywhere, thanks all the same.

The night before the scientists left they sang karaoke in the Hunter's Arms and danced on the bar counter and called Roy a scientific first for the nation. No one could match him in Britain or the States. Even after years of

isolation, South African science was top-notch. Then one
prof grabbed the fringed canopy hanging above the bar
and wore it like a wig and did an impersonation of Tom
Jones. Next morning Pascal said no question but Roy
could be a big tourist pull. Bigger than the dinosaur prints
in front of Levine's General Dealers.

Through it all Roy stayed his normal modest self,
never preening. Quiet, collected and accurate. He gave
everyone something to feel proud about. And that meant
a lot because folks thought they really blew it in the
elections. In other towns they were green with envy!
Over in Eros they put it about that Roy had been trained
by Satanists. And wise-guys in Scorpion Point went and
bought the singing parrot from Beaufort and bragged that
he sang the old National Anthem. So what? He didn't do
tribes, did he? Could that parrot tell the bloody difference between a Zulu and a zebra? No way, José!

So it was that when Elsa opened her door to an early
morning knock and found Mayor Williamson and five
new councillors on the step, she wheeled them straight
into the front room, simply taking it for granted, she told
Baby Vermaak later, that they must want a chat with
Roy. Though she had thought it was a bit odd that they
wouldn't actually look at him and asked her to cover him
or take him outside; what they had to say was for her
ears only. She said they could speak freely, she had no
secrets from Roy who was checking out the visitors and
now gave an initial reading:

'Six Coloureds.'

Running his hands through his thick dark Indian hair
and showing off in his new brown suit and his red silk tie
– bought, everyone knew, since he got to be mayor, for

they ran him out of Zwingli with just the shirt on his back just before the election – Williamson made a speech.

Elsa didn't hear all of it or remember half of it, she later told Baby Vermaak, but Williamson kept looking at her like she had come up from the sewers. His speech was divided into bits about the new Buckingham and the old Lutherburg. Elsa did not remember which was which, but one of them was home to rainbow people, and reconciliation and justice. The other was locked in the past, riddled with racialists, old-style thinking – and Roy. The mayor told her he had consulted the Structures. She wasn't sure what the Structures were but they were important, she knew, because the mayor reported that the Structures were angry with Roy. She had been warned.

Elsa turned to the five councillors then and gave them her look. Just to remind them she knew who they were even if they'd forgotten who they were: heavens! there was old Saul who used to do Dr du Plessis's garden before he took early retirement and moved away; and Amos, who cleaned her car; the others had been through her Sunday-school class. And she absolutely exploded. Great big men ganging up against a tiny bird. What about their precious Constitution? Didn't it say there we had to look after human rights, privacy, free speech for everyone? The mentally ill, the homeless, women and children? Didn't that include Roy?

Roy had been studying the mayor's delegation and now revised his tally: 'Five affirmatives and one coolie'.

The mayor said he was one hundred and one per cent for free speech. But words like 'coolie', 'Jewboy', 'wood-enhead', 'Hottentot' and 'Bushman' had no place in the new Buckingham. As for privacy – well, the bird had been seen by witnesses, it stood in the window and insulted passers-by. The bird broadcast to the street. And the people in the street were determined to put a stop to him – if she didn't do so.

Elsa shivered. It felt suddenly as if the house was full of cats.

When she carried Roy to the window next morning, the first thing she saw was Williamson, wearing his chain of office, standing among the blue overalls of the men off the sewage truck; it was a demonstration. There were maids from the Hunter's Arms in lacy white aprons and tight cerise skirts and frilly mob-caps looking like hot cherry tarts. Schoolkids in uniform and staff from the Volksbank; and Mr Moosah's bunch of professional troublemakers saw Roy and began shouting: 'Death to Imperialism!' and 'Hands off Cuba!' and drew their fingers across their throats, and miaowed like cats but Roy wasn't fazed for a second and shouted right back: 'Twenty-six bloody Hottentots!'

And she had to close the window and draw the curtains because of the racket they kicked up then.

Elsa decided to withdraw Roy from public gaze for a spell and she thought she knew just how it might be arranged. She wrote to the university profs who'd been so impressed, and offered to lend him to science – for a short while.

Bill did not take kindly to being picketed. Then the mayor got hold of him in the pub and told him he was part of the rainbow nation and would he please have a word with his wife? Bill said he was buggered if he'd let some Bombay barrack-room lawyer lord it over him.

'Anyway, I'm an Englishman,' said Bill. 'People expect

me to stand for fair play and all that. I don't like it any more than you do. Why must I sit there being lectured by that fat fraud Le Gros about adapting or dying, and being a rainbow person and seizing the future. I don't give a ratshit about being a rainbow person. And I don't like the future. I want a quiet life, right. So kindly do something about Bigmouth!'

She spoke so softly she could hardly hear her question: do what?

'Put him to sleep.'

Elsa got this chill, like an icy spider between the shoulders, like the day the cobra got into little Twinkie du Toit's crib.

'No thank you very much,' she said quietly, 'I've already made other arrangements.'

A week later she had a letter from the professor who had done his Delilah number on the bar counter of the Hunter's Arms. She had to read it twice before she got the hang of it: it was full of stuff about 'transformation' and 'transparency' and the 'pursuit of excellence with equity' and she got pretty excited especially as it sounded so good, even if it really didn't mean anything to her, and she was formally thanked for her offer; it all seemed fine – until she got to the BUT:

but believing, as we do, that all stakeholders deserve equal access to a level playing field, without reference to race, creed, age, gender, economic circumstance or physical disability, we regret we cannot expose students to the ethnic and linguistic attitudes of the bird in question

The bird in question? They didn't even give him his name! Elsa was suddenly very frightened and though she nearly died even to think about it and kept it from Roy of course, she decided there was only one thing to do. She covered his cage and walked to the graveyard and there among the cypresses which masked the corner where suicides were buried she opened the cage door and held him up to the sun.

'Off you go, darling,' she said, trying to keep her voice steady.

Roy sat on his trapeze and stared back at her, quite nonplussed. With a sob, Elsa pushed her hand into the cage and withdrew him, feeling his heart pumping in her fist, avoiding his reproachful eyes, and held him up to the heavens: 'Fly, sweetheart,' she begged, 'before the wicked men hurt you!'

And shutting her eyes again she flung him like a stone into the sky. She heard his wings, and with a sob she bade him farewell. She kept her eyes screwed shut until she felt a sudden flutter of wings and Roy landed on her shoulder, after a half-hearted circle overhead, and began kissing her ear.

'Oh Royboy – what am I to do with you?' cried Elsa.

That's where Mimi de Bruyn saw her, in the graveyard, and felt instinctively her pain. Mimi was still recovering from the shock of being appointed head of Health and Gender in the new Buckingham Municipal Council. Everyone told her it was a big thing and she must be very pleased but try as she might, she did not enjoy the importance granted her, or approve of it. But she was saddled with it. The new mayor had called her when he and Mr Moosah were parcelling out appointments between the ruling party and Mr Moosah's Communist Party of New Buckingham.

'Mimi,' said the mayor, 'we want you to head up Gender.'

And she asked, stupidly, 'What's that?'

'It means being for women,' said the mayor, 'and allowing us – us men, that is – to start seeking forgiveness for the way we've treated women in the past. Women have been at the forefront of the struggle for freedom; it's time to fight for equal rank.'

'Our policies are to support women, kids and the handicapped,' said Mr Moosah. 'But first comes Gender. And I for one wish to ask you for your forgiveness, Comrade Mimi, for my male proclivities over years. None of us are free of prejudice, I fear. Least of all, my own Asian community.'

'If you know Gender so well, why don't one of you do it?' Mimi suggested helplessly.

Mr Moosah looked shocked. 'I couldn't. It needs a woman's touch to do Gender. Properly.'

'I'd like myself,' said Williamson carefully, 'to do more Gender. But I've got enough on my hands. So, please – you do Gender, Mimi.'

She had done no Gender since her appointment, and the sort of meeting she had just left, which had discussed how to make the sewage service truck a Gender-free working environment, had ended in acrimony when Mr Moosah as leader of SODU, Buckingham's Syndicate of Democratic Unions, said that putting women on the truck would cost his men their jobs and when Mimi asked: didn't he care about Gender then? Mr Moosah got cross and said Gender was all very well, but you had to have Gender with equity and he voted they set up a committee to investigate and everyone agreed.

Why, Mimi wondered aloud, was Elsa Harding in the graveyard urging Roy to fly away?

Elsa wept and said Roy simply couldn't cope with the changes in town.

'Neither can I,' Mimi smiled gently.

'It's his conversation,' sobbed Elsa. 'He says all the wrong words. They'll kill him if he goes on.'

'Who will?' Mimi asked.

'The new men – the mayor and others – they came and they said it.'

'Six woodenheads and a *charrah*,' said Roy.

Elsa began sobbing again: 'You see! He does it all the time.'

Dimly, happily, Mimi saw here, perhaps, a chance to do something. She put an arm around Elsa's shoulders: 'They've got no right to make you suffer for things the bird says. What about people with dogs? Don't they train them to bark at brown people and never at whites? Must they untrain them now? And if they don't will the mayor shoot the dogs next? If anyone threatens you again, come and tell me. Will you promise me that?'

And Elsa promised. Then she went home. She was passing the Hunter's Arms when she remembered that Pascal Le Gros was forever telling Bill to seize the future and become a rainbow person. Before she knew it, Elsa walked straight through the front doors of the Hunter's Arms, not caring whether anyone branded her a loose woman for entering Satan's lair. She would happily have made a pact with the devil – if it meant saving her darling.

Pascal was leaning over the bar; in his white cricket jersey and flannels, he floated over the oaken counter like a woollen moon knitted with large needles. After banishing Roy to the dining room and shutting the door so he wouldn't hear what she was about to say, she begged Pascal, as a man of the modern world with relatives in Miami, to tell her what to do and Pascal said: 'No probs. Seriously. I'll make a list.'

The next morning Elsa sat with Roy at the window, a packet of roasted pomegranate seeds in her right hand, Pascal's list in her left. Together they watched brown council workers passing by and when Roy called out: 'Six Coloureds,' Elsa corrected him, according to the list: 'No, dear – six mixed-race persons.'

But Roy, who had been so quick with ring-codes, tribes, hats and noses, was slow to catch on. Show him a duo of Bengali farmers and, after a long stare, with what sounded like the tiniest sigh of irritation, he managed: 'Two Asians.' That won him a handful of seeds. But a minute later, faced with commuters in a Calcutta railway station, Roy counted: 'Ten coolies,' and lost his seed ration for an hour.

And he was bloody-minded. Show him a shot of a Gay Pride parade. Ask till you were blue in the face: 'How many lesbian and gay persons?' And back came the answer: 'Twenty bloody pooftahs!'

He was better at changing Bushmen and Hottentots into Khoi-San, even if he kept forgetting whether hunters came before gatherers. Anyway, at least they were extinct, thank heaven, and not themselves touchy. But when it really mattered, he blurted out the first thing that came into his head: 'Natives, rickshaw boys, boneheads' – every one marked DNM (Do Not Mention) on Pascal's list.

And she would have to start all over again. First the picture, then the answer, then the question. Slow and relaxed: 'One what, Roy?'

He gave her a look that said he didn't believe he was doing anything so idiotic. But he played along, answering her question in her own voice: 'One – black – African – person. *Good boy, Roy!*'

All this – *and* sarcasm! If Roy felt silly, what the heck did he think she felt? Elsa steeled herself: very well. If he wanted to behave like a baby she would jolly well treat him like one. Thus began the use of the green rubber band, stretched between thumb and forefinger. He got three chances. Show him a dignified Masai tribesperson standing like a stork on one leg, get back 'One kaffir' – and she gave a warning twang on the rubber band. Get back 'Big nig-nog' and a double twang sounded. Three strikes and he was O-U-T. His beak snapped shut with the green rubber band for the rest of the morning. Hurt her more than it did him. But he simply had to learn.

Bill began having nightmares. Led by Mayor Williamson, a crowd of mixed-race persons broke into his garage and smashed up his yacht. He lay in bed beside Elsa, weeping; everything had been ready! The rains were coming, the dam would fill, the mast had been fitted, the breeze was sharp . . . then five years of work was smashed with pickaxes.

He woke, groaning: 'We're sunk. The little bastard!'

Bill went hunting, something he hadn't done since he left the PO. Slinging his American carbine over his shoulder, at the crack of dawn he headed off to the lucerne fields. Came back with a brace of Egyptian geese, badly mangled because he was using heavy 145 grain ammo, probably on purpose, she guessed. He laid out

the blood-streaked glossy-green corpses on the dining-
room table where Roy couldn't miss them. He said some
birds never bloody well learned their lesson. He had
brought down the first bird and pegged it out on the
ground as a decoy. It fooled those overhead who came in
for a look, then he knocked the next sucker out of the
sky. Worked every time.

Bill bent with his lips close to Roy's ear and hissed:
'There's nothing dumber than a duck — except a dead
duck. Right, birdbrain?'

Elsa knew she would have to work faster if she was to
save Roy. She halved his seed and water ration, dropped
his cover over the cage and left him in solitary for
anything from a couple of hours to a couple of days.
Depending. Something like 'Redneck' got him the cooler
for ten minutes. Slander an Englishman with 'Saltycock'
and he drew an hour in solitary. 'Jewboy' earned two.
'Nig-nog' and he was on short rations all day.

Roy hated solitary, clinging to the bars as she shoved
him through the cage door. Crying and keening and
pecking at his feathers. But, then, as she told him,
dropping his cover over the cage, he should have thought
of that before calling Tutankhamun 'One Gyppo'. They'd
done Egyptians all day — hadn't they? So there was no
excuse.

Longest sentence — for calling an amiable bishop 'that
black bastard!' — was three days hard. But she softened
after a day, feeling maybe she'd gone a bit far, horrified
by the dead silence under the cover. In a panic she
whipped it off only to find the cunning little so-and-so
sound asleep.

It was the last straw. Who'd saved him from the
Beaufort pet shop and the mayor and the angry Structures

and Bill's murderous plans? She wasn't giving up now. No thank you very much! From now on, Elsa swore, no more sleeping on the job. He had to try harder.

She began leaving the cover off his cage and the overhead light on. Sometimes all night. Or she put on his cover, seeing how he was aching for rest, only to whip it off moments later when she knew he'd nodded off, and yell: 'Wakey, wakey! Roy – what've I got here?' And slap a Zulu craftsperson or San hunter-gatherer against the bars.

If he said: 'One garden boy' or 'Bloody Hottentot' or anything Not to Be Mentioned, back went the cover and ten minutes later, just as he was sneaking off to sleep, she did it all again.

It worked. He was trying harder. Thinking long and carefully before answering questions, saying less and less. He'd open his beak, then close it again, staring at her forehead until she told him: 'You won't find the answer there, nossir!' And popped him into solitary for a couple of hours.

He came out quieter than ever and the salt and pepper plumage of his neck looked rather ashy. Shaky on his pins, too. But that might have been a play for sympathy. She tried him on Tamil farmers, Israeli settlers, Ibo dancers. Nothing. Ruffling his neck feathers in little shivers, eyes glazed, he just went on hopping from one claw to the other, like a cyclist, dreamily pedalling a rung of his ladder and saying nothing else all day.

She tested him with the official photo of Mayor Williamson, wearing official robes and chain of office. Though Bill said this was playing with fire. Anyone with half an eye would know what he was looking at – just a coolie in a necklace. But Roy, who once could have told you, on the turn, that a Hottie in a hat stayed a Hottie, barely glanced at the mayor and went back to staring at the bars of his cage with weary eyes. He uttered not a peep. Not even when he came face to face with himself in his little oval mirror with the seashell surround. He just gave himself a puzzled stare. As if he didn't know who he was. Of course it was sad. At his peak, Roy could add, subtract and answer the phone, knew every ring-code in fifty miles, each voice in the district, all the tribes in the country. Now he clung to his perch and seldom opened his beak. But if Elsa was honest, it was also an incredible relief. Better safe than sorry. Better no answers than wrong answers.

The rains came. The dam filled. Bill whistled in his workroom as he mixed his alkaline glue. His boat was weeks away from the launch. And he was really friendly now. Back from the pub of an evening, he'd poke a finger through the cage door until Roy hopped aboard and hung on, swaying, and Bill would wink and blow kisses, asking in that high voice he usually kept for speaking under correction: 'Who's a pretty boy, then?'

But Roy wasn't saying.

There were moments when Elsa thought she caught a gleam in his round, dark, empty eye. Something hot. Like embers under the ash of last night's fire. So she kept her rubber band handy. Just in case. You never knew. What would happen if one day, without warning, some person of mixed race, or an Asian, Chinese, gay activist, kibbutznik or African gentleman dropped in, and Roy suddenly remembered he had something to say?

CHAPTER TEN

1956

People could not get over the way Aunt Betsy lost her brother. One moment, Arnaldus and his wife, Ina, had been dancing at a country wedding, next they were dead at Bushman's Bend.

Death on the endless dirt roads was familiar enough. People hit gravel on a bad corner, braked, and took off. Happened all the time. So the shock was not there. It lay in the thought of what Arnaldus and Ina had been doing earlier – laughing, dancing, knocking back a few jars – then the smash-up. Nothing like this would have happened in the old days when you took the wagon to a wedding. But then no one wanted to go back to the old days. You had to deal with modern things. You could not ignore them, or wish them away.

Look at the power of the telephone.

Aunt Betsy had news of her brother's death from a gardener; now that was bad! If she'd had her own phone at least it could have been kept private. Some went so far as to believe that if she'd had a phone – by which they meant, had she attended more to the changes in the world, to progress in the new Lutherburg, to building separate rooms for your servants – the death of her brother might have been prevented altogether.

The town was prepared to be sympathetic to Aunt Betsy's loss, but they wanted a trade-off.

Mayor Joost came to see her and said: 'Look – your brother, he drove an Oldsmobile. Auntie owes it to his memory. This is the middle fifties, for heaven's sake.'

He wanted her to paint her cottage, at least. Everyone was using face-brick now and corrugated iron roofs, but she was still without electricity or running water, living under a reed roof, with dung floors.

'It doesn't look good.'

She was puzzled. 'For who?'

'For us. Not even the brown folk use dung any more,' said Mayor Joost.

Though he had sworn to do so, he did not also tell her folks felt she should get rid of that girl who skivvied for her and, it was whispered, shared her bed, the brown one who never said anything but looked and looked at you with wide eyes until you could scream.

People thought the message was getting through when Aunt Betsy put up on her garden gate a notice painted in indigo capitals:

NO PATIENTS   I'M BUSY.

She began emptying out her consulting room. Storing her medicines in the stable with Balthazar, her chestnut. Everything went – bottles of Horniball's Patent Wonderful Extract; boxes of Fisher's Balsam of Life; packets of Permanganate of Potash crystals against snakebite.

Dr Du Plessis, young smart-arse, said he hoped this was an end to her quackery.

Aunt Betsy said: 'Go climb a tree. You'll lose more patients than I've treated.'

She would be receiving a visitor, Aunt Betsy told Me. This would be his bedroom. She set to restoring the floor of the consulting room, roughened by the feet of generations of patients. Her girl gathered fresh droppings in the goat pen behind the abattoir, tamped them flat, sealed the surface with white clay from the river and polished the new floor to a gleam.

She furnished the room with an old six-drawer mahogany tallboy on which stood a blue pitcher and basin, painted with cosmos flowers, deep red with feathery stems; the bed was covered with a mohair blanket and a springbok skin, from last year's hunting season, was spread on the floor; Aunt Betsy stuffed the new bolster with feathers from the brace of Egyptian geese she brought down in the lucerne fields.

Me lined the drawers of the tallboy with old *Reader's Digest* pages, one of which showed a semi-naked woman.

'Mustn't worry,' said Aunt Betsy, 'he's from the city. They sees that sort of thing constantly.'

A bed of maple wood with leather thongs was made by Ezekiel, the carpenter. A mattress, striped blue and white, stuffed with coir, purchased from Levine's General Traders (Under New Management) was carried to the cottage by Levine's boy, Harry, who draped it over his head so he looked like some fat blue sandwich, walking. When he knocked at the door of the cottage he was singing an old song about a lass who nearly drowned in a waterhole but was saved by a farmer's son who loved her upturned nose.

'A little less foolery, if you please,' Aunt Betsy said.

*

When the boy arrived on the bus from the faraway rail station, Aunt Betsy put on long white gloves, for this was a 'signal' occasion, and walked down Voortrekker Street introducing him. Nico was wearing a striped school blazer, carrying a leather suitcase, a black box with a silver handle sticking out of the side, and a guitar slung across his shoulders.

All the town was prepared to show respect; after all his daddy had been a senator, he'd had the ear of the government and it might be that his aura had carried to his son.

As they were about to pass under the willow, Aunt Betsy warned him that a man with a big beard sometimes jumped out of the tree.

'If he asks you your business, don't fret. It's only Nephew.'

Nico said it was amazing, in the mid-twentieth century, to hear of a man who lived up a tree.

'He's done it for years. Keeping an eye on things,' Aunt Betsy said. 'Now the police's made him a special constable.'

When she showed him round the cottage Nico asked questions which could have only one answer.

'You've never had running water?'

'Don't you miss electricity?'

He was silent before Aunt Betsy's relics of the long night of God's people, ground under the heel of the English enemy; her glass case containing old South African Republican flags, assembled from coloured matchsticks by Italian prisoners of war captured in North Africa; and sketches of bearded Boer prisoners in British concentration camps.

Aunt Betsy walked him into the corner of the garden

and showed him the dark-green wooden outhouse, with pages of *Farmers' Weekly* spiked to the back of the door. His pale cheeks turned pink as if looking too hard made him hot.

Seeing the alcove beside the fire where Me spread her blankets at night, he asked: 'Doesn't she have a real bed, even?'

'She's used to it,' said Aunt Betsy.

'Why do you call her Me? That's a funny name.'

'Because she's mine.'

In his new bedroom, Nico opened the one drawer in the tallboy she worried about. Me shut her eyes because that drawer was lined not with full-colour ads for Ipano toothpaste and the luxurious Wolsey 690. It showed a redhead standing on a balcony in a sheath skirt, gloves to her elbows, quite bare from the waist up except for her breasts, very pointy in fine white cloth, and she was leaning back and saying: 'I dreamed I was a Social Butterfly in my Maidenform bra.'

But the boy said nothing. Aunt Betsy had been right. It didn't faze him one bit.

The next morning Nico came to breakfast wearing black jeans with pockets you closed with silver zips on each hip, and a pink shirt, the collar picked out in white saddle-stitching. When Nico asked for golden syrup on his porridge Aunt Betsy sent Me running to the Co-op for a tin of the green and gold, even though she was always saying it rotted the teeth sure as shooting.

Nico asked why his room smelled of liquorice.

'That'll be the dog's blood bush we stored in your cupboard,' says Aunt Betsy.

Me said: 'You chew a twig of the dog's blood bush if you've a cold or a bad chest.'

'That's not very twentieth century, is it?'

He kept a steel comb in his back pocket and swept his hair in two waves around the sides of his head, closing like curtains above his nape.

Me told him she'd been reminded of the tail feathers of an Egyptian goose.

'It's called a ducktail,' said Nico.

Aunt Betsy nodded hard: ''Tis too. I never saw better on a duck.'

He was appalled to learn they had no radio. He planned to buy a radiogram with the cash his dad left him. And a Pontiac Starchief. Back at boarding school he'd got this Trans-Oceanic standard and short-wave portable radio so incredibly powerful it picked up America. After lights out in the dorm he listened on his special portable earphone, no bigger than a dried pea.

After breakfast Nico nodded to Me to follow him to his room. He sat on the bed, opened the fat black suitcase with its silver handle. From a drawer inside the lid Nico slid a shining black record and laid it gently on the turntable. He took from a little tin box a golden thorn and set it in the silver arm.

'Regiontone. Real English record player.'

He cranked the handle like you did a meat mincer and the record began to spin.

'78 rpm.' Nico lowered the silver arm.

A man started singing fast, loud, blurred – he woke up one morning and looked out the door and his cow was missing. He's sad. He ain't had no milk and butter since she's been gone.

Nico sang too, silently, holding his clenched fist before

his frozen lips, rolling his eyes so far back they vanished under his lids. Clicking his fingers and shaking his head and jerking his hips, his face full of pain as if he was crying and dying. His loving mother and father went and left him just like the old milk cow left her loving daddy. Well, he's leaving now, sings Nico – and she's gonna miss her loving daddy. And if she don't believe it, she can count the days he's been gone.

When the music stopped, Nico was kneeling on the floor, he looked really sad.

He opened his eyes slowly. 'You ever been gone?'

'You mean like your loving daddy's gone?'

Nico said: 'It's not about fathers. He's saying his woman's gone. And he doesn't get what he used to any more.'

'What's that?'

Nico grinned: 'Love.'

'But why does he call it milk and butter? Why does he call her a cow?'

Nico said: 'You gotta listen hard. It's not about cows. It's about a guy missing his girl and what she gives him. If you get it, you get it.'

Then he showed her how to wind the machine and they ran the song again.

And she didn't get it. It was very odd, singing about these cows; because Nico was scared of a cow when she showed him one and he didn't ride Balthazar, and he couldn't shoot for toffee and all Aunt Betsy said was never mind, his pa was just as bad.

'Couldn't hit a barn door.'

Aunt Betsy was overcome by Nico. She waved to him from the other side of the glass when he combed his hair in the sitting-room windows. If Nico broke off a piece of hot dripping candlewax and chewed it, she never asked him to spit it into the box above the fireplace because wax, like wisdom and water, was precious.

He checked over his spots in the glass of her Jesus Feeding the Five Thousand and all she said was that verbena was good for acne and any time he wanted a treatment she would oblige.

And she said to Me: 'Death knocks the shoes off a fellow and he needs reshodding.'

That night, Me lay in her bed above the firewood listening to the music reaching her through the wall that separated her from Nico's room. There was a whirring sound like dove wings as he wound up the machine, a little scratchy whisper as needle touched 78, then the voice, high and quavering: 'Hey c'mon fellahs, let's get *reeeyal* gone!'

The throb of it rattled the reeds in the ceiling and tiny flakes of mud came floating down on her face as she lay in her alcove beside the peachwood logs and watched the firelight making waves on the kitchen wall. Sometimes Nico turned the record and played a song about a heartbreaker. She heard him snap his fingers. She knew he was getting gone. By pressing her ear to the wall she made the music go through her, thudding right to her toes.

It was more fun than clenching her jaw when the church organ played.

People sometimes stopped by the cottage, leaned over the fence and openly watched Nico in his zipped jeans and pink shirt, and he didn't care; he started combing his hair. He liked to surprise them. They stared the way they did at a snow-white springbok or a calf with two heads or the watery-eyed albino from Carnarvon who juggled soup cans.

One day Basson's blue Hudson Hornet pulled into the carport and out climbed the girl Childie they'd seen at the funeral. Nico trotted right indoors and got Aunt Betsy to invite her over. Me knew she'd never, ever do it.

But it turned out that it was fine by Aunt Betsy, even if it meant listening while Bananas told her how obedient, how clean Childie was.

'She is trained to treat my word as law.'

Basson demonstrates. He takes Childie by the shoulders and stares into her eyes. She can go across the road to see Nico, *after* she's done the washing up on Saturday afternoons, and she can stay *until* it's time to cook supper. Whatever Aunt Betsy tells her, Childie better jump. She'd better not even look the wrong way, unless Aunt Betsy tells her.

'I'll be watching, and Mrs Basson will be watching . . . and if you step out of line, God help you, because I won't,' said Bananas Basson.

'Thank you, *meneer*,' said Childie.

On her left hand was a brass ring holding a blood-red glass stone which Me loved. Childie's small breasts shifted under her thin cotton dress. She did not wear a Maidenform bra but she was, Me soon realized, a bit of a Social Butterfly.

When Childie came to visit, Nico dressed in his pink shirt and polished his black leather shoes on the backs of his black jeans. They sat in Nico's room, listened to the cow song; they got gone. Childie tapping her feet, she snapped her fingers, her face creased, she was in pain; she's not in pain. Nico turned over the disc and called her his heartbreaker and Childie smiled.

Sometimes Nico and Childie danced, and when the singer got slower and sounded sleepy Nico would call out: 'Hit me again, sister' and Me would wind the silver handle real fast so the music speeded up, and Nico twirled Childie, Me always looked away because Childie wore nothing under her skirt.

Aunt Betsy said: 'Mustn't worry. If Mrs Basson stands Childie on the milking stool before they set out for town, and makes her soap herself all over, then she don't much need pants.'

Whatever Nico asked Childie: did she want to do something? Or go somewhere? Childie always answered: 'I don't mind, thank you, Nico.'

No matter what it was.

Nico and Childie climbed the pear tree. They sat in the highest branches where they thought of the leaves hid them and Me's job was to keep an eye out for anyone approaching. The leaves did not really hide them. Childie was munching a pear, and she let fall the core, bouncing on the branches, seeming not to notice that Nico had his hand down her dress.

Nico asked if they could all walk down to Sampie's Café.

Aunt Betsy, who never let Me out of the yard alone, said: 'Only with pleasure.'

Nico slung his guitar over his shoulder, and from the first step outside the cottage Me didn't want to go. Walking beside Nico in his pink shirt was like walking with a whole parade. And he made it worse by putting his arms around their shoulders and Me wanted to die.

People stopped and stared and this made Nico and Childie laugh.

It was very dangerous; they were mad.

They were passing under Nephew's willow on Voortrekker Street when, with a crash of green leaves that made Childie scream, a man with a huge blond beard and khaki uniform, holding on to his cap, tumbled out of the branches.

Special Constable Nephew jabbed his finger at Nico:

'I know you! What you doing, out with these?' He jerked a thumb at Childie and Me. 'Us is Herringfolk — not them.'

Nico is puzzled. 'What's this Herring, hey?'

Nephew was amazed: 'Don't you know? You, the senator's son? White folk is; others isn't. End of story.'

Nico thinks it over a while and then he grinned: 'Not Herrings, man! It's *Herrenvolk*. It's German. It means "Higher People".'

'Same difference,' says Nephew. 'It means don't fool about with folks who's not. That's the rule.' He taps his police reservist's badge. 'I'll have to report this.'

'Do it. See if I care.'

Nico must have got mad then because he looked over the road and saw this crowd of men in the stoep of the Hunter's Arms and he walked on a while and when he came to the window of the Dutch Reformed Pantry, right across from the hotel, he stopped, unslung his guitar, leaned up against the window and started singing, really loud.

Me said: 'Nico — they're *listening*!'

'Good,' said Nico. He unloaded his steel comb and fixed his hair. And then he told Childie he planned to hit them again.

Childie said: 'I don't mind. Thank you, Nico.' But she didn't mean it. She was frightened.

Me and Childie sat down on the kerbside and put their arms around each other. Me could feel Childie trembling. In the crowd on the stoep of the Hunter's Arms Me recognized Pop Haarhof; Bill Harding in Western Desert army issue khaki shorts, flapping above his bald knobbly knees; Pastor Havenga, well wrapped in heavy brown serge whatever the weather and sporting a black tie, in case a sudden burial was needed.

Across the road was another crowd; a dozen or so brown men. They always sat on the kerb, hoping some farmer driving by would load them on his truck for a day's shearing. The brown guys whistled.

When Nico got into the cow song again, and promised they'd miss him when he was gone, someone from the white side, probably Pop Haarhof, shouted: 'No, we bloody well won't!'

On the brown side they cheered and whistled. And Me knew it was a cheeky kind of whistling.

The white side bawled at them to shut their fucking faces.

The brown side did a little dance in time to the music.

And the white side got even angrier.

Then Bananas Basson turned up, sun gleaming on the ridges of bone where his hair was shaved above his ears. Childie's golden face turned grey when she saw him and she hid her face in her hands. She tried to get Nico to stop singing but his eyes were closed and he was real gone.

Childie was shaking now and crying and she ran down the road with Me after her. Nico stopped singing and he called after them: 'Hey, stick around!' but Childie was running like the wind and Me had trouble keeping up with her. Behind her came Nico, running slowly because he carried the guitar and cursing.

Me heard someone – perhaps Bill Harding – yelling at him: 'Hey, you – get your bloody hair cut!'

Childie cried all the way home and when they got there she screamed because Special Constable Nephew was standing outside Aunt Betsy's gate fingering his revolver.

'I'm a sentry,' he told Nico. 'This house is under guard.'

Childie snuffled and Me didn't know what to do until Nico arrived and said: 'Drop dead!' and pushed past the policeman.

The house was full of people. Aunt Betsy was staring at Sergeant Roux who was reading a newspaper. He had a warrant to search the house and he'd found this in Nico's room. He held up a newspaper.

'What's the *Memphis Scimitar*?'

Aunt Betsy said proudly: 'Memphis – that's in Egypt!'

'What's the boy been doing in Egypt, hey?'

Sergeant Roux read out the headline slowly: 'Suddenly Singing Elvis Presley Zooms into Recording Stardom.'

Nico groaned loud and low, full of contempt: 'Memphis, *Tennessee*, not Memphis, Egypt.'

He sat down at the kitchen table with his arms folded and Me knew he was thinking this was not very twentieth century.

Bananas Basson arrived now and stood staring at Childie and breathing loudly. Me moved behind Aunt Betsy's chair because, usually, it felt safer there. But she knew nowhere was safe tonight. Childie sniffing hard and wiping her nose with the back of her hand kept the table between herself and Basson, who was padding around it like a lion.

'What's a Suddenly Swinging Elvis?' Sergeant Roux demanded. 'It says here, this El-whatever has got a white voice and negro rhythms.'

'It's not a what, he's a who,' said Nico.

'OK, *ja*,' said the sergeant, 'then I'm confiscating this paper.'

Nico tried to snatch it away and it tore in two. Holding his half he ran to his room, and locked the door.

When the police left, the room was quiet, except for Childie's whimpering. Me waited for Aunt Betsy to act; to say something; to help. But she was perplexed, looking from Basson to the girl. Suddenly Basson lunged and took Childie fast by her hair – Me could see black bunches standing out between his fingers – and began pulling her towards the door.

His voice was thick with joy. 'Do what you like with yours – ' he jerked his chin towards Me – 'but this one's mine. And it's not sitting in no damn gutter, singing native rhythms with some pink gyppo. No way!'

Childie was making a yipping sound like a frightened puppy as Basson backed out of the kitchen, keeping a careful eye on Aunt Betsy in case she cut up rough. But she just watched Childie go and it was horrible.

Nico came out of his room, as if nothing had happened, and asked as if he really didn't care: 'Where's Childie?'

Aunt Betsy paced around the kitchen punching her fist into her palm and sucking her teeth. Then they heard, across the road, Basson's belt coming down with a dead meat slap on bare flesh. Childie's cries floated in the night and Aunt Betsy growled in her throat. For the first time, Nico looked scared. He wound the Regiontone and played the cow song so loud the needle jumped and you could hear it halfway across town. Aunt Betsy rolled up her sleeves, grabbed the axe and swinging it under a creamy moon that made her muscles glisten, she chopped logs off an old branch from the pear tree. Me climbed into her cubbyhole beside the firewood and rolled her blankets around her head to block out the music and the screams and the axe slamming into the pearwood logs.

Me never actually saw Nico go but she pictured it. His guitar slung over his shoulders, hefting his record player. The cops had given him back his newspaper and he sellotaped each page and ironed them flat. In her picture of his leaving, Nico climbed on to the bus and opened the *Memphis Scimitar*, he didn't look back. His music went round and round in her head. She tried counting the days he'd been gone. But somewhere on the other side of ten she lost track.

Gone young Nico might be, but he was not forgotten. Someone began plastering pictures of 'this pinko-weirdo-blokie' – Bill Harding's words – on lamp-posts, walls, bridges all over town. Everyone gaped. But the police, Barnabas Basson and Me knew immediately exactly who they were looking at.

His picture was unmissable, stuck up in the white town proper and in Golden Meadow, on trees and telegraph poles in the back of beyond, right across the huge Lutherburg district. More shameless than election bills, more garish than auction notices of bankrupt farms – on

fences and windmills, boldly he shook himself at the sky;
the guy everybody had heard about but few had seen:
the guy that long-haired senator's son had brought to
town: Suddenly Singing Elvis.

Like the wild-haired Russian tumbleweed after a gale,
he turned up 'abso-bloody-lutely everywhere!' said Mayor
Joost.

Decked out in white suit, black and pink shirt, black
and white shoes the toes of which turned inwards as he
sang, mouth open, eyes closed, dark hair tumbling over
his forehead, fingers poised over his guitar strings, his
pelvis trembling. Even in the photo – it moved! He
looked – why he looked just like the boy Nico, all zips
and quiff, shaking his unmentionables in public – 'like a
bad case of ants in the jockstrap,' said Pop Haarhof.

Some people said: 'It's got to be the Commies'; others
were sure the Roman Catholics were behind it, with their
Italian love of gaudy colours; or maybe Jews; or brown
people or even the English, still smarting after being
booted out in '48. Now determined to destroy Western
Christian values.

Sergeant Nephew was instructed to tear down the
pictures. Dominee Havenga roneoed a letter to his congregation condemning the creeping menace of Egyptian-
negro rhythms from Memphis. He appealed to parents of
teenagers: 'Be VIGILANT!' Warning signs were gaudy
items of clothing; facial tics and, especially, sneers;
sheepsfat in the hair ('like the worst sort of Bushman')
and ESPECIALLY hair grown long and combed behind
the head 'like the tail of the Egyptian goose'.

Mayor Joost and the Municipal Council called on
Party members to keep a close watch on friends and

neighbours, for their own good. Some took offence at this, saying they were quite capable of reporting oddbod neighbours without being told, thank you very much!

The cops did a great job tearing down posters and burning them in the graveyard. But the damage was done, said Mayor Joost bitterly – for far worse than the images of the man in the pink shirt was the steady infiltration of his music; the negro rhythms from Memphis that the boy Nico like a plague-bearer had introduced to Lutherburg had infected an entire community, helpless as some benighted tribe against this foreign virus, the poisoned gift of the decadent, dying West.

Seeing this white negro, glowing like a Roman candle, pinned to the lamp-posts advertising his sexual services so enraged certain citizens that they went home and beat up their wives and servants and while everyone agreed this only made matters worse there was some sympathy because simple, straightforward, normal blokes were bloody sickened by this greasy fairy, stacked like a camel, leering from the lamp-posts. Women and servants were liable to fall for negro rhythms and ducktails and pink shirts – just like bloody that! And what then?

However, as martyrs proved to be the lifeblood of the early Christian Church, these punishments only spread the faith. Soon it had lodged in the hearts of the very Party members to whom appeals for loyalty were addressed. And when reported by concerned neighbours for listening to the white negro rhythms from Memphis, the guilty persons made lame excuses like: 'Oh, we only listen to the slow numbers,' or 'I didn't know it was Him.'

That was partly true: he was all the harder to fight because of the frightening rapidity with which he became part of the inflexions, gait, rhythms of Lutherburg life:

one moment people had honestly never heard of Presley; the next they found themselves singing, whistling or humming snatches from songs picked up like flu. It confused the hell out of things to find that Presley sang sacred music too and when the pastor tried to address this by saying: 'OK if you're singing hymns he sings. But none of the white negro stuff – right?'

But people took this as permission to go right ahead and start buying records and players and pink socks.

Quite why the fever should have struck Lutherburg and none of the neighbouring towns, no one ever knew. Other places had their passions: the biannual tug-of-war over in Pumpkinville; the pig-sticking competition in Zwingli; finger wrestling in Eros; brandy and incest in Abraham's Grave and of course rugby everywhere. Some enlightened conservatives like Pop Haarhof said: 'Look, I'm open-minded. I like Frankie Vaughan. I'm even prepared to tolerate Johnny Ray – but this is like a disease.'

People over in Abraham's Grave compared it to the adoration of idols in the temple of Baal; and they'd no sooner said so than a huge effigy of Elvis Presley, traced in white stones, pelvis thrust forward and quiff rearing over his forehead, appeared on Spook Hill. The astonishing thing was that whoever had built this giant had used the very stones that had once spelt out the name of Lutherburg on the hillside. There seemed something indecent, profane even, in using your own name to worship a strange god. It was like the bloody Israelites, they joked in Eros, Lutherburgers would be making golden calves next and worshipping them . . .

Even more alarmingly, white people and brown people sang the same songs with the same words to the same rhythms, snapping their fingers and waggling their lower bodies. It was enough to make a Hottentot honk.

'Seen from behind,' said Dominee Havenga, 'you can't tell them apart.'

When it became clear that there was no stopping it, mayor and municipality and churches and police agreed it would be sensible to give the phenomenon proper direction and shut the mouths of the clever dicks in towns like Zwingli, where Lutherburgers were seen as no better than a tribe of South Sea islanders obsessed by some sort of bloody cargo cult. Not that Zwingli folks had anything to feel proud about. But it was embarrassing, nonetheless, to be mocked by a bunch of randy sheepshaggers . . .

The pastor preached a thunderous sermon warning that anyone who listened to Presley was no Christian. Yet still the fever grew. Mayor Joost himself had been heard by reliable witnesses whistling 'Old Shep'. Soon the very people who condemned the gyrating and the finger-snapping were humming and whistling, and before long Presley was on the lips of people who had never sung anything other than the psalms and the National Anthem.

Me pressed her nose to the garden gate and heard every day about the milk and butter that went missing when the old cow left and she remembered Nico and Childie and Mr Basson's belt. Now there were many other songs about mean women and teddy bears and the blue moon of Kentucky and something being alright, Mama. You heard them shaking the walls of Sampie's café, and in the Co-op, and even in the churchyard. You heard them from shearers and fence menders and gardeners, and from shopkeepers and councillors. You heard the music not just in town, but down on the farm, where people who never saw another face from one month to the next would still greet visitors in the traditional way, with coffee and rusks and prayers – then once the curtains were drawn, with a quick, sly wink, a 78 was shyly slid from its brown papery sleeve and polished on a trouser leg with the proud explanation:

'This is our "All Shook Up". Like me to sing it for you?' Some people bought records even if they didn't own gramophones; you didn't have to go to heaven to believe in paradise, did you? Even those too poor to own a single record knew each new number to hit the charts, because a net of users began exploiting the very latest technology: the new party line. You cranked up your gramophone and, by holding the receiver next to the loudspeaker, the music was relayed simultaneously to dozens of remote farms where anyone wanting to join the party simply lifted the phone.

As suddenly as it had started the phenomenon began to fracture. As with movements of faith which develop far from their source, since no one had ever seen more than a record sleeve or a fan magazine shot of the King, strange variations on the original orthodoxy inevitably manifested themselves. The town split into schismatic sects each claiming to be the true representatives of the faith; some claiming salvation was possible only through works, others holding it took faith alone.

The former held that only those who made the pilgrimage to Memphis would one day see him face to face. And special monthly savings clubs, like Christmas clubs and burial clubs, formed for this purpose; though no one ever left Lutherburg, several citizens were rumoured always to be about to depart on pilgrimage.

Others held that to wait patiently was enough and one day he would come and dwell amongst them. When a child minding goats out at Scorpion Point on the Zwingli road claimed the King had appeared to him and promised he would soon be landing at Cape Town, and then make his way to Lutherburg, dozens of believers spilled out on the Zwingli road, singing and snapping their fingers, sporting guitars and pink shirts and ducktails in a frenzy of welcome; and for three days and three nights, camped in their tents, anticipating with dancing and singing and *braaivleis* and gramophones blasting his songs into the high and rocky crags the promised arrival.

When big E didn't pitch, it dented their faith not one bit; they simply said he had his reasons and one day he would come.

Increasingly, newer sects developed their own ideal versions of the true King, and they held he was exclusive to them alone. There was only one true Elvis and they were his prophets ready to fight to the death for their faith. And it was really good to see how people like the Dominee and Mayor Joost who had once condemned him bitterly, far from calling him a randy greaseball and a white kaffir and a grave threat to Western Christian civilization now went about hailing the King as the first man to understand entirely the concept of separate development because his music had peculiar appeal to different groups and they predicted that the new music, in the right hands, would advance the cause of group freedoms in Lutherburg, under the inspired leadership of the Party.

English speakers maintained Presley had a real sense of

fair play, and believed brown folks and white folks should be allowed to live apart, in a free and natural way; unlike the mayor and his neo-Nazis who believed in ramming segregation down people's throats in a cruel, unnatural way.

Traditional Calvinists, for their part, steered clear of politics and rejected all debate about secular and negro connexions in their ideal Presley, preferring to concentrate on the simple faith of a Christian boy from the South who loved his mother, sang gospel and understood the need for separate but equal freedoms.

The miners over Nickleton way had their vision, too. They believed that Elvis was the patron saint of bare-knuckle fights and they sang: 'I'm evil!' a lot, before traditional punch-ups on Saturday nights.

Over in the brown town they believed Elvis Presley was mixed race, right? And if ever he visited Lutherburg they'd have to change the law that made brown folks ride on special buses, use separate lavatories, carry a pass and get kicked around by the cops.

These dreams and these variant faiths might have continued but for the strange business which Me always thought of afterwards as the Lake of Basson's Ear. With it came her discovery of something inside herself which began to free her from her old life. The day when she came across the Lake of Basson's Ear it was as if, without knowing it, in all her time with Aunt Betsy she had been an explorer lost in a region for which she had no names, no landmarks; she travelled far and with great difficulty until she came to a great new place, the sight of which changed her for ever: a moment when the old world came to an end and a new one struggled to begin – and with it, a new person, a new Her, a new Me.

CHAPTER ELEVEN

1994

Mimi puzzled over things people had once sworn to do, or die, and simply didn't mention any more. How life had adapted! And what they had done loudly, boringly, fatally all their lives, now had never happened; and what they had sworn to die rather than do, they did with gusto, called it duty and pleasure, and wondered why she couldn't see it.

In the beginning, she asked: 'Have you no shame?'

'Shame! Pride is what we have, Mimi.'

'But what about – *before?*'

'That was then – this is now.'

It seemed to her that before Change politics had been a matter of faith. After the Change, faith was a matter of politics.

And nothing summed this up better than the second shock to overcome Pascal Le Gros, who had barely recovered from the treachery of the ex-spy when he encountered the adaptable faith in the Israelites.

Vince and Shirleen de Lange were British Israelites over in Nickleton, an old mining hamlet a good half hour from Buckingham, on badly rutted dirt roads. A couple of dozen prefab miners' houses, a community hall which became the Israelite temple and three iron windmills: that was it. A pit of a place but they were waiting for the end of the world and, since they didn't have a date, waiting had to be cheap.

Just a trickle of them settled at first. Soon it was an invasion. Provincials up from the coast in rusty saloons, suitcases wrapped in plastic bags, hand in hand with bewildered children. Or fancy folk in flight from the big cities, with tales of rape and gunfire in the new South Africa.

When people thought about the Israelites at all it was to wonder how they paid the bills. They weren't saying they were good and they weren't saying they were bad; though everyone agreed they were crazy to live in Nickleton, not a shop, or a school, and the high velocity wind blew sand at those little tin-sided old miners' shacks and rattled them worse than windmill blades.

Israelites were sometimes in Buckingham for groceries, or to scrounge firewood and cheap cuts of meat from Mr Bok the butcher at Karoo Choice, and to drop their kids at the new white school. Which raised eyebrows because they were always broke and the white school cost big bucks. They'd hang about telling people what they should do to be saved. You'd see them in Sampie's Café; in the bar of the Hunter's Arms; in the farmers' Co-op. Bright smiles and guitars and city shoes. Then they'd vanish, quietly as they'd come, back to Nickleton and go on getting ready for Armageddon.

Vince was a big, sandy fellow. The heat got to him. He gave out moistness like steam off a hot road after a summer storm. There was an air of retreat about him. A sense of making off. It was there in his slippery handshake; slide-away sultana eyes. But affable and easy to like. Selling insurance, that had been his game – his neck of the woods, he called it – back in the big world. Before he came to live in dusty Nickleton. Before he became an Israelite.

Shirleen wore a lot of white that set off her dark hair; white leather bolero; white ribbon in her jet hair. The dimple so centred in her cheek you felt it couldn't be real. Bright lips and gales of scent. Where Vince backed off, Shirleen came forward. She was outward, friendly: soft smile and a warm handshake. She'd been on a make-up counter, back in the big world. Before she had her vision. It was hard to imagine any vision persuading her to settle in dusty, stony, pinched, parched countryside, miles from anywhere, being herself so very plentiful, with a roundness she tucked into a pair of white jeans, and high-heeled cowboy boots and the dimple puckered in her plump cheek like the button in an eiderdown.

Israelites hadn't much to do while waiting for the world to end. They were not Christians and they did not talk about God. It was Yahweh this and Yahweh that. They would be saved by Yahweh. Flood, fire and boils lay in store for those Yahweh hadn't saved. How they lived no one knew, but they were always saying their needs were few. A guitar for making up new hymns because hymns were scarce. And a copy of their second sacred text after the Bible, Pastor Tezer's book telling them of good and bad noses in the Holy Land.

They might have been religious but they weren't old-fashioned. They brought their city ways to the Karoo. Shirleen in her boots and her Walkman and her dark twinkle. Vince and his guitar. Modern people. Out and about people. Streets ahead of the bumpkin factor, the khaki shorts brigade and the posses of wrinkled lemon frocks, the beige safari suits and electric blue shorts which were high fashion in Buckingham.

That was the thing about the Israelites. They had style: the world might be about to collapse in fire and flood, but they dressed for it.

Pascal Le Gros took to Vince and Shirleen from the start. Real cognoscenti – and one hell of a change from the bumpkin factor in town. Tolerant too. Israelites didn't want their followers to be British. Or even to speak English. And certainly they didn't have to come from Israel. Broad-minded, travelled people. They'd been to Mauritius, so they were qualified to talk faraway places with Pascal, who had daughters in Miami. Well connected, too. As Pascal told it, the Israelites had left the Holy Land way back when and drifted over to England, and become part of the Royal Family. No wonder the bumpkin factor didn't like them. But then what did one expect from the BF? Minds narrower than needles, two-faced yokels who bragged they never set foot in the pub – devil's cockpit, seat of Satan – then hit the bottle in their back gardens. Oh, yes! Like there was no tomorrow.

Now Vince and Shirleen, they called themselves saved, chosen of the Lord and all that – yet they weren't too proud to drop in at the Hunter's Arms for a civilized snifter. He, for one, welcomed that, as he told Mike and Maureen.

Maureen pointed to their bar card, unpaid for months. She'd welcome some cash. Saved they may be; they were also seriously broke.

Curious souls sometimes visited the Israelite temple in Nickleton on the Sabbath and heard Vince talking about being saved, and warning them to beware of black women

CHRISTOPHER HOPE

who lured white men into bed, determined to steal their genetic codes. Yahweh, the Israelites preached, had voted for separate races and separate tribes, of which they were the first fruit, and anyone who'd seen the violence and lewdness and interbreeding of the cities, since the elections, knew the world was about to snuff it.

Some people liked what they heard and signed on.

It pained the new pastor of the Dutch Reformed Church, young Pastor Niemand, brought in to replace the schismatic Dominee Greet. Buckingham already had too many churches. A Dutch Reformed Church for brown people and a Dutch Reformed Church for white people and a New Reformed Reformed Church for Specially Pure White People, over in the old Anglican church.

'We already have a religious war in town,' Gerrie Niemand protested to Maureen. 'Who needs another?'

Half his flock had already swanned off with the mad defector Greet, and taken up residence in the little old deconsecrated Anglican church, beyond the abattoir. Now he was losing youngsters to these Nickleton soulsnatchers who were eating into his remaining congregation like a plague of bloody locusts.

Maureen gave him short shrift. What did they expect? His own church deserved it! After making everyone live as they did for yonks – no drinking, no racial mixing, no smiling, no raffles, no nothing – now they pretended to be champions of tolerance. Bloody cheek! She adjusted her towering blonde hairpiece, shifted the little parabellum pistol on her hip and started referring to him as minister of the 'Much Deformed Church'.

Maureen was also getting more and more testy about Pascal, or 'the fat crook', as she called him now and when

Mike said that wasn't very nice, she shook her great head of hair: 'He's giving too much credit to the Israelites.'

She stuck a notice to the bar slate where drinkers ran up their tabs: NO CREDIT BY ORDER OF MANAGE-MENT (i.e. Maureen).

This came as a surprise because everyone had believed Pascal Le Gros was a one-third partner in the hotel as well as the brains behind the place, source of culinary inspiration, chief, strategist planning to beat the bumpkin factor. He was going to restock the country with Bush-men; he got wall to wall coverage in the *Zwingli Advertiser*; he was travelled, connected, smart.

He was planning to theme the hotel bedrooms:

'Myths and magic of the old Karoo. A trio of themes. Memories of empire. Traveller, farmer, hunter. Bushman, Boer, Brit. Special wallpaper.'

He was planning to make Buckingham a hub. Persons of the world, at home in Mauritius and Miami, would flock to town. Springbok hunter and philosopher, weary tycoon in search of his soul and rural raconteur would meet and mingle over old-fashioned mulligatawny in the restaurant or stoups of mulled wine in the library.

'What profit?' Pascal demanded when folks asked him was it true – did he own nothing of the hotel? 'What profit if you own the world but lack vision, generosity? If you don't know quality when it stares you in the face?'

And nothing told more surely of Vince and Shirleen's quality than the way they became Israelites.

It had happened one morning in a sports shop in a town called George while they were shopping for run-ning shoes. 'Nike, if you please,' Le Gros would nod when he told the story. 'No tat. My kind of people.'

Vince and Shirleen had been chatting to the saleswoman, as people do back in the big world, about rugby and the politics and armed hold-ups and who got carjacked in their street, when suddenly the saleswoman looks Vince straight in the eye and asks: does he not seek the kingdom of Israel?

Leaving their running shoes unbought Vince and Shirleen hurried home, opened the bible and there it was: Yahweh's order to Moses to seek the promised land. Within weeks they had given up their jobs, sold their house and moved north to Nickleton. It had been a vision. People with vision impressed Pascal, tremendously.

Maureen announced to Mike that she had had a counter vision. In it Pascal appeared as the Big White Bwana. And the Big White Bwana was messing up. Wasn't he? And to Pascal's surprise, Mike said, yes, bloody right. Messing up something chronic.

Until then Mike had been hedging his bets. He and the fat man went back a long, long way. Big, round Pascal in his tennis whites. Little dark Mike, slight and sharp. When you asked Mike what he was, he said he was a sidekick. And Pascal was the brains, the business end of the operation that brought the three of them to the Hunter's Arms. But Mike was hooked up to Maureen now. Widowed Maureen whose late husband had worked on the copper mines in Zambia. One minute Rusty was there, the next it was toodle-oo, she told Mike when they got together.

Maureen of the big bucks, of the huge hair, and the tiny pistol and the doddering, incontinent Dobermanns, Brad and Bruce, whom Pascal hated worse than Bill Harding hated his wife's budgerigar. Maureen threatened to shoot Pascal if he harmed her dogs but it was Mike who did the real damage; he told Pascal that his menus were the pits. Who'd want Sole Bonne bloody Femme in a desert town where they thought good cooking was roasting half a sheep on the fire and pouring beer down your throat while turning the spit with your bare toes?

Maureen booked a weekend away and, in case he didn't take the hint, she told Pascal they were sick of minding the bar while he propped it up with his belly, claiming to be owner and sole proprietor of the 'best damn little pub in a hundred miles'. Sick of Big White Bwana, wafting about like a noisy cloud, spouting ideas. He sailed by and they got wet. Who was doing the work? Throwing out drunks; talking staff into staying on when Pascal screamed at them for not knowing how to flambé bananas? Poor little brown people ordered to pour half a bottle of brandy over the pudding, worth a month's wages, and setting fire to it. No wonder they messed up! The sight of good hooch going to waste got too much to bear and they tried to snuff out the bloody flames with their bare fingers.

Maureen hoped, with a good deal of heavy sarcasm, that he'd take the hint. To get some much needed R & R, she and Mike were off to the coast, Friday through Sunday.

Pascal did not take the hint. He felt the break would do him good and hired Vince and Shirleen to mind the hotel. They got close instructions about checking the receipts in the public bar where Henry the brown barman and his predominantly brown customers roistered until the small hours; and they got instructions about the karaoke machine and to make bloody sure that only

respectable persons were admitted to the ladies' bar.
Brown was fine. So long as it was *respectable* brown. Shoes
were to be worn at all times. No spitting. Anyone effing
and blinding could do that sort of thing in the public
bar.

Maureen asked how they could trust strangers to keep
decent till receipts.

Pascal shook his head sadly.

'If you can't trust a British Israelite, whom can you
trust? When you've made your peace with Yahweh, when
you're set for Armageddon, you do not fiddle the
accounts. Finesse replaces pettiness.'

Just looking at Shirleen told him she was full of finesse.

Maureen began telling Mike that 'the fat crook' was
sneaking into Nickleton at night and banging Shirleen.
Mike put it to the guys in the pub: could they picture
Pascal, in his baggy cricket flannels and white jumper,
rearing from chin to knee, cresting over his belly like a
wave of milk, huge Pascal stepping nightly on tiny feet
in sparkling tennis shoes down Nickleton's single street,
passing the old station, the rusting minehead workings,
and sailing invisibly into Shirleen's little tin-sided house?
Which was only a little bigger than he was. You might
as well believe the moon grew wheels and waltzed about
the sky and no one noticed.

If this wasn't entirely credible, Maureen believed,
alternatively, that if Pascal wasn't doodling Shirleen in
Nickleton then he was doing it at home. Which was an
even weirder idea – Shirleen in her cowboy boots
clippety-clopping into the Hunter's Arms and slipping
into Pascal's bed. Maureen had said once that the only
thing bigger than Pascal's belly was his opinion of
himself. His idea of love would be to go to bed with

himself. Yet, still, something told her he was banging Shirleen.

JJ, the ex-cropsprayer, mumbled into his beard in the corner of the bar that it was like hothouse gasses. When Bill Harding bought him a beer he explained. People pumped carbon dioxide into the atmosphere. Damaged the ozone layer. Right? Got back bad ultra-violet rays that gave people cancer. OK? Well, likewise the elections. Hot air. Poisoned promises gave people diseases of the head. Dreams of free houses and electricity and phones sent farm workers loopy. Bamboozled them into choosing a brown mayor. Dominee Greet ripping off his toga because ten brown people walked into church. Setting up in opposition to the old firm. The arrival of the British Israelites fleeing the 'horrors of the Great Whore'. At first he'd thought they meant the Great War, but they weren't old enough for the last bloody war. Then Pascal, Mike and Maureen buying the Hunter's Arms, which hadn't made money in years. Some people reckoned the three of them must be sleeping together. Crazy, right? Now Maureen's run mad. Let Mike the Spike try logic on Maureen. Just ask her this question: if Pascal was doing what she said he was doing, why go away when Shirleen was minding the bar on Friday night?

Maureen screamed when she heard about three to a bed and said she'd rather kill herself. But she had an answer to JJ's question: because, somehow, in ways which she did not fully understand yet, Pascal was pulling a fast one, that was why.

CHAPTER TWELVE

1958

Two whole Christmases had passed since she heard the big belt coming down and Childie weeping in the night and Nico left.

On Christmas morning, Arletta Basson gave Aunt Betsy a progress report.

'If little miss Smartypants acts like a common farmgirl, then on the farm she stays. Not so? Barnabas tells her: for Pete's sake, get yourself some self-respect. You're worth more than two-and-six and a bag of monkey nuts. He's always kind to her, my Barnabas. But then men don't see like us, do they, Aunt Betsy, or he'd know that little madam's no better than she ought to be. Turn your back for a sec and she's off, doing things.'

'What things?' Aunt Betsy asked.

Arletta arched her eyebrows, a heavy, careful, compact woman with a good square forehead and what Betsy regarded as a quite unrealistic respect for her husband. If you asked Arletta about the weather, said Aunt Betsy, she did not give you an answer till she'd checked with Basson.

'Things with – ' Arletta lowered her voice – 'm-e-n. She's been sneaking out to Bushman's Drift. There by the shearers' camp. And for why? You know what those boys there are like! Me, I'd have thrown her out. But Barney says: she's just a kid. So he locks her in the barn for three days, for her own good. He's a real softie is Barnabas Basson.'

'There's men who does things too.'

'Oh yes?' Arletta looked shocked and went home to prepare lunch.

Christmas Day languor hung over Lutherburg and in the summer haze mirages here and there made the white stones in the wide sandy flow of Voortrekker Street, and the church steeple and the old slave bell, tremble like watery reflections; the day was wound up like a clock. With the arrival of the new Lutherburg it was felt that there should be no walking on a Sunday, and no sport and no outward movement of any kind, though citizens with cars sometimes took them for a spin around the showgrounds, the dam and the graveyard, driving very slowly, and men wore suits and ties and women wore hats and sat there without moving; the important thing being stillness, even in motion.

Christmas was like Sunday, but twice as holy.

So great had been the advance of freedom in the past ten years that it had been decided that every group should enjoy its own, separate version. Decent people should stay indoors on Sundays and religious holidays, and never stray, but remain in their own traditional areas. For Lutherburgers proper this was not too hard – respectable folk never set foot in the brown town.

The trouble was the other side. The number of people in Lutherburg proper employing brown servants increased steadily and, as a result, about the same number of brown people wandered the streets on Sundays and religious holidays as did in the week, because there was the same cooking and scrubbing and washing and baby-minding and gardening to be done.

But somehow on Sundays and holidays, in the great silence of lunchtime or the sunny indolence of mid-afternoon, or amid the echoing darkness of Sunday night, these temporary sojourners seemed fewer, perhaps because they had learned to move with great stealth, or perhaps because sensible people had learned to overlook them.

By lunchtime, the hush on Voortrekker Street grew profound; everyone was gathering around the dining-room table, and the servants in the kitchens were sweat-ing over roast lamb and potatoes; gem squashes, cinna-mon pumpkin, creamed cauliflower and buttered carrots; porcelain gravy-boats full to the brim were making their uncertain way into the dining room where the family were resting their heads on their hands, saying grace. It seemed as if everyone in the world was either praying or eating, this Christmas Day.

Everyone except Me who was in the front garden tipping a watering-can over Aunt Betsy's monkey flowers which were protected from the hot dry winds blowing over the plains from the Snow Mountains by a curtain made of silver paper gathered from boxes of de Rezke filter-tips. The flowers yawned in the heat, their butter-yellow throats reminding her of thirsty puppydogs, so greedily did they lap up the water.

Her peace and her pleasure were interrupted when Mr Basson's truck pulled up with a screech of brakes outside the bungalows across the road. He must have been out on his lands, for he did not run his beautiful Hudson Hornet on farm roads but reserved it for very stately trips around the village on Sunday afternoons, with Arletta beside him.

Basson swung down from the driver's seat, wearing khaki shorts and a khaki hat and a big sheath-knife strapped to his belt. Me could not pull her eyes away even when she felt the last of the water sputtering from the can, and she stood there, feeling naked and foolish, knowing it was just her and Mr Basson, not looking at each other looking at each other in the hot sun and the silence. Bananas Basson lifted his head now and stared at Me, the blind, incurious stare of a buck seen through her rifle sights, miles off but uneasily aware of her presence. He seemed drunk, rooted, looking this way and that and she could have sworn he trembled. Though he was not seeing her, she felt trapped. At last he shook his head like a man waking from a dream and walked over to the garden tap. As soon as his back was turned, placing the watering can quietly on the ground, she ran indoors, hearing behind her the sharp gurgle of the rushing water and she knew he'd been docking lambs' tails against the scab and the worm and now he was sluicing off because the lambs bleed and make a mess on hands and boots.

In the kitchen Aunt Betsy was preparing fish. A large smoked snoek, thin-lipped, black-eyed, pungent, lay on the table. She was the only person in Lutherburg to eat fish on Christmas Day and the fact was widely resented. What riled people most was that Aunt Betsy had got that fish off the smous, whom they thought they'd seen the last of. It made people madder still to be told that Aunt Betsy had ordered her fish on religious grounds.

'I want it for Christmas because Jesus was a fish.'

'I thought he was a lamb,' said the smous.

Aunt Betsy got out her library book, *A History of Christianity*, and showed him a picture of the Roman catacombs: 'Before He was a lamb He was a fish.'

She'd been taking out library books ever since Nico left. 'If that boy can know what he does about Memphis, then I can wake up to the world, even at my age,' said Aunt Betsy.

The smous was no happier than anyone else with Aunt Betsy's order for Christmas fish.

'It's not my line no more.'

He did not use donkeys any longer; he did not peddle; he was a businessman; he drove a Studebaker Transtar truck and if some kids who remembered the old days ran after him in the street shouting: 'Slowcoach, slowcoach – here comes the cock-a-roach,' he told them to please bugger off.

'I travel now,' he tells Aunt Betsy.

'You always did.'

'Commercial traveller. In the bar business. Beautiful cork beer mats, perfect miniatures of your favourite spirits. Music if you need it. Drinking birds with felt heads who pluck from your glass a drop for their parched tongues, as if by magic. Book matches. *Anything* but fish. And anyway we're too far from the coast for fresh fish.'

Aunt Betsy thought this over and then she went into the lucerne fields and bagged a fat Egyptian goose. 'Swop you,' she said.

So the smous brought her the smoked fish she craved.

It was nearly ten years since Aunt Betsy had walked over to Silver Street with her stones of cold water soap. Ten Christmases and always the excitement of their presents. Often the girl's was something she had made herself. A catapult, the tongue cut from springbok hide, the rubber thongs from an old inner tube; or an ingenious little tractor made from a cotton reel, notched for traction with Aunt Betsy's dragon-faced red clasp-knife, using a sliver of candle wax to lubricate its stabilizing winding arm which let you tighten its rubber band spring. It crawled halfway across the house when fully wound.

First Christmas after Nico left Aunt Betsy gave her a wind-up Regiontone record player, and when the passion ran through the town she gave her Presley 78s; and Me sang them to herself, but none ever moved her as much as the old milk cow who went away. Aunt Betsy's gifts proliferated after the night Childie got beaten and Nico left: a hunting knife with a bone handle, her own .22 rifle. Their range and luxury made Me feel uneasy, grateful but uncomfortable; they seemed to her a kind of language for things Aunt Betsy simply could not say herself, they were too rich, too sweet, like talk made of chocolate.

Now, beside her plate, out of pink tissue paper there emerged a hand mirror of light blue wood and a silver surround. Me studied her face, broad, with a slight slant to the dark brown eyes, and cheekbones that rose just a little, curly dark hair over which a pink plastic hairband arched like a magic horseshoe. Last year's Christmas present.

Me gave other things in return: she rubbed Aunt Betsy's feet for an hour with arnica oil until she was dozing happily; she cut a double pile of firewood; she shone the old stove until the scratches in the ironwork looked like fine eyebrows. But now as she sat down to Christmas lunch, try as she might, she could not eat the fish; it was oily, too salty, it stuck to the roof of her mouth.

And so it was that when the shot rang out close by, Me acted quickly, spitting the mouthful on to the side of her plate and following Aunt Betsy out of the door and across the street and into the Bassons' garden. Something like a siren wailed inside the house, growing louder with every step. Everything else looked just as it had when Me came indoors, away from Basson's blind stare. There was the Ford pick-up in the driveway, its paint ticking quietly in the fierce summer sun. A pool of water glinting in the mud beneath the garden tap where Basson had sluiced off his boots.

Aunt Betsy did not stop to knock, she simply pushed open the front door and they burst into the house.

Arletta Basson sat at the dining-room table still wearing her Christmas hat, a green crown with silver glitter on its points, and she was screaming. Mrs Basson's scream was all one way. Pushed out of her chest. Hanging there, a terrible thin song, so long Me wondered how she could keep going without breathing in.

The astonishing thing was that although they were in the house in seconds, they were not the first. A dumpy woman in a red headscarf was holding a small boy with one hand and she was stroking Mrs Basson's face with her free hand. Aunt Betsy knew her: old Ma Williamson with two sons, Baba and Little Boy. Mrs Basson's scream flew like a bird. The remains of a leg of lamb lay on the carving board; the pumpkin was still warm and steamed gently. On the polished parquet floor lay broken cups and saucers, spilt milk, scattered sugar.

Mrs Williamson flicked her eyes towards the bedroom,

and so they walked in and there, stretched out on his back on the pink candlewick bedspread, lay Bananas Basson, staring wide-eyed at the yellow plastic candelabrum with its three cardboard tapers cunningly weeping yellow wax. He was also wearing his Christmas hat, a black Egyptian fez with a red tassel and he was holding a revolver in his right hand. There was a dark patch at his right temple and a smell of burnt paper and singed hair. Leaking from his left ear was a steadily spreading lake of blood.

Ever afterwards on her private map Me set her bearings by the Lake of Basson's Ear. It clarified the way forward. She looked into the dark mirror and saw herself. 'I am here,' she said. 'They are there.' After that, she was never the same.

More and more people off the street were crowding into the house, staring at the woman and the remains of the Christmas lunch. How could a street, empty a few minutes before, produce such a crowd out of nowhere? Perhaps, feeling her audience growing, staring, waiting, Arletta Basson had stopped screaming though she still wore her Christmas crown and she sat at the table as still as ice.

Mrs Williamson went on stroking her head. Her son, Little Boy Williamson, thinking no one was watching, reached out, tore a piece of meat off the joint and stuffed it into his mouth.

Ma Williamson spoke softly, comfortingly: 'What happened, in heaven's name?'

'Mr Basson,' began Mrs Basson, speaking of her husband

as if he were only slightly better known to her than to the others, 'came home for lunch. I was just making the gravy . . .' Here she began weeping.

'Go on, *mevrou*,' prompted Mrs Williamson, 'you were making the gravy?'

'Then I heard his truck. Just like always. And then the garden tap and I knew he'd been docking sheep's tails. I called to him: "Why wash your hands in the garden, man? Come inside."'

Arletta took off her hat and wiped her eyes with the crumpled green tissue paper and sobbed for long minutes while Ma Williamson stroked her head and murmured: '*Ag*, no, shame, hey!'

And the watching crowd echoed her, drawing out the sympathy into a long groan: '*Ag*, no, shame!'

'And then he ate?' asked Mrs Williamson.

Arletta Basson nodded. 'Sat down and said grace and we ate lunch. He even asked for more potatoes 'cause he loves potatoes.'

'Yes, *mevrou*,' said Ma Williamson. 'And then what?'

'He said he must go and do something.' Arletta Basson looked helplessly at the broken tea things, the spilt milk. 'Then he did. I heard the bang.'

She started screaming again and still screaming she got down on her knees and began sweeping the smashed cups with her bare hands.

Ma Williamson shook her head, a movement so amazing that it far outweighed her words, which were pretty shocking in themselves. She looked down at the weeping, sweeping woman and said, plain and clear: 'Well, I'm sorry – that's just not good enough.'

Aunt Betsy spoke now for the first time, very quiet: 'Did he do lots of sheep this morning, my dear?'

Arletta picked up her crown, smoothed it and began to tear it into strips. Very neat, and very concerned. More like her old self now, pleased that there was a proper person speaking to her at last and not one of these folk from the brown town. The strangers were peering through the bedroom door where her husband lay staring at the three-branched candelabrum. It wasn't nice. She smiled now, opened her mouth but nothing came out; and her ripped paper crown melted in her tears until it looked like green mashed potato, sticking to her fingers.

Aunt Betsy's eyes went blank, the way they did when she was turning over something difficult. Like calculating which direction the springbok would run from; or gauging where underground water might lie in a dry field.

'He wouldn't have done this – ' Mrs Williamson wasn't letting go – 'not if it was just sheep's tails.'

The watchers shook their heads: 'Not if it was just sheep's tails.'

But what was it he'd been doing if it wasn't sheep's tails? That's what Aunt Betsy was wondering with her gentle questions; that's why her eyes had gone all shadowy and she seemed a million miles away and Me could see that she had a pretty good idea.

Sergeant Nephew burst in and when everyone ignored him he drew his revolver and began yelling: 'Out of the way, you lot.'

The watchers stared at the bedroom door so hard that Nephew had to go see for himself. He marched right in and came right out again, white as a daisy and licking his lips. He put his gun back in its holster and looked as confused as everyone else.

Me knew then what made the watchers so brave. For

once it was white folks who were in deep trouble and as for the brown folk, shocked as they were, they were enjoying it. There was no denying it or hiding it.

Ma Williamson repeated: 'A man doesn't do *this* because of sheep's tails.'

And each time she said it Arletta Basson shuddered as if she'd been struck but she kept on smiling at Aunt Betsy like she was a lifeline, a saviour, a proper person to cling to, amid savages and sneerers. Someone who'd stay by her.

Aunt Betsy had that impatient air she got when she was planning a trip and Me knew that just as soon as she decided where she was going, they'd be gone in a puff of dust.

Sergeant Nephew spread his arms like a man coralling geese and began to urge the watchers towards the door. They moved quietly. Slowly, too. They were going, but they were doing it in their own good time.

And when he thought no one was watching, Little Boy Williamson stole another piece of lamb.

CHAPTER THIRTEEN

1994

In fact, it was Vince who minded the bar on the Friday night. Pascal, Maureen and Mike left for the coast. Propping a big Hebrew Concordance against the cash register, doling out the beers and doing a gentle sell on Israelite beliefs. No one much liked the religious stuff. But Vince was unpushy and a good quick barman. You never needed to ask twice.

And Shirleen was free to mingle. There was about her a directness, turning on the speaker a clear fixed gaze and you knew she really cared about hunting springbok; or the best way of docking lambs' tails and not getting blood on your boots; or why the dam was empty again this year. She was a fine audience. Her scent was full of flowers. There was something friendly in the creak of her white jeans when she crossed her knees and nodded and leaned forward, full of understanding, that made it a pleasure to explain things to her. To offer her a drink. Sliding a bill across the counter with a wink at Vince: 'Same again for my friend here,' or: 'Give your good lady a refill.'

She had this way of matching drinks to the speaker. Sensible port and lemon with Mr De Wet, the inspector for the Volksbank, up on a night's audit, who said he'd never had such a man-to-man talk with anyone in Buckingham; Babychams with Bill the last Anglican who told her jokes about lunatics. Plain beer with Mr Williamson the new brown mayor, who was a democrat and hated fancy habits, and asked if she'd thought of serving on the town council?

When she protested that she simply couldn't keep up with the serious drinkers and she'd wait till her thirst caught up with her, thanks all the same, they patted her arm and said: 'Not to worry,' and: 'Tomorrow's another day,' and told Vince to put the cash in the till – for later.

Vince smiled, very relaxed, setting up the drinks with lazy ease and paging through his Hebrew Concordance. How many people knew, for instance, that 'Adam' was an old Hebrew word meaning 'red' or 'ruddy' and referred to the colour pink, as we experience it when we blush? And who were the only people in the world to blush? Europeans, white folks. That's who. We were the original Adamites, children of the ruddy countenance, pink people, the chosen of Yahweh.

And everyone was pretty impressed. They couldn't recall a Friday night like it. Shirleen listening, Vince reading Hebrew while he kept the beers coming. Even Mr Bok the butcher, who had once called the Israelites a bunch of wankers – religious? his arse! probably fleeing their creditors – now found himself telling Shirleen all about slaughterhouse techniques, and he said well, maybe Vince had a point because, in his experience, black guys didn't blush.

It was JJ, deep into sweet sherry, after sharing with Shirleen the story of how, after the war, he and a few friends built South Africa's first iron lung from spare airplane parts and saved countless polio victims, who summed up the general feeling when he raised his beer and thanked Vince and Shirleen for a wonderful, wonderful evening.

On Saturday night, it got even better. The bar was crowded soon after opening time. The entire rugby team came down after a hard game away, against neighbouring Zwingli. Big boys called Dion and Darryl and Danie, their ears rubbed raw from the scrum, smelling of their showers and Brut aftershave, and planning on an evening of snooker.

Normally the older customers kept well clear. The young were inclined to get rowdy after a few beers and dance on the snooker table. Or, after the gymkhana, to ride horses through the swing doors of the bar. Whereupon Pascal in white flannels and cream sweater would rise above the bar, wax full and fat and furious, and wag his finger, spots of darkest red glowing on his cheekbones, and threaten to send them to the public bar where the brown guys drank, and they jeered him good-naturedly and called him Old Man Moon Rise and Moon Doggie and Fool Moon.

But this Saturday night, Shirleen was soon reaching out to the young around the pool table, saying she felt really silly not being able to play, but she simply couldn't learn. After that, she and the boys got on like houses on fire. Pressed to the pocket lip, she leaned roundly over the cue, shining, in her white bolero and leather pants, with Danie or Dion putting their arms around her shoulders to steady the shot. Cheering when she potted her chosen colour. Happily stumping up for her next Campari and orange.

And when she cried that she simply could not keep up

with them, they said: 'Not to worry,' or: 'Night's young, isn't it?' – and told Vince to put the money on ice till Shirleen's thirst caught up with her.

On Sunday night Vince and Shirleen again opened the bar, something Pascal never did because Sundays in the old Lutherburg belonged to God and you didn't even go for a walk and old habits died hard. But the bumpkin factor faded when Vince opened that Sunday night and the new Buckingham was up and running. Farmers from miles about and even a few women. Normally, no respectable woman walked into the Hunter's Arms bar – not by the front door, anyway.

Maybe the women came because they'd heard tell of Shirleen's natural friendliness. But they soon put their doubts aside. Shirleen gave her attention to everyone, without exception. She was working hard, trying to be pleasant. Like a really professional hostess. She was much friendlier than Maureen who never left the bar, always packed her pistol, sometimes drank more than the guys and when her perspiration flowed you could see her thin grey hair beneath her loosened hairpiece.

The bar was humming; you could hardly see across the room for the smoke and bonhomie and it must have been pretty late in the evening before anyone began to register that, from time to time, Shirleen – who'd been listening astonished to the rocketing prices of good bull semen – suddenly vanished.

She was never gone long. Ten minutes – maybe five. Then she'd be back, slipping effortlessly onto a stool, picking up her Drambuie, and listening to tales about the days when wool sold so high that you drove around the veld pulling scraps off trees, or why you could never tame a wild Bushman.

It took a further little while to realize that when she disappeared, so did whoever she had been listening to last.

People got it at more or less the same time. Everyone except Vince apparently, busy pouring shots for customers or collecting the price of drinks waiting on Shirleen's thirst to catch up with her. And saying happily that if you were an Israelite your needs were few and Yahweh would provide.

Everyone began chewing over the space between their ears. Men were wondering: was *this* how Yahweh provided? Women were trying to recall where their husbands had been all night. Everyone knew the Israelites were broke and, sure, groceries and school fees and firewood had to be paid for somehow. But *this* broke? When they got it they looked around for someone to blame. It was a bloody mess, that's what it was. It could hardly get worse. Especially if you were a busy guy, a clean liver, a hard worker and a good Christian, and you hardly ever set foot in the pub. And your wife never ever did, until tonight and now you found yourself hobnobbing with a woman who went upstairs with guys and sold her body.

It got worse. They were the guys she went upstairs with.

Vince went on talking in the silence, explaining how all you needed to be saved was the Adamite complexion: pass the blush test, Vince urged, and join the British Israelites. He gave his shy, affable grin. Yahweh would provide.

Once more, it hit everyone at more or less the same ghastly moment that Vince wasn't the innocent he seemed. He not only knew what Shirleen was doing –

he approved! He *ran* her! This wasn't a bloody scandal, it was business. Vince had been marketing his wife as a rare, once-in-a-lifetime offer. Each guy, as he slipped from the bar, had believed himself specially chosen. It was easy enough to fix. The Hunter's Arms had plenty of empty rooms – each with an identical white candle-wick bedspread, clean sheets and everyone an identical set-up.

It looked as if Yahweh not only provided, he doubled your money. While Vince banked the bucks for Shirleen's untasted drinks in the bar downstairs, she was rolling the customers in the bedrooms above their heads.

It was Mr Bok the butcher, draining his beer and downing the glass with a firm slap on the counter, who spoke for all of them: 'Me, join a bunch of Jews? No ways!'

Shirleen reached for her Tia Maria and studied the ceiling. Vince flushed and said he could not allow that remark to pass. It was a lie. The Israelites were not Jews.

Bill the Anglican, who had gone upstairs with Shirleen first, wanted to know in a very loud voice: 'If not – what?'

Shirleen crossed her knees and said, 'British actually.'

The creak of her white pants sent shivers around the room when she added: 'Through and through.'

She talked about how the Queen of England descended from Abraham. Beneath her throne reposed the Stone of Scone – which was actually the Tablet of the Law Yahweh gave to Moses.

JJ, who had borrowed off Mr Bok to go upstairs, was mad as hell. If British Israelites were the real thing, then who were the guys in Israel? Fairies?

Vince began hurting. Sweating. The others in Israel were fakes. Interlopers. They'd seeped into the Promised

Land from Semitic sewers further east and forced true Israelites overseas.

'Look, guys – ' he held up Pastor Tezer's *Book of Noses*, and turned his face sideways – 'check it out. Ours are straight. And we blush.'

'So you ought!' someone yelled from the back of the room, and got a big laugh.

Mr Bok said that if Israelites weren't Jews then they gave a bloody good impersonation. And when Vince asked: what did he mean by that, the butcher threw a 'you know what I mean' glance at the cash register and stomped out, and they all followed him. Fearful men watched closely by frowning women. Dreading the interviews to come. Wondering how long it would be before the news was all around town. Vince started yelling about the ire of Yahweh scorching those who mocked his Chosen People. But no one really cared. Seriously, what more could the Israelites do? The damage was done.

When he got back next morning Pascal found not a lot of love around. People wanted someone to blame. And it was all his fault. If he hadn't pulled her in, if he hadn't gone off to the coast, if he hadn't been the one who was supposed to be banging Shirleen in the first place – then maybe none of this would have happened.

Pascal tried to put a good face on it. He said: 'I, for one, refuse to be held responsible for the full-scale adultery of an entire town.'

He checked the till. Receipts doubled; cash accounted for; takings present and correct.

Considering how wrong Maureen had been about him,

she might have given Pascal a break. But now she implied that maybe he wasn't up to it anyway. All froth and no champagne was the way she put it. After all, everyone else had been screwed, the hotel included. Why not him? She scorned his profitable accounts. What about drinks paid for but never poured? What about the mattress money? Vince and Shirleen – Brothel Keepers of Distinction – had made big bucks. The hotel would never see a cent of it.

Mike the Spike knew he was supposed to feel bad, for Maureen's sake, but he just couldn't keep his admiration to himself. It bubbled out of him. He went on about what a rip-off it was, and a scam, a bloody cheek! Only to start asking, again: 'Hey, but listen – did the mayor *really* go upstairs? How many bedrooms did Shirleen use?' Hell, they'd never filled that number. And he sat up late working out Vince's average nightly takings, muttering: 'Jesus, classy stuff!'

Come Monday lunchtime a bilious silence was settling like fog over the town where people had done what they shouldn't and no one knew how to handle it. That was when the invasion began. A cavalcade of old cars from Nickleton carrying every British Israelite – young and decrepit, pensioners, kids, babies – came clattering into town and formed up outside the whitewashed, thatched Municipal Council Buildings in Democracy Drive.

They must have worked all night long to organize their banners: 'True Israel Is Us' and 'Yahweh Rules' and 'Jews Can't Blush'. They'd also made a huge blow-up of the important drawings of Jewish noses from Pastor Tezer's *Book of Noses*. At a signal from Vince, the Israelites tapped their noses to show how straight they were.

The cops slipped out of the station and would have

closed down the show but Mr Williamson, the new brown mayor, reminded them of the big change since the elections. We could disagree in public now. It was a healthy sign. So long as we did not incite racial hatred. No one was sure if this was racial hatred. It was difficult, to begin with, to see what the Israelites were so mad about – until the crowd, led by Vince and Shirleen, marched down Democracy Drive to Joffe Brothers and Sons and milled around the front stoep, yelling for the Jews to come outside and do the nose test.

That's when Mayor Williamson went over and explained to Vince and Shirleen that the Joffes' sons sold up and headed for the diamond fields forty years before. All that remained was the name.

But they weren't giving up. They marched down to the old synagogue on Leibrandt Street where they began chanting: 'Adamites United Will Never Be Defeated'. The old synagogue had been for decades the dinosaur museum, full of dusty fossils and clawprints fixed in rock.

When she saw the marchers, the curator Trudy du Plooy, a timid woman who wore pink, and was wife of the headmaster – one of the first to go upstairs with Shirleen – burst into tears and ran out of the back door and all the Israelites cheered.

After that things calmed down. The Israelites went back to Nickleton and got on with their lives. When Shirleen appeared in town, in her bolero and boots and wide smile, women looked right through her; men looked the other way.

To Mimi de Bruyn it seemed, as the months passed, that something perfectly clear had come out of the wholesale conversion of the town to the charms of the Israelites; for Shirleen was evidently and rather proudly pregnant. There were rumours that Vince had not taken the news well. If the child wasn't his, then there was the interesting possibility that any one of a dozen or more men, from the new mayor, Mr Williamson, to one of the boys in the rugby squad, might have fathered it.

But it was difficult to know what was happening because, with the paternity question hanging over their heads, no one said a word about Shirleen's condition on the dual principle that what you did talk about hadn't happened, and what you did not talk about was no one's business but your own. And you weren't talking.

There were a couple of isolated incidents in the weeks following. A swastika was spray-painted on the wall of the old synagogue. And in the far corner of the cemetery reserved for Jews, behind a screen of cypresses, two headstones dating back half a century were kicked over and yellow paint daubed on the fallen stones.

It went all the way to the new Council. In the old days there would have been prayers for guidance like there were prayers for rain and rugby and for smiting the enemies of the Lord. But opening prayers before meetings had been replaced after the election by the multi-faith Minute of Meditation and Mayor Williamson asked councillors to meditate on the right of all to protest, so long as it did not offend any section of the rainbow community in the new South Africa. It was then agreed that the swastika be removed from the town museum, because defacing public property could not be permitted. The desecrated graves were more of a problem. But after a long debate they reached what the mayor called the judgement of Solomon – until Mr Moosah, the Moslem member, objected and it was changed to the judgement of democracy.

It was decided to do nothing. The daubed, tumbled stones behind the screen of cypresses were left where they lay, on the grounds that, as there were no Jews left in Buckingham, there was no one to offend.

CHAPTER FOURTEEN

1959

Aunt Betsy nodded to Me, and they left.

Behind them, Arletta Basson, as pale as the *witgat* tree under her Christmas crown, with nothing to say to the women who stayed behind, stroking her shoulder and murmuring: '*Ag*, shame, hey!'

Behind them, Sergeant Nephew's cry: 'Get the hell outa here, can't you!' – increasingly shrill, because the witnesses let him see, clear as sunrise, that they were going but in their own sweet time, thanks very much.

Behind them, the Lake of Basson's Ear. And a miracle. A double miracle because Basson's death made the formerly important people of Lutherburg proper shrink into their skins and grow as pale as ghosts. And turned the previously invisible ghosts of the streets into flesh and blood and impudent eyes, taking their own sweet time.

It made Me think of church and Dominee Havenga up in the white leatherette pulpit saying that Jesus died that others might live. Well, so had Bananas Basson.

Back at the cottage Aunt Betsy saddled Balthazar, all the while growling and punching herself on the chin – and they hit the road out of town. Me did not dare to ask their destination though, somehow, when they swerved off the Beaufort road and took the track between squat ugly koppies freckled with shards of sun-blackened rocks lying like smashed dinner plates amongst the thorn bushes she suddenly she knew where they were bound and it gave her swimming feelings in her belly; Aunt Betsy was taking her back to the place where she'd begun, before she'd even been Me.

Basson's farmyard, deserted but for a few chickens peck-ing in the gravel outside the kitchen door, was no longer the place she remembered. The wool boom had bought an expensive new house of yellow brick veined with blue, steel-framed picture windows, a corrugated iron roof and a tall wireless aerial stabbing the crystal sky.

Aunt Betsy breathed through her nose, hard and long, just as she would do when calculating the direction from which the geese would fly long before they appeared, swimming out of the sun, like spots before the eyes. Or timing the jittery, prancing run of the springbok through the thorn trees and lifting her rifle with exquisite preci-sion. Nothing was worth more than one shot, ever, said Aunt Betsy.

She barely glanced at the blue Hudson Hornet parked in the garage. The new house was of no interest to her; presumably her instincts told her it was empty. Now she swivelled in a slow circle, sniffed hard and quick, like a dog, until she locked on to something beyond the windmills and the water tank, and off she went, with Me running behind her to keep up.

Well hidden by a shield of vast bluegums, like an invalid or a prisoner, in the shadow of the water tank and guarded by two creaking windmills, they found the original farmstead. It had been abandoned when the

Bassons built their smart new place: bushes grew from its roof, ants marched in columns through sand-blown bedrooms. Me remembered where in the yard – midway between the hen run and the chopping block – she and old Daisy had waited for the Boss to decide what to do with them. On the red stone front stoep she saw his white rocking chair, where the Boss tilted comfortably, lobbed his empty bottle of cherry brandy into the sun, and swung his rifle to his shoulder. She remembered bullets pecking at their feet and splintering shale stinging their ankles as My Eyes and Blind Daisy took the road to Lutherburg.

Here the servants still lived, except there was no one to be seen this Christmas afternoon. She wondered about Childie and as if she knew her thoughts, Aunt Betsy said: 'Now where is that kitchen maid – can you tell me?'

In the dip where the stream ran once a year stood the tumble of whitewashed labourers' cottages where she'd lived with Daisy: they had not changed a bit – their fat-bellied baking chimneys flaking, windows stuffed with rags. An elderly woman wrapped in a red blanket, slow and rheumy-eyed, was stirring a three-legged porridge pot. Into each of these cottages in turn, still without a word of explanation, Aunt Betsy darted, then reappeared muttering louder than ever. Something was gone and its absence hurt and puzzled her.

She stooped over the old woman:

'Where's the Boss been working today?'

The answer was slow and sure. The Boss had been working over Bushman's Drift. Now he was gone to town 'for the Christmas'.

'Nothing more to tell me?' demanded Aunt Betsy sharply. 'Where's the kitchen girl?'

The woman shook her head. She was very, very sorry that she could not be of more help to Madam – and the 'little Missy'. She glanced at Me with respectful eyes and turned again to stirring her pot.

Without a word Aunt Betsy suddenly grabbed her stick. The old lady cried and tried to snatch it back but Aunt Betsy held it high over her head, then carefully wiped in on her pants and Me saw that it was not a stick at all but a whipstock, splintered near the head, and the braided leather lash had been wound about the fractured stock like a splint

Now why, Aunt Betsy wondered aloud, would someone be stirring her porridge with a whip?

The old woman began crying, pulling at the corner of her blanket to wipe her eyes. Then she lifted her sleeves to show bruises, fresh and still suffused with blood; she parted her greying grizzled hair to show more cuts and bruises. The Boss beat her! Like this! And the old woman collapsed into herself, rocking to and fro, cringing and wailing so that Me could see the blows raining down. Basson must have beaten her with the whipstock, so fiercely that it snapped.

'Then he cried – ' the woman gave out surprisingly realistic gruff masculine sobs – 'then he threw down his whip. And then he rode off in his truck.' She mimicked the engine gathering speed. 'Very, very fast.'

Aunt Betsy held out the whip: 'And then?'

The woman reached out to take back her whip and quick as a butcher-bird striking, Aunt Betsy pounced again, grabbing her wrist and forcing the fingers back so fiercely the woman shouted with pain. On her index finger, cruelly twisted in Betsy's grip, Me saw that she wore a ring of red glass mounted on brass wire, hasped in tin, a very lovely and utterly familiar ring children lusted after, sold in the Co-op or Sampie's Café for twopence. Me knew it instantly – Childie's ring.

Ignoring the woman's shrieks Aunt Betsy wrenched the ring off her finger, threw it into the air, caught it, looked at it hard as it nestled in her palm, balled it in her fist, tucked her fist under her armpit and walked around in circles for some time, then she sniffed and spat into the dust.

'Where did you steal this?'

The old woman threw herself full length on the ground and grovelled at Aunt Betsy's feet. She had not stolen the ring. After he had beaten her the Boss had pulled it from his pocket and thrown it in the dust with the broken whip.

'Oh, oh, oh,' said Aunt Betsy to herself. 'The lousy, lying *smeerlap*; the *pietsnot*; the bladdy *skellum*!'

Again the sharp nod to Me to follow, and she unhitched Balthazar and they mounted up and set off across rough country as they would on a dowsing expedition. Me holding to Aunt Betsy's waist felt her icy calm. They left far behind the old farmyard with its circle of protective bluegums and the woman at her pot, and they moved across the sheep camps on the hillsides, and here and there a knot of grazing *Doppers* lifted their black heads at the sound of Balthazar's hooves on the rocky hillside and bolted in a panic of backsides; fat ewes closely followed by sturdy lambs who showed a circle of darker wool where their tails had recently been.

Me glimpsed the four windmills near the dam. They skirted the old graveyard where generations of Bassons lay under stained white headstones, fenced against jackals and lynxes; a notice wired to the rusting iron gate:

RESTING PLACE OF GOD'S DEAD. To their left was
the skeleton of an even earlier dwelling: the original
eighteenth-century homestead of thick mud walls, built
by the pioneer Bassons who paid a couple of Rix dollars
rental to the Dutch East India Company when nobody
owned these lands but the Bushmen. The cab of an
ancient truck, cleanly severed from its body, was nosed
up against the front door of the house and seemed to
shove its snout through the old mud wall, as a sheep will
poke its head through a fence.

Now Me began to whimper; for they were close to the
southern edge of the farm, where it fell away into a
gorge, and her flesh froze. They were on a narrow track
littered with fractured shale plates and leathery bushes.
Sensible persons avoided this place for its horrid air and
bad dreams, but Aunt Betsy was not skirting the dreadful
gorge, she was descending. Me heard her breath coming
in hard pants like a dog, and she tightened her arms
around Aunty Betsy's waist as they moved ever deeper
down to the old, dry river bed where the rocky hillside
plunged to a mass of boulders and thornbush, among
curtains of tall, wheat-coloured reeds so fine and fragile
they rippled in the slightest breeze like waves of brass.

Bushman's Drift. A place where the ghosts were sad
and angry and always searching. This had all been
Bushman country, until the coming of a certain Mr
Vorster and his wife and two small daughters, who
camped here with their beasts and were murdered by a
'band of !Xam' from the Sak River who made off with
thirteen hundred sheep and ninety oxen. At this stream,
while watering themselves and their stolen herds, the
avenging Boer commando struck, shooting three hundred
in a massacre so swift and absolute that there was not

time to bury them and the small corpses were tossed into the drift and more or less covered under an avalanche of boulders. Everyone knew, if you listened at night, that you heard their voices crying out for burial.

Ignoring her muffled sobs, Aunt Betsy roughly broke free of Me's desperate arms around her waist and dismounted. Leaving Balthazar on the edge of the kranz, she went sliding and slipping deeper into the gorge and when Me hung back, called sharply: 'Come, girl. I need your eyes.'

Tearful, wiping her nose on the back of her hand, she followed Aunt Betsy who was already deep in the drift, scrambling over the boulders and through the reeds, darting here, pausing there to check the ground as if she was shooting rock rabbits. Me did not know what she was supposed to be looking for but she was closer to the ground. That was her advantage, if that was what it was, for she had not gone more than a dozen paces when she saw it quite clearly, sticking out of a tumble of rocks which were grouped around it as if to frame, or hold, or hide it. She made no sign, no sound, she simply went down on her haunches and stared.

The foot was small, the sole calloused, there were traces of sand caught in the whorls of yellow skin on the ball of this foot. Aunt Betsy arrived panting and crouched, chewing her lip, then very slowly began to lift the stones away and a leg was uncovered and the beginnings of a pink dress.

Me remembered Childie high in the branches of the pear tree, seeming not to notice that Nico had his hand down the front of that very dress.

Sucking in her breath like she'd been running a long way Aunt Betsy unpacked more stones and every stone lifted revealed more of Childie, and just as in the old days when Mrs Basson stood her on the milking stool before leaving the farm for Lutherburg and made her scrub herself all over – once again, she was not wearing pants.

But that was not why Aunt Betsy was sucking in her breath, or why Me began to shake and scream as loudly as Mrs Basson when Bananas blew his brains out – maybe louder – because Aunt Betsy was also screaming alongside her now. What Me saw was worse than ever it was when Childie and Nico danced to the song of the missing cow who left home and didn't give no milk and butter any more; and Basson dragged Childie home by the hair and beat her with his belt. For now Childie was not only beaten, and her breasts which had made Me think of the Social Butterfly were purple and blue and bloody; not only was she not wearing pants; but Childie was also missing her head.

Strangest of all is what this did to Aunt Betsy who knew more and better than most. Me saw the effects when, next day, Pop Haarhof's wife, Breda, brought her blonde twins who'd got bad pink-eye and Aunt Betsy prescribed cold tea in an egg-cup, morning and night, and Mrs Haarhof said: 'Awful business. But we must stand together – isn't it? She's the one who played with your brother's boy – not so?'

Aunt Betsy did not answer, as surely she must: 'What's to stick to? The girl was killed by him, sure as shooting.' She said nothing.

She had said nothing since replacing the stones on the body to guard against hawks, and riding back to the

Basson farmstead, lifting the receiver and twirling the handle and, for the first time in her life, making a phone call to the cop shop.

Oh, she had made a stab at normal behaviour. She had been shooting and bagged a brace of fat geese; chopped a mountain of firewood; mooned about the yard pulling at her lip and spitting occasionally into the African daisies that crowded the water tank.

But it was for what she *didn't* do that Me began to loathe her. For saying nothing, for her helpless shrug, for getting on with things: for ignoring Basson's Ford pick-up in its spanking blue paint right there, across the road, where he'd parked on Christmas morning. You couldn't miss it; it was like a sentry which challenged all passers-by: it said: 'Well, what do you think?'

Aunt Betsy said nothing and went on saying nothing until Me thought she'd like to kick her ankles, bite her fingers, anything to make her speak. To make her do something. Aunt Betsy would not go back to Basson's farm where Childie's head waited among the reeds and the boulders of Bushman's Drift.

'We'll never find it,' said Aunt Betsy.

When the rains came to Lutherburg and battered on the tin roof, Me dreamt of Childie's head bobbing like a tennis ball among the swirling waters of the drift.

The town was deeply divided by Childie's death.

In Golden Meadow it was said that this sort of thing happened all the time and what did you expect? The farmers got away with murder. Maybe, though, this time it was different – everyone knew who had killed Childie. It was up to the police now.

In Lutherburg proper they insisted that this sort of thing was almost unheard of – and no one must jump the gun. You couldn't blame Basson 'before all the evidence is in'. Until her head turned up there could be no sure proof that Childie was dead at all. And if she was dead it didn't mean Basson had killed her.

Then the district surgeon, young Doc du Plessis, reported this about the girl: she'd been pregnant when she died.

Then a young man from Fryingpanfountain turned up to claim the ring. He said that he and Childie had been walking out. Childie's admirer was a tall young shepherd, with a head shaped very much like a peanut, pinched at the temples, and he told the police he'd been waiting for Childie in the old Basson farmhouse beside the deserted graveyard on Christmas morning but she never arrived.

'She couldn't – could she?' Me said. 'She'd had her head cut off.'

'Hush, child,' said Aunt Betsy.

'It's not good enough,' said Me.

There was relief in Lutherburg after the young man came forward to claim the ring. 'That's who made her pregnant,' they said.

But a little more thought showed them that it made things worse than ever because folks in the brown town went around saying if the shepherd from Fryingpanfountain was the father of Childie's baby, it meant either that Basson had killed her because he'd made her pregnant – and that was bad enough; or that he murdered her in a jealous rage because she was two-timing him with the peanut-head – and that was worse.

And people in the brown town demanded justice.

Though for whom they did not say. But Me understood. They wanted something to be done.

A lot of farmers took this badly. They gathered at Mayor Joost's place and drank brandy and threatened to torch the township if this sort of shit went on. To suggest that a white farmer so lusted after his coloured maid that he was prepared to kill her was totally unnatural, as well as illegal; it was also – well, so bloody outrageous that only a politically motivated bunch of brown bigots would even think of it. And in the following days, quite a few labourers got beaten up.

And then there was the problem of Basson's funeral. If it was conceded that he had killed himself then Pastor Havenga would be obliged to bury him in the section of the graveyard set aside for suicides, beyond the screen of cypresses adjacent to the Jewish quarter. It was very awkward: people over in Zwingli and Eros were saying that old Bananas had been going with this Hottentot girl and put her up the spout. So he did her in. Then he blew his brains out on Christmas Day, between the roast lamb and the cabinet pudding. And now he was going to be buried there by the Jews in suicide corner.

'That's Lutherburg folks for you – stuck up, you bet, but randy as rats.'

Arletta Basson solved the funeral problem. Her solution was as elegant as it was unexpected and so quiet no one knew about it until it was all over. She buried her husband among a batch of unmarked graves in the cemetery in Golden Meadow.

But she wasn't stopping there. Next she arranged Childie's funeral and invited Aunt Betsy, who said no thanks, she didn't think so.

And Me spoke up: 'I'd like to go.'

She went, dressed in the clothes Aunt Betsy had made her for the funeral of Nico's parents, and she went without even asking. And still Aunt Betsy said nothing.

A crowd turned out for Childie's burial. Ma Williamson came with her sons, Little Boy and Baba, and so did many of the people who had crowded into the house the day Basson shot himself. They followed the white coffin, loaded on a tractor, to the graveyard where it was lowered by rope into the shaft, and Dominee Grootboom called on God to show mercy to the innocent. Then spadefuls of sand landing on the coffin-lid made a plume of dusty red smoke as if a fire burned below.

Afterwards the rope was coiled and slung on the wooden cross: CHILDIE – REST IN PEACE (–1958) it said, because no one knew when she had been born. Though everyone knew how she'd died.

It was strange to think of Childie and Basson lying in the same ground.

After the funeral Me walked around the township. She knew people were staring at her and their eyes widened when she asked directions. But she didn't care. The streets had numbers not names and she got lost now and then, but that didn't matter because she knew where she was when she found what she was looking for.

That night Me slipped beneath the covers with Aunt Betsy, warmed her hands with arnica and began to rub the bony feet, the calloused soles, the blue veins that ran like wires behind her calves, until Aunt Betsy was snoring gently and the heart-shaped blue flame in the paraffin lamp shuddered like a leaf, then she swung her feet onto the cold floor and wearing only her nightdress, sewn by Aunt Betsy from two sacks of Blue Ribband flour, she walked down Voortrekker Street, away from town, to a point where the tar ended and the dirt road began and then she struck left across the veld towards the grinding groaning voice of Golden Meadow.

In the dim streets there were no streetlights and paraffin lamps flickered behind cotton curtains and the smoke from a thousand cooking fires still hung like storm clouds over the chimneys. A dog barked, somewhere a woman screamed. Me stood before a brick house, indistinguishable from a dozen others, and knocked and kept on knocking until a woman, scratching her head sleepily, opened a window and called loudly into the smoky moonlight: 'Go away! It's late.'

'It's me,' says Me.

The woman at the window thought a moment then clapped her hands.

'My Eyes!' cried Blind Daisy, 'I am so happy to see you!'

Aunt Betsy did something, at last: she marched right over to the police station where Sergeant Nephew kept her waiting. When at last he saw her he was being very lordly; worse, he was being modern.

'Why does Auntie want her back?'

To which she could give no more than her old reply, even to her ears now somewhat thin and unconvincing: 'Because she's mine.'

And then to her horror she began to weep.

Sergeant Nephew swivelled back in his chair, staring at the pale cream ceiling, across which a small green lizard curled and uncurled like a rubbery eyebrow.

'This is the late fifties,' said Sergeant Nephew. 'You can't own anyone any more.'

'I paid for her, fair and square.'

'I may not like it; you may not like it – but times,' Sergeant Nephew pursed his lips and nodded, 'is changed.'

Aunt Betsy went into the veld with her old Mauser and she shot targets all day, increasing the distance by fifty yards and still getting good heart shots. Nothing wrong with her eye. She'd cut from brown paper a man's torso and ringed the heart with charcoal, black as sin, and she got some satisfaction from her accuracy.

But it didn't help all that much because what was the good of accuracy when she should have done the proper thing with it – and shot the cause of her misfortune? Basson had got his own back. When he killed his kitchen maid, he killed Me, too.

In her place was another person, a woman who walked down Voortrekker Street each morning on her way to the Town Hall where her job was to write down details of every brown baby born in Golden Meadow; she was the new Clerk of Births.

Some said she got the job because she was almost white and some said she got the job because she was responsible brown and others felt it was worrying to watch a person changing places, going from Lutherburg proper to Golden Meadow, from white to brown town, without so much as a by-your-leave. There was something alarming about it. Something unnatural.

Mayor Joost said what everyone thought: 'We're here and they're there. Isn't it? And you don't go there from here.'

She was taller now, as if she'd grown inches in a few weeks, and she called herself Mimi.

Aunt Betsy asked Arletta Basson, because she saw her from time to time: 'Why Mimi?'

Arletta reported back: 'She says – because there's more of Me now.'

More? Different certainly. From her bedroom window Aunt Betsy watches her passing the cottage, and she does not glance left or right: she wears dresses of soft blue and dove-grey. Clothes Aunt Betsy has never seen before. But then this is no longer the girl she raised – this serene, dreamy woman walking down Voortrekker Street.

Aunt Betsy peers at her through the muslin curtain and asks herself: 'Can that really be Me?'

And is strangely comforted to know that it cannot be. Nor is she particularly curious about this other person, this Mimi. No, the pain, which she nurses inside her like a rock, is for the child who has gone. Not since the loss of the Good Doctor has Aunt Betsy felt such grief. Or been so overwhelmed by change.

She straightened her back and fought her grief. She chopped firewood, she shot for the pot; she flexed her biceps and spat in the dust, she went out water-divining, she clung to all the comforting old ways and things.

But every now and then she rode over to Bushman's Drift and searched among the boulders for Childie's head. She felt that if she found it, then maybe Me would come back to her.

Then she watched the new woman walking past her cottage, looking neither right nor left, and knew that even if she found the head where would she find the Me to give it to? And the pain began again, the stone grew inside her, the hurt there was no curing.

*

Arletta Basson was another queer one. Basson's death also changed her. Once a shy farmer's wife with pots of money, she had changed into the Keeper of the Morgue and Layer-out. There was never a funeral she missed — but she went now always to the brown church; she was the only white face at the wake. The solitary angel at the graveside, greying hair pulled back tight into her neck, as pale as a peeled pear.

Her husband was the first white man to lie in the cemetery in Golden Meadow. And it was all her doing. As if Arletta felt that her Barnabas, having failed to deliver in life, wished to make amends in death. A man who never in his life set foot in the brown town, now lay there for eternity!

In Golden Meadow they felt it was some kind of compensation: you can't play fairer than burying your spouse amongst the enemy, now can you?

In Lutherburg proper it made them distinctly uneasy to think of old Bananas down among the coloured folk and they wriggled their shoulders to show just how awkward it was.

Other things were changing too. The shot Bananas Basson fired into his brain had also stopped the party. The passion for the King was fading. Except here and there, a couple of people kept the faith.

When good rains broke the drought, the giant Elvis began to come apart as the stones out of which he had been formed rolled about in the wet and the mud. Until only his quiff remained, a jutting triangle of stones.

It was amazing how quickly people forgot. Within a few years hardly anyone knew very much about the figure on the hill. He seemed to belong to another age.

Visitors to town would ask: 'What's *that* up there —

some sort of fertility symbol? Like those neolithic figures you get overseas – like Cerne Abbas or Uffington? And what on earth's that pointy thing – his pizzle?'

The Moosahs, first Asian family to settle in Lutherburg, in '61, a mere three years after the Lake of Basson's Ear and the War for Childie's Head, could go around saying, without anyone challenging them, that they espied a certain Hindu symbolism in the pattern of the stones and suggesting ancient Asian builders alone would have had the skill to assemble such a monument.

Others said, let's face it, it had to have been whites who did it. Not so? Non-Europeans lacked the technical expertise to assemble a colossus on the hillside.

Still others took the view that in Lutherburg, the whites could barely cross the road unaided, and only indigenous tribes – long vanished themselves – Bushmen or Hottentots, had the energy, the artistic ability, to draw gods in stones.

Soon there was nothing left of the mighty figure on Spook Hill, except remains of his right knee and his quiff of hair floating like a sail over the town, and a little night music floating up from the tin shack they used as a morgue in the brown town.

Arletta Basson, who wouldn't have known a Suddenly Singing Elvis from a bar of soap in the old days, started the tradition when she sang 'Return to Sender' while she laid out the body of her late husband, Bananas Basson.

When people heard Arletta singing they knew they were in for funeral weather. Someone had died – of the heart or cancer; domestic stabbing; suicide or the drink; paraffin fire; carbon monoxide poisoning. When the case was especially bad she favoured 'Love Me Tender', sung with a generous vibrato.

Sometimes the new Mimi helped her.

It had been that way, ever since the two women followed the tractor bearing Childie's coffin to the graveyard. When they teamed up, the tin walls added a lovely shivery bass to the lower registers of 'Peace in the Valley', with which they traditionally wrapped up an evening in the house of the dead. You always knew when they were working together because you could hear them singing. Slow and sweet to start and generally finishing up with something catchy like 'All Shook Up' as they washed their hands in Dettol and removed the dabs of Vicks from their nostrils.

People thought it was a bit weird. But they said nothing.

Basson and Childie were chapters better closed. If the girl wanted to live in the Brown Town and call herself Mimi, she was mad. Then again, Aunt Betsy had had her six cakes worth.

There was a certain sympathy for Arletta. If you couldn't trust a stray you'd plucked from the street and fed and clothed and raised — what price some little farm slut who didn't wear pants and had the hots for a man twice her age and lured him to destruction? And there was a groundswell of support for Bananas Basson, and what he might have been driven to do.

Though what that was, no one said.

Mayor Pompie Joost spoke for the town when he muttered to himself: 'No more silly stories, no more Hottentot hogwash. Just ordinary plain decent Christian living. Back to normal!'

But it wasn't. Sergeant Nephew received a report: Balthazar had been spotted dragging his reins over the koppies, out Bushman's Drift way. No one would have noticed otherwise. Since Me left, Aunt Betsy spent more and more time out in the veld; she had become an invisible person. But now they knew where to look.

They found her among the reeds of the old river bed, rifle beside her.

Shooting duck – Nephew suggested – when she collapsed.

Heart, said Dr Du Plessis and for once he was right.

Mimi tried not to consider how she felt. She had not seen her mistress since that night she had walked away. When she heard that Aunt Betsy had been found in Bushman's Drift she knew it was not really Childie's head she searched for; she had been looking for Me.

But Me was gone for good, and she warned herself: 'Mimi, keep out of this.'

Then the mayor walked into the town hall and stopped by her desk in the Births office and asked – didn't she want to make the arrangements, hey?

Too shocked to be anything but polite Mimi said no, thank you.

Mayor Joost was shocked right back: 'Shame! Wasn't she your sort of mother?'

And Mimi said: 'I was a bargain.'

'Listen here, man. She's got no kin; so who must do the necessary?'

And with Arnaldus dead and Nico gone, she knew he was right.

Mimi asked Arletta to help and she said: 'Only a pleasure, my dear.'

They laid her out at home because somehow that seemed more appropriate and Mimi, for the last time, eased the yellow feet out of her boots; and for a last time brushed her hair which was full of spring though now as white as the feathery snow that sometimes falls in the winter in the high Karoo, and they call bed-feathers or *kapok*. She took from the wall the picture of the Good Doctor in his heavy frame, doffing his black homburg and smiling, and placed it on Aunt Betsy's breast and before they sealed the coffin she added the pair of sheepshead slippers she found in Aunt Betsy's cupboard and realized she had kept for all those years the shoes of the child she'd bought for six bars of cold-water soap.

'What shall we sing?' Arletta asked.

Mimi didn't know. The only thing that ran through her head was the song Nico taught her, about the old milk cow and how she was going to miss her loving daddy when he was gone. How many years ago had Nico been gone? Three? Four? She had stopped counting.

She shrugged: 'You choose.'

'Shall we give her – "Just a Closer Walk With Thee"?'

Without waiting Arletta started off and they sang two verses, high and quavery, that being mostly Mimi's fault because she found her voice strangely trembly, and all the time Aunt Betsy lay quiet as quiet, as she got when something serious was about to happen: before her dowsing wand smelt water; or when she lifted her rifle and shot the pants of the smous; or when her feet were rubbed with arnica oil and she dropped asleep, still as a stone in her box-bed; as quiet as she lay now, with the Good Doctor on her breast and the sheepshead slippers at her feet; her jaw clenched so you could see the muscle. Just as Mimi had seen her lie a thousand times or more, over the years when they had slept together.

As if nothing had changed.

For that was the way of the cottage. Everything was as

Me had left it when she walked away and became someone else. Her bed over the woodbox; her chair at the table; her enamel cup with the red rim, her tin plate and knife with the ivory handle, yellow as butter. All in their old place, except for the girl who had been her. She was gone and now Aunt Betsy was gone and that world was gone and yet the things insisted – we don't change, we are faithful, we are the same. All that is missing is you – you were once everything to us.

Aunt Betsy was buried in the cemetery in Lutherburg proper and this was a problem. What to do with Mimi?

Mayor Joost was especially cross. As he told the Pastor: hadn't it been bad enough when the old auntie was alive? Mimi had really no business to be causing trouble, again. You never knew what to do with her. If she had been Aunt Betsy's child then she would have stood at the graveside. If she had been a servant she would have stood at the gate. She was almost Aunt Betsy's child, she was at any rate her only surviving kin – Mayor Joost admitted this. But she was also almost a servant.

Rules were rules.

'If we let just anybody stand by the grave, half the brown town will be at every funeral,' said the mayor.

'They'll be wanting to buried here, next,' said the Pastor.

So a compromise was reached. Mimi stood halfway to the gate, under a huge bluegum tree and Arletta went and stood by the grave while Pastor Havenga read the prayers.

'I'll be your witness, OK?' said Arletta.

Mimi really didn't mind standing some way off. Any

closer and she would have felt Aunt Betsy's speechless reproach. Better to be standing back, towards the place the servants would have waited – if Aunt Betsy had had servants – and to feel free.

TWO

LUTHERBURG–BUCKINGHAM
1995

Change, or rather the lack of it, was the bastard, Mayor Williamson decided, and signalled Maureen for another lager.

The bar was crowded, and through the big wooden windows he could see a bunch of farmers on the long stoep, clustered around a man flogging something from the back of a Nissan. Hotel maids in apricot hot pants trotted out trays of coffee and beer. One of Pascal's Farmers' Fiestas was on the go – together with karaoke and Pilgrimages in the Veld, another step along the road to making Buckingham the Hub of the Karoo. The ten o'clock sun beat down and, across the road, the guys sitting on the pavement where Freedom Street intersected Democracy Drive shifted around the corner of the wall of the Dutch Reformed Ladies' Pantry to catch a little shade.

The mayor was waiting for his Festival Committee. It had been carefully chosen to represent what Pascal called 'all the key players'. In fact it was so representative it got nowhere. Pascal Le Gros and Mimi de Bruyn had been voted rotating co-chairs; Bill Harding, grizzled and puckered about the lips but still feisty, represented the English remnant, Dr Romeo Angel, the new district surgeon, was co-opted as an international observer from the People's

Republic of Cuba; Baby Vermaak was official translator, and also represented women's groups; others elected were the three Calvinist ministers, brown and white and renegade: Pastors Grootboom and Niemand and Greet. Pastor Niemand spoke for farmers, and Dominee Greet for the white right and the breakaway church; Mr Moosah represented the radical young cadres and the Structures in Golden Meadow.

The British Israelites had declined to take part. But then they were badly split at the moment as Shirleen de Lange was known to be pregnant and Vince denied he was the father. The men of Buckingham watched Shirleen waddling into town – eight months gone – and smiling in that sleepy, sultry way of hers and they thought it served her right for doing as she did that weekend, drinking in the bar of the Hunter's Arms and going upstairs with just about every bloke in town while her husband raked in the shekels. Only one thing stopped them from cheering: the knowledge that one of them was almost certainly the father of her kid.

Surprisingly, Mr Moosah had been appointed to represent British Israelite interests; he hated the Israelites but he hated Zionists even more, and so did the Israelites, and they decided to pool interests. Pascal called it another seismic shift.

Mike the Spike was honorary treasurer; Maureen was catering manager. The mayor's brother, Baba, was business adviser because he'd done pretty well in a joint venture with Pascal: a dozen bungalows on the old golf course were modernized and turned into the Buckingham Country Club, where they planned to flog time-share holidays. Now Baba was working on Pascal's plans for a Bushman Park: they called their project 'San City'.

Festival Committee members present and correct were Mr Moosah sipping water, and Maureen and Mike having words with Pascal about the Bushman in the scarlet jacket who sat on top of the Yamaha loudspeaker.

They called the boy Chinkie, on account of his slanting eyes and apricot complexion. Just a month before, Baba Williamson had brought the little guy into the karaoke bar at the Hunter's Arms and said to Pascal: 'Here's a sample.'

The boy wore a loincloth, a bow across his shoulder, a springbok skin kaross or cape was tied around his neck and a quiver of small arrows dangled from his waist. Standing up straight, he reached no higher than the bar counter. He looked about ten.

When they'd first got him Mike the Spike was all for throwing him back. Too young to keep, said Mike.

Pascal reckoned he was older. Maybe sixteen even if he looked a kid.

'They age,' he said, 'quite quick.'

He sat the boy on the speaker to get a good look at him and there was about his narrow eyes, set in an almost triangular face under whorls of crisp black hair, a sadness which would have stunned the hearts of lesser men.

'Get him to say something,' Pascal told Baba.

'He doesn't talk.'

'Not a peep?'

'At home I suppose he does. But only in Bushman. You know – full of clicks.'

'How'm I supposed to communicate?'

'What's to say? He's a sample. If we like him we order others, and they'll talk, for sure.'

'Where'd you find him?'

'Kalahari.' Baba showed him the invoice. 'See, it says

genuine wild Kalahari Bushman. I got a contact up there and he supplies.'

To everyone's surprise, Pascal got along pretty well with the boy; he'd lift him from the speaker and say: 'Chinkie, fetch my biltong from my room.'

He designed a uniform: red fez with black tassel, scarlet coat with gold buttons and red shorts. Chinkie became hotel mascot, doorman and page rolled into one. And he really took to the life; he smoked cigarettes and hummed along to Jim Reeves, Dolly Parton, Gypsy Kings and Tom Jones, though he still said not a word.

And he really admired Pascal; his little wizened face broke into smiles, as Mike said, like eggs cracking, whenever the fat man showed up. Pascal conferred wealth, status, prestige. Chinkie gained in importance through his connection to Pascal's booming, florid, sailing presence.

Maureen said he was bound to pine.

Pascal said: 'Well, how can I help that? I only got permission for one Bushman for my park. But when folks see how well San City does, they'll be begging me to import dozens. Because it'll put Buckingham right up there, among the best.'

Making Buckingham visible, or at least identifiable, was exactly why the mayor had formed the Festival Committee. It was long overdue. For God's sake, even Zwingli, a centre of reaction and race prejudice, was selling itself as the Rainbow Capital of the Karoo. A year down the road from Freedom and it was time to celebrate – right? So what about a giant bash, a carnival, jubilee, street party? Anything that reached out to folks, gave them a lift, drew them together.

But it was easier said than done. Finding an idea everybody would like – popular in Buckingham and Golden Meadow, among the grassroots and the Structures and the radical cadres, with the white right and the farmers and Dutch Reformed Church, acceptable to women, children, gays and lesbians, the handicapped, pensioners and supported by the English remnant – had not been easy.

Bloody difficult, actually. Because it was to be a celebration of change and a year down the road there was little sign of it. Except in matters of power.

Mr Moosah said: 'We won the national elections. And then we were "transitional". Now we've won the local elections and so we're permanent.'

'You mean democratically elected,' said Mayor Williamson.

'Same difference,' said Mr Moosah. 'It's our turn now.'

In fact all that had changed were the tunes, the names, the codes, the words for not saying what you meant. The privileged minority, alias white folks, still lived in the town proper and the traditionally deprived majority, a.k.a. brown folks, were stuck out in Golden Meadow – and the jobless sat all day in front of the Dutch Reformed Ladies' Pantry for the Poor and Indigent, on the corner of Freedom Street and Democracy Drive, just as, in the old days, they had waited on the corner of Voortrekker and Leibrandt for some farmer to stop by and offer a bit of shearing or fence mending.

'I want to reach out,' said the mayor.

'Sure,' said Mr Moosah, 'I'll reach, as long as those guys don't try any of their old nonsense.'

That was the trouble. Any number of Festival meetings, any number of ideas – all of them pretty bad. A

Shakespeare Festival, Bill Harding wanted. Not on the rates, said Mr Moosah, speaking on behalf of the tra-ditionally deprived majority – if the bourgeoisie want fun and games let them pay for it. But how about a Karl Marx Read-in? Certainly not, said the farmers. What about importing bicycles from Germany or Holland and giving them to the deprived community who don't have cars? – suggested Bill Harding. Why should the deprived majority not drive around in BMWs, asked Mr Moosah, just like the privileged minority?

Listening to them, Williamson had to ask himself whether people in this damn dorp didn't have about as much chance of understanding each other as Pascal had in communicating with his Bushman boy who sat on top of the Yamaha all day pulling at a Coke.

Dr Angel walked into the bar accompanied, as always, by Baby Vermaak and they sat drinking Daquiris.

Buckingham had been the first town this side of the Snow Mountains to get a doctor from overseas, and it seemed like change of a sort. Dr du Plessis did a bunk just ahead of the enquiry by the Medical Association into the mortality rate amongst his patients. Mr Moosah said it was time to think global and applied for a doctor from the first Cuban shipment and Buckingham imported earnest, olive-skinned, crinkly-haired Dr Romeo Angel, in beige safari suit and big steel glasses, direct from Havana.

That was pretty bloody modern. Everyone remem-bered when they didn't allow Cuban cigars into the country.

Mr Moosah's Hands Off Cuba Committee decked out the streets with Cuban flags for Dr Angel's arrival. It

looked like a real change but then Bill Harding dis-
covered a problem.

'Jesus! Eleven bloody official languages in this country
and Pepe don't know a word of any of them. Nip in to
see the quack with a sore throat – and chances are he'll
whip out your appendix.'

Mr Moosah attacked him for absolutely typical old-
style negative thinking.

'Instead of always seeing problems, why don't we make
a virtue of this? Why not learn a third language? The doc
and the whole town? Something midway between Dr
Angel's lingo and ours. What say – French? We all get
together and give it a go. Isn't that great?'

Only Dr Angel and Baby Vermaak learnt to speak
enough French to understand each other. That meant she
was always present at consultations and closed her eyes
if you undressed. But some patients were super bashful
and refused point-blank to take off their clothes with a
woman present. Then Baby sat outside the surgery,
listening while the patient shouted out his symptoms
which she translated through the keyhole to Dr Angel.

Mimi de Bruyn turned up now, with that quiet, almost
apologetic air that so disconcerted people, just as
Maureen was denouncing Pascal as a fat crook *and* the
meanest man she'd ever met. That made a full committee.

Mimi accepted a cup of coffee. 'Surely he can't be that
bad?'

She'd grown fond of Pascal, rather as you might grow
fond of a rogue elephant who has never gored you.

'Wanna bet?' Maureen walked over to the Bushboy on

the Yamaha and tried to lift him. 'See? He's stuck Chinkie on top of the speaker – with strips of bloody Velcro. Sewed into his pants. 'S bloody cruel to keep a wild creature cooped up in a hotel, eating bad food when he should be spearing game and digging for tubers.'

'I can't just turn him loose,' Pascal protested. 'Not until the reserve is ready to receive him.'

'Why not? Out is home. Under the stars. At this rate he'll have every disease known to science by the time your place is up and running. At least stick him out in the backyard. He'll think it's Christmas – ' She turned to the Bushboy – 'won't you, sweetie?'

The boy stared wildly at the little parabellum in the white holster at her hip, and the towering hive of her hairpiece.

'For heaven's sake!' Maureen was perplexed. 'You'd have thought he'd never seen a pistol before. He looks nips.'

'Wouldn't you be feeling the nips if you'd been shot to extinction? Imagine if you'd been brought straight out of the bush into this degree of sophistication?'

Pascal's generous wave took in the buttoned pink leather bar, studded along its full voluptuous length with gilded little apples; the mournful mounted buckheads on the walls, the old clock with the spidery hands taken from the old church before they pulled it down; the dusky drum-major on the Jameson Whiskey mirror, the Bank Notes from Around the World, glued like violent stains on the ceiling; the velvet hoopoe with the bald orange head, who dipped his beak into a glass of water and raised it, as regular as clockwork, all day long.

Maureen had never forgiven Pascal for the British Israelite bordello nights run by Vince and Shirleen. The

Bushman boy brought the warfare between them into the
open with Maureen saying that the fat man was out to
lunch and Mike the Spike, caught in the middle, between
his one-time partner and mentor, and his mistress, hoping
he wouldn't cop a bullet, drinking more and more flaming
Kümmels late into the night, then sleeping it off till
noon.

Pascal said: 'Arab sheikhs who race camels Velcro their
boy jockeys to the saddle. That's where I got the idea.
He wanders, otherwise.'

'They're supposed to,' Maureen said, 'they're natural
bloody wanderers.'

'Yes, in their natural habitat. But not in the bar. I've
got the committee here and Chinkie's forever whipping
things. Bladdy little magpie! He pinches the spoons. I
find him with his nose in the sugar. I want him where I
can see him but I promise,' Pascal spat on his fingers and
crossed his heart, 'as soon as we got the reserve up and
running he can roam to his heart's content. But, for now,
I got to protect him.' He glanced fondly at Chinkie on
top of the speaker. 'One day Buckingham will be crawling
with the little bastards.'

Mimi de Bruyn looked at Pascal and smiled, warm and
full.

But then, thought Maureen, remembering the night
she'd found the deputy mayor virtually embracing the fat
crook, Mimi would, wouldn't she?'

Mayor Williamson wanted to say: 'Never mind saving
the San . . .'

Williamson didn't think of himself as particularly
prejudiced but when he considered the whites of Buckingham what struck him was not their successful brutality
but their uselessness. Centuries of rule had not impressed

their serfs. Seeing them now, struggling to come to terms with even tiny changes, was enough to make him weep. If they could not shoot it, kick it, fuck it or eat it, they went home and beat someone up. That was about the sum of it. Pascal should set up a white man's reserve, where they could be protected from themselves.

But instead he called the meeting to order.

The Festival Committee met in the bar on the basis that 'if we keep it informal, we keep it fun; we keep in touch with the grassroots; we listen to the people.' Now they sat around a corner table under the old church clock and Williamson asked for ideas on the festival.

That was when the screaming began in the street outside. The boy on the speaker shut his sad eyes and trembled so violently you could hear his Velcro crackle.

'It's only a tape,' said Baba Williamson reassuringly.

'He doesn't know that,' said Pascal, 'he thinks it's real.' He got up and patted the boy on his fez. 'Hello, my friend. Don't be frightened.'

The Bushman kept his eyes closed tight shut under Pascal's patting pudgy hand. The screaming got louder and so Pascal put on Jim Reeves to calm the little guy.

'Let's go, Chinkie,' said Pascal, unzipping him from his perch, 'and see for ourselves what the trouble is — OK?'

And of course the committee also trooped out to take a look.

Fritz, a hunter from Namibia, was giving the farmers a show. Mounted on the roof-rack of his Nissan 4 x 4 was a loudspeaker and around the car were about twenty large farmers in khaki shorts and hats, drinking coffee served by the maids in hot pants.

The volume was up to tops and the speaker was

screaming. When you thought it must stop it grew into a bloody bubbling agony; its sobbing, champing voice sounded every now and then quite human.

Fritz explained: 'Listen carefully and you can hear the jackal's soft barks.' He turned up the volume. 'Now that's the actual sound of a rabbit being eaten alive!'

Maureen said: 'God! How long does it go on for?'

'It's a loop,' said Fritz. 'It doesn't have an end. Buy the tape and the speaker, I throw in free clamps for the roof-rack. My revolutionary method of vermin disposal is simple. Drive out into your lands one night, park your *bakkie* where you know there has been jackal activity; set up the speaker, run the tape on the car sound system and go to ground with your rifle. This baby brings the jackals running. Boing! It's a dinner gong. They can't resist.'

'Well, blow me,' said Mike. 'Look at Chinkie. I thought Bushmen were keen on this sort of thing.'

The Bushman boy had buried his face in Pascal's ample stomach.

'Damn. You've got yourself one pretty soft Bushman there,' said Mike. 'Damaged goods.'

'He's only a sample,' Baba Williamson said crossly. 'On appro. If he doesn't perform we send him back.'

The committee went inside and got on with the meeting, only this time Dr Angel was muttering and there were tears in his eyes. Pascal Le Gros asked Baby what the trouble was.

'It's the Cubans. They call him back to Cape Town once a month,' Baby explained. 'On the bus, mind you. They make him stand guard at the embassy, and take his salary off him because they need hard currency and send him back here with pocket money and his bus fare. He's very unhappy.'

Pascal wasn't having any of it. If the doc felt like crying – fair enough. But would he please do so in private?

'What must visitors think if the first thing they see is our GP in floods of tears? They're not to know he's a homesick Cuban pining for rum babas and hand-rolled cigars.'

When the meeting finally kicked off, Mimi de Bruyn took the minutes and Mayor Williamson called for suggestions for the Event of Great Joy, which Baby translated for the doc as 'Beaucoup de joie!'

The ideas were awful; they had been awful since the first meeting. Bill Harding said why not a nice pig-sticking display at the showgrounds, with mounted police officers spearing beer cans at full gallop; Pastor Niemand wanted a tractor parade; Minister Grootboom wanted a mixed-race tug-of-war, everyone pulling together; and Mike the Spike wanted a Ken and Barbie doll look-alike competition. Pascal wanted *Aida* staged in the open air at the showgrounds. Mr Moosah, speaking for the British Israelites, wanted hymns and readings from the Hebrew Concordance. Next, Mr Moosah, speaking for himself and the township Structures and interested cadres, wanted a Heroes' Acre to be built on Spook Hill, preferably by the North Koreans, with black marble tombs and lots of graves, like the one in Zimbabwe.

'A monument to our uprising.'

'Come off it,' said Bill Harding, 'what uprising?'

'The comrades were ready,' said Mr Moosah.

'Sure, the comrades were trained and waiting, certainly, the AK-47s were hidden in a cellar under the sports hall – everyone knew that – and plans were laid to seize the post office, police station and bottle store and render Lutherburg ungovernable; and yes, these guys drove up from Cape Town in souped-up Volkswagens arriving after dark and knocked on the windows of certain houses known to be the hiding places of the comrades, and told them to be ready for the call. Then they went off and downed litres of white wine and sang marching songs and waited for orders that never came. Some army!'

'We won,' said Mr Moosah.

'The other side gave up,' said Bill Harding. 'You guys couldn't have won a bloody raffle!'

Mr Moosah said he resented a white man insulting the heroes of the struggle.

Through Baby Vermaak, Dr Angel chipped in then: what about a freedom fiesta with steel bands, giant floats and dancing in the street?

Pastors Grootboom and Niemand and Greet objected. Calvinist friends found the concept of street dancing foreign to their culture. Farmers did not know Latin rhythms.

Dr Angel explained that it was just a case of moving your body as the spirit took you. He demonstrated.

Watching him shimmy across the room, the pastors pointed out that undulating movements of the body were not popular among Calvinists.

Mr Moosah raised another important point: 'Any fancy dancing and the Israelites will think it's foreign and cosmopolitan – and that can mean only one thing.'

'Which is?' the mayor asked.

Mr Moosah spelt it out: 'J-E-W-S.'

'For crying in a bucket,' Maureen objected, 'the Calvinists and the Much Deformed Church have run our lives for long enough. If they don't want to dance at our party – fine. It's a free country. They can sit it out. Wallflowers of history. Once again. We can't be hindered by the old ghosts of yesteryear.'

Mike the Spike said: 'Anyway, for Christ's sake, there's no bloody Jews left in Buckingham.'

'Maybe,' said Mr Moosah. 'But perception is the thing. If the Israelites perceive a Zionist presence in the fiesta they will not dance. And I, for one, would not blame them. And we want all stakeholders on board for our party, do we not?'

'Terrific,' said Pascal bitterly. 'So far we don't have Calvinists, Jews or dancing at our festival. Why not go the whole hog? Cut out booze, too.'

'Suits me,' said Mr Moosah.

'I concur,' said Pastor Grootboom. 'We must stay dry.'

Baby Vermaak translated for the doctor. His face crumpled. He shoved his fingers into his dark hair, he rubbed his nose with the back of his hand, he stamped his foot; and holding out his hand with stiffly extended forefinger and pinkie he made little stabbing motions at the pastors. Then at Mr Moosah. Then he wept.

'What's Pepe say?' Mr Moosah demanded.

'He says – ' Baby swallowed – 'that he's reminded of Havana. At political rallies he cheers his leader: "Viva Castro!" But in his heart he says: "Die, you bastard!"'

The committee stared but Dr Angel was oblivious. He raged on through his tears. Baby struggled to keep up with his tirade.

'"May your mother fry in hell!" At least that's what I think he's saying. His accent's awful,' Baby confessed.

'We'll put it down to a mistake in translation,' suggested the mayor, 'and not include it in the minutes.'

Baby smiled gratefully, because Mr Moosah was chair of the Hands Off Cuba Committee and in a position to make big trouble for Dr Angel.

Mimi de Bruyn, laying aside her pen, chose this

moment to speak. Her voice was soft: 'I propose Elvis
Presley – a Celebration.'

It was, quite simply, an idea of such brilliance there
was nothing more to say. The farmers would like it, said
the Pastors Niemand, Greet and Grootboom, because
they could concentrate on Elvis the country boy; Mr
Moosah reckoned that the British Israelites would buy it
because Presley was pure Caucasian; on the other hand,
progressive forces would like it because he was working
class. Mike the Spike said he'd wear stovepipes for the
occasion and gave the bar a blast of 'All Shook Up' on
the karaoke. Dr Angel blew Baby kisses and said Elvis
was a great American! Mr Moosah murmured that after
the appalling way the States treated plucky little Cuba, it
would be best to position Presley as a citizen of the
world, like Karl Marx or Kwame Nkrumah, available to
comrades everywhere.

It was agreed then that:

(i)   Gala celebrations to be held in the Town Hall
in a month's time.

(ii)   Grand prize for the most authentic entrant.

(iii)   Points awarded for costume, performance and
musicality.

(iv)   Event open to all groups, classes and genders
– unemployed, pensioners, the handicapped,
children and women.

(v)   Independent international judge.

The meeting agreed it on a show of hands and Mayor
Williamson, though he was too young to remember very
much, made a speech which got the heart of things
exactly:

He painted a picture of a golden age when tiny kids off the street gave you a pretty good cover of 'Hound Dog'; mothers soothed their infants with 'Love Me Tender' and 'Wooden Heart'; and old men rocking on their porches hummed 'Crawfish'. Happy days. He pointed out that this was a highly revolutionary act. Years ahead of its time. When Eros and Zwingli were still stuck in the accordion age and even Cape Town was still fixed on Mantovani and Nelson Eddie, in an era of wide khaki shorts, demob suits, short back and sides, long thick yellow socks, pass books and police brutality – Buckingham led the way! You might see people of all races, in stovepipes and leather and pink candy-striped socks and slim-jim ties, hair slicked back in the biggest baddest ducktails anywhere, dancing in the streets.

It wasn't exactly true but it sounded wonderful.

Pascal was so overcome he put his arm around Mimi's shoulders and said she should have a prize.

And Mimi was so overcome she wept – which surprised everyone. She didn't know why she thought of the idea; it had just come out.

And all the time the Bushboy in his cherry-red jacket sat on top of the loudspeaker, fiddling with his brass buttons, looking from Pascal's face to the tear-streaked cheeks of the woman who smiled at him, while he smoked one of Pascal's cigarettes which he usually stole in neat handfuls from the box of fifties beside his bed; just as he stole brandy, biltong and cash, whenever he came across it; not in a spirit of wickedness, but as a form of praise for a man who had so much of it.

When it came to advertising the event, republicans like Pastor Niemand had a problem with the term 'the King'. And Mr Moosah, speaking as a democratic socialist, agreed one hundred per cent. Also the Israelites, he warned, would not wear any King but Yahweh. Eventually the committee accepted a compromise:

HOMAGE TO ELVIS:
FIRST CITIZEN OF ROCK AND ROLL

Later that day Pascal went into Beaufort to see the printers about the posters, and while he was out, Maureen found Chinkie stealing booze from the bar. To be precise, he was knocking back the mix in the jug where Mike rinsed the tot-measure: Maureen banished him to the backyard where instead of drinking totwash, she said, he could be re-educated into the life of the wild.

Pascal returned to find the howling boy up a tree with doddering Brad and Bruce, slavering at the foot.

'Call off those carnivorous horses or I'll fix them!' he yelled. 'They're a health hazard.'

Maureen ran into the yard. 'Back off or you're dead meat.' She took her pistol from its holster: 'Do me a favour, Pascie.' She pointed it at his great crushed beet nose: 'Lay so much as a finger on them. Go on.'

People had all sorts of theories why Pascal did what he did next. He was running scared; he was up to something; he'd got religion; he was as mad as a bloody Englishman. Anyway, what he did was – he pulled the little guy out of the tree, took him by the nape of his neck and walked him down Democracy Drive, right to the end of town, whistling 'Heartbreak Hotel' and smiling; and when Pascal smiled like that, Maureen said, you'd better get insurance, or legal advice.

227

He walked to Mimi's place.

After the Change, Mimi had been the first of the
Golden Meadow crowd to move back into town. Good
move politically. Send the present incumbents a message
– the original owners are on their way back. Fine. But
why choose the very house where you were a virtual
slave? Of her previous life with Aunt Betsy, Pascal knew
a little, but he found it too queer to comprehend.

He stood outside the crooked wooden fence with its
thicket of cacti and its African daisies and the bright
yellow monkey flowers in pots on the front stoep. The
walls of the cottage were of baked mud, the old iron roof
sloped over the front stoep in a lip or skirt designed to
sluice away the harsh winter rains that fell infrequently
and violently. The edges of the roof were frayed with
rust.

He knocked and called out: 'Where is the brilliant
Miss de Bruyn?'

When the top half of the green stable door opened
with its rusty creak, a rush of old herbs, candle wax, mud
walls and dung floor, mixed with the slightly salty tang
of leather *riempie* chairs, enveloped him.

Pascal thought: 'Jesus, it's out of the ark!'

Mimi appeared framed in the upper half of the door
against the sepia shadows of the room behind her.

'Here. Take him.' Pascal pushed the boy at her.

And when with delight in her eyes she said she
absolutely couldn't, he added: 'Please. Till I'm sorted.
Otherwise, he's going to the dogs.'

CHAPTER SIXTEEN

When the Bushboy moved in with Mimi de Bruyn, time seemed to go into reverse.

Rumour said she'd taken Chinkie away on health grounds. Power had gone to her head. It wasn't enough being deputy mayor, head of this and rotating co-chair of that: 'She's confiscating kids now!'

The timing was bad, too. Just as the town united in the preparations for the Elvis Evening, and plans were laid for a great First Prize of a Week in Memphis, plus visit to Graceland, all expenses paid, and the president of the Elvis Presley Memorial Society (Western Cape Division) had agreed to judge the Evening – and he was said to be a man of international standing. Just when people needed Le Gros to concentrate on getting his act together – because who the hell else was going to be greeter-in-chief when the president arrived in Buckingham? – Pascal started playing silly buggers with Bushboys and chasing after the deputy mayor who seemed to have turned very strange.

What disturbed a lot of folks, older people, especially, was that just when they'd put all that sort of thing behind them, a middle-aged woman was to be seen once again walking down the main street, passing Nephew's willow,

with a small figure trailing behind her. Narrow your eyes
and it might have been yesterday. And who wanted to
be reminded of yesterday? Except now the child wore a
red coat; and, once upon a time, it had worn sheepshead
slippers. If you were progressive, it made you angry. If
you were old-fashioned, it made you sad. If you were
English, it made you feel redundant.

Mimi had no business disturbing everyone like this.
Nor had Betsy. When she died, it turned out she'd left
the cottage to Mimi in her will. Actually, she'd left it to
Me. And Mimi had to appear in court to prove that she
was also Me. She had explained how she'd taken the de
Bruyn part of her name from old Blind Daisy, but Mimi
was her own. However she was, unquestionably, also
Me.

Arletta Basson had appeared as witness and everyone
remembered her memorable confirmation: 'She is Me.'

It had seemed pretty funny at the time. But it hadn't
been funny, after the Change, when Mimi moved into
the cottage. Not even her own side was very pleased.
They said she really ought to get something more
modern, more in keeping with her position, something
more suitable. You didn't want your deputy mayor living
like – well, like a poor white.

And now the San child was also living in the cottage
and followed her along the street like a pet. Those born
after the fifties thought it was crazy. No one took their
servants walking any more. No one had servants; they
had staff, employees, personnel.

Anyway, Chinkie was not a servant, he was the bar
mascot.

*

Increasingly Mimi forgot about Health and Gender; she
forgot about Church and Party, she forgot politics and
she gave herself over to making Chinkie happy. For the
first time since she'd walked away from Aunt Betsy's warm
bed smelling faintly of arnica oil, on that night long ago,
she now allowed herself to remember without guilt. Or
not to remember at all.

And why not? It was a fair trade: she'd given the town
Elvis, a Celebration; an idea with a big future. And Pascal
had given her Chinkie who was a kind of future too. A
future for her past.

That she and Pascal seemed to have something going
baffled people as much as her attachment to the Bushboy.
The fat man had been in and out of her cottage like a
yo-yo ever since he handed over Chinkie.

Pascal couldn't believe anyone lived without electricity
or running water, the oil lamps throwing waves of soft
yellow light on the portraits of the vanished Boer
patriarchs, and the dead eyes of long-gone prime ministers, the garish jewels of the old Boer flags picked out in
coloured matchheads and psalms written in seashells.

And he was fascinated by the way Mimi inhabited her
former prison, in which nothing had been altered, except
that the new mistress slept in Aunt Betsy's cupboard bed,
recessed into the wall, curtained with the apricot silk
hangings – and not in the alcove beside the fireplace
where the wood was kept.

As to why Pascal had donated the kid, it was the talk
of the town. Some said he was looking for a new home
because Maureen was gunning for him. And his planning
application for the San reserve had bitten the dust when
Mr Moosah's planning committee had booted it into
touch. So maybe he was courting influence?

Certainly Pascal was heard yelling at Baba Williamson that he was supposed to look after the black end of this joint venture, right? Supposed to be in touch with the grassroots, OK? But the bloody grassroots had bloody well gone and kicked them in the teeth.

Baba Williamson said it wasn't so much the grassroots: it was the Structures. Mr Moosah had consulted the Structures and they had iced the idea of San City; they didn't fancy lots of naked San on the premises when they had jobless enough in Buckingham.

Maureen enjoyed reporting the conversation between the fat crook and the mayor's shyster brother:

'Jeez, Baba, these Structures – it's like the ancient Greeks consulting the oracle at Delphi. Do they always tell Moosah what he wants to hear?'

'Not quite,' said Baba. 'He tells them what he wants to hear.'

Mimi also took to visiting Pascal – to report on progress or, rather, her lack of it, for Chinkie had not transplanted easily. However much taking the boy into her home satisfied some inner craving to heal the wounds of time, it did not prove to be easy.

The Bushman resented her arrangements from the start. Where he had stolen from Pascal with pride and a certain affection, he raided Mimi's cupboards with vengefulness and spite; he scooped fat handfuls of honey from the honey jars leaving sticky puddles, and dozens of sugar ant trails followed his dribblings through the house; she found his thumbprints on the butter; he lapped milk from the jug; he refused to sleep in the room she had made ready for him, Aunt Betsy's old dispensary, Nico's fateful room where Childie and Nico danced and Me wound the Regiontone. Instead, he caused her more pain than she could have anticipated by sleeping stretched out beside the fire, in the wood bin, her old bed all those years ago.

Mimi dressed him in shorts and shirt, just like an ordinary little boy, but he didn't like it.

'He wants his uniform back – but,' she shook her head sadly, 'it doesn't really work in my house. Then there was his hat – I couldn't bear it.'

And Pascal heard with astonishment for the first time, since no one ever talked about it, of the death of Bananas Basson and the killing of Childie.

'The last time I saw a fez with black tassels was on the head of a man who had just shot himself and a great lake of blood was flowing out of his left ear . . . what do you say to that?'

And though he had no answers to her question, or perhaps for that very reason, Pascal became the recipient of memories she had not dared to turn and face: nights in the sheep pen with Blind barking Daisy, Nico who had gone and the War for Childie's Head.

When she began sobbing, Pascal would slide a box of tissues down the bar counter and pat her hand. But he said nothing and that was wise, turning his flat white ear like a radar dish into her stream of confession; because into the space he provided for her, Mimi projected not only her pain, but also her admiration.

Perhaps if they could have known the impression they made, when Maureen popped her head around the door of the karaoke bar – the grave and rather severe Mimi de

Bruyn in careful blue skirt and matching scarf and Pascal standing opposite her, trying to hold his belly in – they might have been more discreet.

The first time Chinkie ran away, Mimi drove to the Hunter's Arms in a panic, to find him in his customary position, perched on the loudspeaker drinking Coke.

Maureen said: 'Pascal's ruined him. He just wants crisps and Coke and the karaoke. They're supposed to eat ants in the wild.'

'I've tried everything,' said Mimi, 'but I can't get through to him. I don't want him drinking that stuff.'

She yanked the can from Chinkie's hand. The boy looked at her with fury, then threw back his head and gave the most uncannily accurate, horribly real impersonation of the dying rabbit on Fritz's tape.

A week later he was gone again and this time when she got to the hotel he was not on the speaker in the karaoke bar. A search of the town revealed nothing.

'You can't tame them, that's the problem,' said Mike. 'The old farmers around here, on a raid, they generally shot the parents. Too wild, see? And they took the kids. You had a fighting chance, taming the kids.'

Mimi turned on him. 'I don't want to tame him! That's a horrible idea. I want him to have a home.'

''Scuse me for breathing,' said Mike. 'I was only trying to help. Maybe you should have tied him to a tree.'

Pascal felt almost as badly as she did when the little bastard went AWOL – but for different reasons. For one thing he was extremely pissed off with the Bushman. It seemed to him the height of ingratitude. He had set a lot of store by the gift to Mimi. It wasn't, as the town suggested, a bribe; neither a sweetener nor a wish to curry favour. No, this time he was engrossed, for reasons he did not understand, in Mimi's pain. He felt he had looked into her heart when she showed him her house and he imagined a want supplied, a loss recouped, the return of, or to, some happy state she desperately missed, a love of sorts. A child in the house where she had been a child. True, Chinkie was not a child – but he was young, and we all had to settle for what we could get, not so? If the Bushboy didn't know he was well off, he thought bitterly, then maybe he deserved to become extinct. No damn good in the old or the new Buckingham.

A lot of people were pleased when the Bushman walked. It was time Pascal got his come-uppance. Bill Harding said:

'You're not going to be much good trying to run a park full of San if you lose the first one you're given, hey?'

Baba Williamson was very gloomy: 'I signed a receipt for him. He was only ours on appro. A sample. What'll I tell my supplier?'

For days Pascal searched the district between Eros and Compensation, as far as the Snow Mountains. He waxed confident with Baba.

'Not to worry. He'll make it back. Like dogs – they got terrific homing instinct, Bushmen.'

The curious thing was that though he didn't give a sheep's fart for the boy, he felt Mimi's loss and he blamed himself when she mourned and said she'd gone and lost Chinkie by not giving him a proper home.

His concern, his patience with her tears, his search for Chinkie, these things moved her greatly. Mimi wondered at Pascal's generosity. The spirit of self-sacrifice is power-

fully connective; the glow of good feeling it arouses in
the selfless giver plus the reciprocal admiration it enjoins
in the beneficiary. It could be said that it was from this
time that Mimi fell in love with Pascal Le Gros – if love
it was. The boy had gone, the gap remained and Pascal
solved the problem in a way which strengthened them
both, or so it seemed; for in place of what she had lost,
he proposed putting the most valuable thing he could
think of – himself.

There was also an official side to their courtship. When
he started stepping out with Mimi de Bruyn, Pascal did
so in his capacity as rotating co-chair of the Freedom
Committee. And rotate he did, big, white and lunar.
Round and round and round he swanned. From the
Hunter's Arms to Mimi's cottage was his iron orbit. Mimi
de Bruyn was his co-chair, his twin moon; they came out
after dark and shone brightly.

It was a miracle made in committee.

Mayor Williamson and others tried to put a positive
spin on it, even though they worried like hell. Not since
the ex-spy married Marie Smit over in Golden Meadow
had a white guy hitched up with a brown woman and,
amid the suspicion of his motives, there was a grudging
admission that Pascal knew what he was about; those
who'd looked at his library books in the reading room
knew he was alert to currents of history. As a good
Hegelian he believed in the big idea and, once again, he
pointed the way to the future by this rainbow love affair
with Mimi de Bruyn. It meant Buckingham was moving
in the right direction, plugging into tomorrow.

Once again, it came late in the day – lesser, duller
places, like Eros and Zwingli, had seen white–brown
liaisons in dozens since the Change, but one had to start

somewhere and, anyway, it was no secret that love across
the colour line in Eros and Zwingli meant screwing your
servants, which is basically what they'd been doing for
years. Only now they called it progress.

Mimi was unaccustomed to anyone paying court to
her. There had been a deacon years ago but he had gone
off with the telephonist who ran the paraffin exchange.
A Party worker or two. And, briefly, Mr Moosah, until
he put Party before pleasure.

In fact, when she thought it over, Mimi was just as
puzzled as everyone else. It seemed a most improbable
thing. What was it about the big round man in the
cricketing flannels and the purple and black chevrons at
the throat and the tiny feet in shining white tennis shoes
beautifully double-knotted that took Mimi de Bruyn's
heart and put it through the mincer?

Sometimes she thought it must be that Pascal reminded
her of Aunt Betsy, the same sense of certainty, the same
overwhelming confidence and the same capacity to float
above the objections and wrangles of the town. Then
there was his willingness to find the missing child. First
Chinkie and then Childie.

For Mimi love was finding another heart to hold. It
was a way of fighting off the shadows of losing three
mothers: being three times an orphan. Fathers were,
perhaps, more reliable, she had always believed, and it
was a belief that drew her to Pascal for reasons he did
not understand and that was just as well. For, as if there
was some special rhythm to it, shortly after Aunt Betsy
died, Blind Daisy went too. Pains in the chest and crying
in the night and Mimi had run for Doc du Plessis who
gave her pills and said he'd come in the morning and, by
a miracle, he did but it was too late.

'I see you, My Eyes,' Daisy had whispered, and Mimi knew it was over.

Now this love affair. It was not something she had ever expected and though they made the best of it, she knew it was not very popular with her people, her comrades. For them it smacked of foolishness. Why do it: with a fat white man? Why bother? Why him, of *all* people? It was not very progressive, no. It was not really politically very astute. In fact, to some it was really not very patriotic. Just when we've got them on the run – why team up? That was the question. Why not kick them into touch? It was old-fashioned, this love of hers and Pascal's, there was something uncomfortable about the mating of the modern with the past, with the *passé*.

She took him down to Bushman's Drift and there they made love, witnessed by a passing fence mender, who came across this couple in the bottom of the gorge: the man looked like a cloud come down from heaven, said the witness when he told his story back in town of his vision; a cloud that covered the woman as a white woollen kaross covers the wagon seat, as a field of daisies covers the earth, their white heads softly waving, as the feathery desert snow called *kapok* covers the naked earth.

In his wooing, again the curious delicacy, despite his bulk, and novelty, together with a lightness, odd and paradoxical in a figure over six foot, broad as an oak, with feet the size of acorns and purple as a turkey in the face. People couldn't believe it. The fat man and the deacon, head of Gender, Comrade de Bruyn.

Pascal ran into trouble on all sides when he began searching for the head of Childie. In Buckingham proper they said there was no proof that the head had ever been in the gorge and these were the superstitions of simple minds – like the belief in watersnakes. And Golden Meadow asked: did we really want to drag up that business all over again? It was not in the interests of reconciliation between the communities.

But Pascal was, by now, as firmly under Mimi's spell as she was under his, and in trying to soothe her obsession with the sundered body of her friend he rushed in on tiny feet where no sensible person would tread.

He accosted Arletta Basson and asked her if she knew what her husband might have done with Childie's head. She looked at him with her dull brown eyes and said please, he mustn't talk nonsense, she knew nothing of Childie or her head. And when Pascal said her husband shot himself, didn't he? Arletta just went on looking at Pascal, much as she looked at the bodies on the table down in the morgue, and said that one day Barnabas had been docking sheep's tails and the next he was dead. That was all she knew and if he wanted to know any more he must ask Mimi because the girl who died had been her friend, and a right wild young thing she had been, always snaring men.

From that moment there commenced a cooling in the relations between Mimi and Arletta Basson, who took the view, prominent in the town, that if you wished to accomplish something, like an act of repentance, for example, then you washed the dead and laid them out and sang 'Just a Closer Walk With Thee' while you did so. You did not talk about why you did something, as Mimi de Bruyn increasingly tried to do. You did not wish to bring back the dead: it was enough to know what you had done; it was pain in full measure and needed no words.

And so, shortly before the great Elvis Presley Festival, the duets ceased. No more did the Angel of Death call upon the Recording Angel to help her down in the morgue. No more did the singers make the tin walls of the little hut shiver with their beautiful blending of 'Peace in the Valley'.

Pascal did not even hear the warning bells when he questioned the mayor who, Mimi said, had been in the house the day Bananas blew his brains out; Little Boy Williamson, holding his mother's hand. Was it true that he had stolen a piece of mutton from the Sunday roast?

The mayor flushed angrily: 'We were hungry. I'd never seen so much meat on a plate in my life.'

But, no, he had not peeped into the bedroom and seen Basson lying on the pink candlewick bedspread: 'All I saw was the meat – big leg of lamb in a half inch of blood and gravy, steam rising . . . There was salt, a black ridge of it, running from the crown to the knucklebone. I ached for that meat, my stomach cried for it.'

More he could not or would not remember.

Pascal was to be seen beside Mimi laying a wreath at Childie's grave. He told Mike the Spike that only when Childie was reunited head and body would reconciliation and forgiveness be possible among the people of Buckingham.

Maureen was openly hostile now and each day Mike trimmed back his allegiance to Pascal, weighing which of his patrons offered more long-term security. And it came down to Maureen – she owned the hotel; she could throw Pascal out any time she chose.

He tried to warn Pascal.

'I got this woman once,' babbled Mike the Spike, 'and romanced her rotten. Flowers, Babychams, Sun City and before I rubbed the shit out of my eyes she'd taken me for forty grand. Maur's different. Now I gotta say to you, Pascie, this is a real good chance here, for you, me and Maur. She's a class act. I gotta chance, like you gotta chance. And all because Maureen puts up the whack we need to make the Hunter's Arms a real going concern. Don't mess up on this one, Pascie. Don't pull this one through your arse. Or who knows where you'll end up.'

'You're bloody lucky you ended up with me,' Maureen spoke up from the far end of the bar. 'Otherwise you'd still be flogging time-shares at the coast with our fat friend here.' She flicked her pistol at Pascal. 'I know just what you're after with that Mimi who does the bodies and sings in the church. It isn't love or even sex – it's favours. Politics.'

'Everything, my dear, in this country begins as love and ends in politics,' said Pascal.

'I don't know,' said Maureen, 'some things end in jail. Hopefully.'

What had seemed an unbreakable combo was coming apart at the seams: fat Pascal and little Mike the Spike, whippet thin, keen as a stiletto or a sharpened bicycle spoke or a pointed stick, to which was tethered balloony, pale Le Gros. The moon and the flick-knife, the abbot and the assassin.

Pascal warned Mike: 'Leave me, and you're finished.'

Maureen told him to go and screw his hand. For good measure she warned him against trying to drive a wedge between her and Mike.

'He's here to service the fridge and me, not necessarily

in that order and not always satisfactorily. If you don't like – take a hike.'

From then on he slept at Mimi's place, behind the apricot silk hangings. She watched him struggle out of cricket flannels and sweater; it was, she thought, a bit like watching a hard-boiled egg unpeeling itself; Pascal was now in this crazy orbit around her; he was her plump, pale satellite. He called her his shining light, his sun, his earth, his world: she called him her moon landing and her explorer and her soldier in arms and drawing the curtains behind him went flying.

Mimi marvelled at how so much body could accommodate itself in such a snug space.

Pascal explained: 'I'm fairly bulky but I compensate by possessing an almost India-rubberiness of limb; I can contract and bend and squeeze myself into almost any space.'

And he did, he did.

Lying under him she should have been pinned to the mattress, but she felt no weight; it was like floating over the sea not on, but under, a big billowy air cushion. She was unbruised. Unlike exposure to the sun, which burnt the skin, Pascal's love-making left her touched but curiously cool; not sunstroke but moonburn.

Maureen barred him from the hotel.

Pascal was angry. He wrote to the mayor resigning from the Festival Committee. He was sorry that his 'extensive arrangements' for the event, and for welcoming the president of the Elvis Presley Society to Buckingham would now 'no longer come to fruition'. However, he was left with no option because 'unbalanced, armed amateurs' had made his work impossible.

Mimi let it be known that if Pascal was resigning then so was she.

'But with both our rotating co-chairs gone and the president arriving on Friday, who will greet?' cried Little Boy Williamson.

'Mike'll do it,' Maureen promised. 'He's a born greeter.'

CHAPTER SEVENTEEN

The pink Fairlane came swaying down Freedom Street, tailfins proud, full-blooded brake lights blinking, bumpers polished to an eye-blinding glint and two large fake leopard-skin furry dice suspended from long leather laces swinging from the driving mirror above a strip of pink fur running across the top of the dashboard, stretching like a perfect beach on some distant star where all pleasures were hairy. A large green butterfly rode on the prow of the Fairlane's bonnet, and through its plastic wings the afternoon sun showed a pattern of beautiful veins. An honour guard of soldiers lined the route as the limo turned majestically into Democracy Drive and pulled up outside the Hunter's Arms where the speakers were pumping out 'Ready Teddy'.

Greeter-in-chief Mike the Spike was waiting, in skin-tight black jeans, loads of zips and a lot of wave to his hair, and in the lapel of his long white sports coat a pink carnation, despite the fact that Maureen had warned earlier:

'That's Pat Boone, sweetie, even I know that.'

The Acappella Choir from the brown church, under the baton of Pastor Grootboom, lined up on the second floor stoep of the Hunter's Arms, gave out a smooth rendition of 'Let's Have a Party'. The spectators cheered and the drum majorettes began scooting about with drinks.

These arrangements were Pascal's, like so much of the forward planning – put in place before his break with Maureen and Mike. He had dressed staff in short frilly white skirts and boots and spent days training them to ride roller-skates, and now they whizzed about offering people this special Welcome Cocktail he'd invented for the occasion: the Big El – two measures of gin, a jigger of crème de menthe, a dash of Budweiser and a maraschino cherry.

The driver of the Fairlane was a short round guy: peppery moustache, big wide hat and creamy suit, and a string tie knotted under his chin in a big brass P. He looked a bit taken aback when Mike did his official greeting bit:

'Call me Mikey, my old *chommie*.' Mike pressed a cocktail on the president. 'In the meantime – cheers!'

Maureen, wearing a black dress and a good string of pearls and her pistol slung on a very pretty white belt of cross-stitched hide, thought he looked a little short to be presidential material. She just hoped the fat crook had not sold them a pig in a poke. He was supposed to be international. She invited the president to hop on a chair so the crowds might all get a decent dekko.

Hoisted on to the chair, the president had his first hint of trouble. Some of the younger rugby mob, who'd been hitting the Big Els, broke into: 'Why was he born so beautiful, why was he born at all!'

Maureen told them to shut up: 'Bunch of bloody paw-paws, it's not that sort of party.'

The president declined a Big El: 'No thanks, Mikey, a cold lager is just the ticket.'

Then Mayor Williamson formally welcomed to Buckingham the President of the Elvis Presley Memorial Society (Western Cape Division). He tried to sound positive – but the fact that fighting had broken out at such a crucial moment amongst members of his committee had depressed the hell out of Little Boy Williamson. A moment of rare concord, and then this! Mimi and Pascal had resigned. Dr Angel was missing. His outburst at the last meeting had not gone unnoticed. He had been summoned to return to his embassy for shipment back to Havana.

'For re-education,' said Mr Moosah.

'Prison, you mean,' said Baby Vermaak who was also absent from the welcoming party.

The three pastors, Grootboom, Niemand and Greet, in their togas, said a prayer of welcome: another of Pascal's ideas, a benediction based on a tripartite alliance – American values, ecumenicism and civil pomp.

Then the honour guard lifted their AK-47s. The guard was composed of former fighters from the liberation army, under the command of Captain Nephew. The Stars and Stripes was unfurled from the roof of the Hunter's Arms.

'A single volley,' hissed Nephew.

The honour guard probably meant to do as he said but the excitement got to them and they couldn't stop firing. The president, up on his chair, looked a little bleak as he pulled at his lager and watched them empty their magazines into the sky. Everyone understood the soldiers' excitement – through the long war of liberation they had never got to fire a shot in anger.

Captain Nephew screamed: 'Hold your bloody fire, you stupid bastards!'

Maureen whispered to the president: 'Time you said a few words – folks are getting frisky.'

All Buckingham was on the street now, milling around his Fairlane – and the president, who'd done this job as a favour to Pascal's lawyer down in Cape Town, began to wish he hadn't come. He looked at the little sharp guy in the stovepipes, the woman with the gun at her hip and the big wig and white gunbelt, the crazies with the AK-47s, the brown choir, the girls on skates; he stared at the faraway rock-freckled conical hills standing like breasts on the flat brown skin of the Karoo; and he muttered 'Keerist Almighty!' and steamed into his speech.

The president came from Woodstock and his usual accent advertised the squeezed vowels and clipped consonants of ordinary everyday Cape Townian English. But he spoke now with a twang modelled partly on that of the American Vice President, whom he'd had the privilege of observing at close quarters during his South African tour, blended with a touch of Bill Clinton whom he had studied from tapes. OK, it wasn't Memphis, maybe – but it was Southern wasn't it?

'First name's Vernon, folks – which was Elvis's daddy's name, as I'm sure I don't have to tell you. And when the King was just a kid he ran with cousins back in East Tupelo. Called? You got it – Smith! That's me, Vernon Smith at your service, and looking forward with all my heart to sharing in this great event, the Elvis Homage tomorrow night. My friends, we're the same people, your country and mine, and we in the United States salute South Africa, sister democracy and rainbow nation. Glad and privileged to be here. May the best person win! Goodbye and God bless you all.'

The Acappella Choir came in now with 'Yanky Doodle

Dandy', the drummies scooted round with more Big Els and all who heard the president's speech felt it was so good you couldn't have told it from the real thing. Some said they even preferred it to the real thing, because American accents you got on the box sometimes had such an edge you couldn't follow two words in three.

Spectators were milling around the Fairlane, breathing on the side-mirrors and squinting through the windows and trying to caress the paintwork until Vernon Smith said: 'For Chrissakes, keep those folks off my limo, can't you?'

The honour guard waded into the crowd. Strangely enough no one seemed to object to being pushed back with rifle butts; quite the contrary – there was a feeling of pride about it. After all, if you were going to have a real American president as your guest of honour you must expect to be knocked around by his body guards.

The welcoming party now moved into the dining room, its San motifs concealed for the night under pink curtains, together with a black carpet, the King's colours, and they sat down to burgers and fries, with Mike proposing toasts in brandy and Coke and saying what an honour the president had bestowed on the town by his presence and thanking him for giving his time.

Over the chocolate fudge icecream Vernon Smith drew Mike aside and said he wasn't giving his time. Pascal had promised a fee. He named a figure.

Mike told the mayor and Williamson said he didn't have that kind of money on him and would the president take a cheque?

'Cash,' said Smith, 'or I split tonight.'

In the end they gave him most of the money from the bar till and the mayor placed in the drawer, at Maureen's insistence, an IOU drawn on the Municipality. Then the president announced he was hitting the sack. 'Big day, tomorrow.'

Mimi had taken to driving over to Nickleton most days and Pascal was pretty puzzled by this interest in the Israelites. When he asked what she was doing she said she wanted him to understand something. She took him down to the old cemetery in Silver Street and showed him the children's graves, small wooden crosses gnawed by ants and twisted in the wind, hidden among the stiff grasses of the encroaching desert. She told him about her old job as the Recording Angel, and how, if you thought about power, it exceeded anything dreamed of in Health and Gender.

'The first test in life,' said Mimi, 'is to be born.'

Those who failed this test lay beneath tiny white headstones scattered like grains of rice. But those who survived faced a bigger test: life and its three primary colours – brown or white or black. When she'd been Clerk of Births, that was the fundamental fact Mimi decided when she wrote you down in her book. It made the day of judgement look pretty pale – didn't it? At the last trump you'd be judged by your past life; but Mimi, recording angel of Lutherburg, had the power to decide, by the stroke of her pen, whether you'd have a life worth living before you'd barely begun! What she wanted was to put something in the place where she'd been.

'If I could save a child, I'd have a future.'

Pascal looked as if he understood. His shaggy, grand eyebrows rose like floating doormats; his red round mouth grew rounder still and smaller till it resembled the lips of a bottle, which he tapped with his plump finger sending gentle shock waves fluttering through his jowls.

Perhaps he thought she was talking about Chinkie. At any rate, he nodded. That was the mistake.

Or perhaps Mimi wished to believe he understood. And so she acted.

On Friday evening when Mike greeted and the drummies whizzed by with silver trays of cocktails at the Hunter's Arms and the president of the Elvis Presley Memorial Society got up on the chair and made the speech about the King, East Tupelo and Sister Democracies, Mimi and Pascal lay in bed pressing passion upon and from each other, like fruits in a compote, very slow and very sweet and slightly sticky. Until from the room next door Pascal heard something: a whimper, like a puppy or a cat.

'What the heck's that?'

With a smile as beautiful as it was terrifying, Mimi pulled him out of bed and she led him through to the spare bedroom, Nico's room, the old dispensary, Chinkie's room, which he wouldn't use. Beside the window was an old yellowwood cradle and in the cradle was a sleeping baby. Mimi reached down, touched the child's cheek and it sighed and slept.

Finger to her lips she led Pascal back to bed.

'Whose is it?' he asked.

'Mine.'

She gave the terrifying smile again: 'He can be *ours* – if you like.'

It took him a while to realize that he had been made a

unique offer – fatherhood and marriage in the same breath – and he was appalled. Worse, he knew it showed.

He lay there thinking that babies do not come from nowhere. Judging by the cradle and the clothes, Mimi had been preparing – correction, *someone* had been preparing for the arrival of a child. And then, quite suddenly it came to him why Mimi had been driving over to Nickleton almost each day.

'Shirleen!' Pascal said, 'That's Shirleen's kid.'

Mimi shook her head. 'He's mine.'

For a moment he thought: she's pinched it! But Mimi didn't feel like a child stealer; she was too confident, too pleased – more of a proud owner. He saw it now. Shirleen didn't want it. Everyone in town dreading the result of Shirleen's pregnancy. Maybe Vince pressing his demands for paternity tests? And suddenly, bingo, along comes Mimi and takes it off their hands. And now she was offering to share the kid with him. The *only* guy in town who couldn't be the father!

Pascal said: 'You must be crazy!'

She carefully drew away from him. Then she jabbed him in the windpipe with fingers extended. The sudden violence of her attack horrified him. He gagged.

'Shh!' said Mimi fiercely. 'You'll wake him.'

Mimi hadn't finished. She moved away from him, her back braced against the wall, drew her feet up and kicked him until she ejected him through the curtain and he fell to the hard dung floor and bounced, not like a ball, but like some too-ripe fruit that flattens with a thump when it hits the ground.

Mimi attacked Pascal as he lay on the floor, winded and bruised, and she did not stop. Lashing out, her fists sinking sometimes a few inches into his flab with the sound of mosquitoes being swatted with cupped palms. She savaged him as if he were everyone she'd ever hated. Her mother who sold her for six cakes of soap, and Aunt Betsy who ran out on her and Childie who was dead and Nico who got gone and Chinkie who vanished.

Pascal held on to the bedside curtain, hauling himself to his knees, and it came loose with a roar of tearing silk. Then wobbling uncertainly, he staggered from Mimi's house, still holding the torn curtain.

It was shortly before dawn, the last of the darkness lay on roofs and windows like wet paint, when Maureen had been woken by the sounds of someone dropping pans in the kitchen downstairs. She heard the fridge door slam and muffled curses and heavy steps descending the front stairs.

She ran out on to the moonlit verandah that fronted the Hunter's Arms like an iron breastplate. Pascal, shining like a sheeted ghost, was carrying something large and pale slung across his shoulder, heading for the red Nissan pick-up parked below her. She cursed herself for not changing the locks on the hotel doors and stripping him of his car keys, and screamed at him to stop right there – this bloody minute! or she would unleash Brad and Bruce. But Pascal simply lifted two derisory fingers and slung the body into the back of the truck, and she knew from the detonation as frozen bone hit metal that it was a mutton carcass. He'd helped himself to half a sheep from the deep freeze and, no doubt, the cash tills and CD racks and bar shelves.

She ran back into the bedroom for her gun, but she

was too late; the truck accelerated into the night and it occurred to her as the sound of Pascal's engine died away that he had been wrapped in some kind of silken curtain or veil. That explained his milky luminescence; cold white flesh; because under his veil he had been quite naked.

CHAPTER EIGHTEEN

Mayor Williamson stood before the stage curtain of the Buckingham School Hall. Above him, spelt out in golden script, pasted in looped parallels to the heavy crimson curtains just below the proscenium arch, was the legend:

HOMAGE TO THE KING – BUCKINGHAM 1995
(Karaoke equipment courtesy of the Hunter's Arms)

For the mayor this was without doubt the worst of times. Everyone had been to see the mayor first thing that morning. Maureen wanted Pascal arrested. 'Running around in the night, bare as can be!'

Baby Vermaak wanted him to protest about Dr Angel's expulsion.

Mayor Williamson said he could not interfere in the domestic affairs of a friendly country.

Baby said he was being untrue to the memory of Elvis Presley. 'He hated commies. He'd never have done this to Romeo.'

Mimi de Bruyn called and showed him her child. And when he asked where it came from, she said, 'Ask Pascal. And when you see him, tell him to stop writing to me. I don't want to see him ever again.'

Pascal had camped in one of his own time-share bungalows at the Buckingham Country Club, nursing his prodigious hurt. He had been plying Mimi with notes, via Captain Nephew, who had asked for Maureen's half-sheep to be returned. Pascal fired off counter claims; her theft of his intellectual property – 'My cocktails, my gloss, my style, my small but essential touches, my *class*! Claims I shall pursue through the highest courts in the land.'

And then he wept and asked Nephew if he thought Mimi would take him back and Nephew said: 'Damned if I know. She was a funny girl from the start. I knew her when she was worth just six bars of soap and I remember what she did to old Betsy.'

When he visited Pascal, the Mayor asked: 'Where's the child from?'

Pascal thought hard, before answering. 'It's a miracle.'

Mayor Williamson understood. 'The Israelites will think so.' And he gave him Mimi's message.

'I love her,' said Pascal.

Williamson felt it again, utter helplessness before the demons of the place. He wanted to comfort Pascal but he could think of nothing to say. He shivered with the bitter, familiar way it was. The same bright pain he had felt when Old Blind Daisy died and Arletta Basson said: 'She was our cook, once, y'know – and I always wondered if she was as blind as she made out.'

He hated Arletta for saying that and thought, sometimes, that people like her were savages. And yet he liked her. He liked Pascal. In every good thing cruelty sharpened its tooth. He had felt it keenly as he readied himself for the contest, as he sprayed himself with Brut and polished his chain of office on his shirt front and slicked back his hair – a dollop of vaseline making a luscious fat black wave.

His committee turned up. Everyone, that is, except Pascal.

Mimi de Bruyn was pale as a lily – looked at no one but smiled in a strange, wild way. Baby Vermaak sat at the far end of the aisle leaving about six seats between herself and the next member of the committee, Mr Moosah. Dr Angel had been repatriated that morning.

The president, Vernon Smith, was seated on a little podium at the back of the hall before a card table on whose green baize surface rested a glass of water, pencils and paper and an Anglepoise lamp. His eyes were scratchy from lack of sleep and he kept mumbling to himself.

The mayor knew what Smith was whispering. The first thing he'd seen when he arrived at the hall was the pink Fairlane parked right outside the back door, under a police guard. It had been there since the early afternoon and when he'd stopped by the judge's podium to greet the president, Smith refused even to acknowledge his presence, put his head down and repeated to himself: 'Dear Christ, get this fucking show on the road, and let's get the hell out of here.'

Mike the Spike, in velveteen maroon jacket and stove-pipes, kept trying to break into this monologue but Smith waved him feebly away like a sick man scaring flies.

The British Israelites kicked off the show by standing one and all and singing a hymn to Yahweh, dealing death to Semites. The Israelite Presley was given, as only to be expected, a kind of English accent, a rather full figure of a man heavily made up with a black wig over his usual reddish fuzz and gold-flecked sports coat falling to the backs of his knees.

The mayor recognized Vince de Lange; and he launched into 'Rip It Up' with a pretty solid rhythm but an unfortunate tendency to over-emphasize the pelvic thrusts, offering jerky and rather obscene belly bumps like a man trying a hula hoop for the first time, or nudging a pinball table with his groin. But looking relieved and, sure enough, there was Shirleen in his back-up, he'd know those white boots anywhere.

Next on was the affirmative action Elvis – a black guy bussed in from Zwingli who fancied the Little Richard look but now more closely resembled, say, Chuck Berry; he did pretty well, too, and there was heated discussion around the hall: given the white negro Presley was, did you want whiteness tending to negro – or vice versa?

A Gay Pride Presley in pink leather pants on a big Harley Davidson followed with 'Lonesome Cowboy'; a moody, close-cropped and excessively butch Lesbian Presley tricked out in Army khakis swung through a very Dietrichesque 'Wooden Heart'.

Then came a choral Elvis from the Buckingham accappella group, the only artists to dispense with the karaoke and give out 'Treat Me Nice' for twelve voices – though there was some argument as to whether the person of Presley was indivisibly one, or was he there whenever one or more gathered in his name?

The hall had caught the spirit now and relished trouble taken and knowledge lightly worn; Buckinghamers began clapping softly to the beat and their eyes glazed and they were gone. Applause rang out when some specially pleasing subtlety caught the eye: the black bolero the

Gay Pride Elvis wore over his pink pants – the bolero jacket had been a favourite of the King's as a young man, and pink and black were his sacred colours; or the Martin D-28 guitar which was the King's first and best when he began to make some money.

There was also some nice improvisation. The official Calvinists under Pastors Niemand and Grootboom brought on a clean upstanding fresh-faced Elvis, a kind of khaki choirboy with a ducktail who leaned into 'Just a Closer Walk With Thee' – only to be cruelly barracked by the breakaway Reformed Calvinists who replied with their unorthodox but inventive Aryan Elvis in black leather boots and dark glasses, skull and crossbones tattooed on his cheekbones, SS badges on a peaked cap and a chest glinting with Iron Crosses.

But you did not need money or equipment to move the audience. One of the strongest performances, a disabled Presley in a wheelchair, given by a kid under ten, drew a lot of applause for sheer spunk but he blew it because his dressers made him wear a little cap, probably based on the famous shot of the boy Elvis, aged eight, sitting on a kerb somewhere in Memphis wearing this little round number on his head.

The Israelites started yelling: 'He's wearing a yarmulka!' followed by hissing and Hitler salutes.

The Israelites didn't make trouble; they were too relieved for words by the miracle: a child that didn't get born. Yahweh was rooting for them.

And so it went. Mimi swaying slightly as if to some other music and crooning softly; and the mayor wondering who was minding the baby; and Arletta Basson who knew the words of all the songs from 'Old Shep' to 'In

the Ghetto' better than most, was quite silent; and the
president scribbling notes; and Mike the Spike clapping
every act to show he was even-handed; and Baby sobbing
quietly when she thought of the look on Dr Angel's face
as they loaded him on the bus and how she ran beside it,
leaping into the air to peer through the windows, hoping
for a last glimpse of her friend.

Everyone thought it was over and the president would
be giving his verdict now and Captain Nephew had the
honour guard ready to protect his limo because Smith
had warned that once he gave his verdict, he wasn't
staying: 'pronouncing and flouncing' was the way he put
it.

Then without warning he rolled on stage. Wobbling
slightly on those tiny feet, fleshy bulk strapped into his
jumpsuit, white as innocence.

This was not the vision anyone really cared to know,
though they recognized of course which of the sover-
eigns was here represented: the King of the last days, of
the Las Vegas comeback, the satiny jump suit, the
outrageous flairs so wide they covered his white sand-
shoes like silken tents, the curiously high collar towering
above the rolls of fat on a neck thick and red as a polony,
and plunging dizzyingly down almost as far as his belly
button in a naked vee, choked with black chest hair out
of which there sprang, like a frightened bird, as he began
to sing, a chunky gold medallion; then there was the
diamanté-encrusted white guitar and when he turned his
back, there it was, the corset that hugged that huge belly
into some semblance of waist and hips, seen in all its iron
discipline; two ridges showed how it stretched from
shoulder-blades to coccyx.

Here was the King of whom someone said it all when she begged: say whatever you like, but don't say he was fat!

It was appropriate that he should break into 'Heartbreak Hotel'; and as he moved his fleshy lips, vermilion in the spotlights, his customary white outfits at last seemed to make some sense; as if this was what he had been rehearsing for all the time.

A paradox. He was the aged King – but for a few moments, say around two minutes thirty seconds, he was also the twenty-two-year-old Presley singing straight to his best girl, Dixie Locke, on the night of the South Side Junior Prom, 1955, in Memphis. And such was his brilliance that not only was he someone else, he persuaded all who heard him that they were someone else.

But he didn't do it for the audience. It was plain to all in the hall that the singer had one target only. All his artistry, the majestic shrug of the pelvis, the lazy flick of the dark curtain of hair across his forehead, the long lazy sneer of the full wet lips – all was aimed at her. For her he conjured up the hotel of heartbreak; the desk clerk dressed in black. It was not just a great song – it was an aria of grief and sadness.

It was also ill-suited, improbable, mad ambition.

Pascal had become the monarch run to seed, the overblown, wobbling, pill-popping, swollen gargantua of the last terrible years – and he brought him to life as surely as he now reduced the hall to silence with the echoes dying away on Lonely Street and the hall was on its feet. Whistling, screaming, stomping ... And the mayor knew the guy had it all his own way. Except for Mimi.

Mimi didn't look at him. Maureen shouted something

but the noise of the crowd drowned it out. Mike was impressed, you could see that. So was the hall. It was wonderful stuff. There was really no one to touch him and everyone knew it when the president stood up and pronounced. Vernon Smith got his American accent back and he said they had a worthy winner, not only in the departments of rhythm and authenticity and sheer rock-and-roll genius but also in peace and love and reconciliation. America and South Africa were sister democracies and the people of Buckingham were the pot of gold at the end of the rainbow.

Then he handed over the prize to Pascal and hightailed it out to his pink Fairlane.

Only Mimi didn't move.

And after standing a moment, drenched in sweat and longing for her to look at him, Pascal took the money and ran. Right out to the Fairlane, back wheels spinning and the president opened the door for him, laid a lot of tackie on the gas and gunned it out of town.

For weeks Maureen went around telling everyone about the sheaves of sheriff's warrants arriving daily; it seemed Pascal's life was one long confidence trick followed by flight. Charges against the fat man poured in from all over the Karoo: roofing-felt fraud or ripping off time-share punters in Margate. He'd been married four times and his ex-wives were suing him:

'Jointly and severally,' said Maureen. 'If he as much as shows his nose back here he's inside for good. Unless I shoot him first.'

Mike the Spike stood by her and lamented the sad end of a guy with 'big brains and a sharp business sense who just couldn't get his act together'. But he could not keep out of his voice his admiration when he remarked that old Pascal's bum and a barrel of butter were made for each other.

'He falls into a shithole and comes up smelling of roses.'

But no one really minded. In fact, far from feeling that he had in some sense robbed them of the prize, people were increasingly glad that if anyone had gone to Graceland it had been Le Gros. It relieved them of the responsibility of having to come up tops in Memphis — and quite a responsibility it would have been, since there were plenty of folks in Buckingham who'd never been as far as Zwingli.

Life soon got back to what it was, guys sitting day in day out in the bar of the Hunter's Arms. And day in day out guys sitting on the corner of Democracy Drive and Freedom Street, waiting for some passing farmer to offer them a day's shearing and on both sides of the road, they took a pride in Pascal's travels.

Maybe he was that very day sitting in Graceland?

Was it as big as the pictures? And did it have long white columns out front? And pink satin sofas and a black bedroom suite edged with white leather trim? Was Pascal looking over the King's eight-foot bed and genuine milk-bar right inside the house where the King sat around drinking shakes?

The more they talked the clearer it became that they could have sent no one better to Memphis than Pascal Le Gros who, after all, looked a bit like Colonel Tom Parker, didn't he? He was sassy and streetwise and smart; whatever those damn Yanks threw at him, the fat man could handle. Yes, they were happy he was in Graceland.

And Mimi was happy. After the loss of Childie and Nico and Chinkie she had a grasp of the future; she wheeled her child down Freedom Street. She peered into his face as he lay sleeping on her breast after feeding; and she thought, yes, he looked like his father who had gone to Graceland.